"A brilliant debut of black girlhood and mental health."
—**Elizabeth Acevedo**, National Book Award winner and *New York Times* bestselling author of *The Poet X, With the Fire on High,* and *Clap When You Land*

"It's rare to find a book that aptly balances the comedy and tragedy of being human."
—**Nic Stone**, *New York Times* bestselling author of *Dear Martin* and *Odd One Out*

"As a weird, depressed, Radiohead-obsessed black post-teen myself, it's clear Morgan ripped my heart out and splattered it across the pages of this book. It's perfect."
—**Samantha Irby**, *New York Times* bestselling author of *We Are Never Meeting in Real Life.* and *Wow, No Thank You*

"In this wildly smart novel—about depression, high school crushes, faith, and being black in America—Parker has created a voice that will be a touchstone of stories about growing up and growing wiser. I love this book."
—**Julie Buntin**, author of NBCC John Leonard Prize finalist *Marlena*

★ "A funny, clever, wild ride of a story about growing up and breaking free."
—*Kirkus Reviews*, starred review

★ "This fresh read provides a positive and inclusive take on mental health and wellness and offers readers some tools to survive on their own."
—*Booklist*, starred review

★ "Drawing on her own teen experiences, Parker adroitly touches upon matters of respectability and 'presentableness,' stigmas against discussing mental health issues in the black community and among young adults, and internalized and societal racism."
—*Publishers Weekly*, starred review

"This sometimes humorous, sometimes heartbreaking story explores the topic of adolescent mental health in a fresh and truthful way."
—*The Horn Book*

"Parker offers a hilariously honest and heart-opening experience. It's a wholly necessary debut by an award-winning poet."
—*BookPage*

BOOKS BY MORGAN PARKER

Magical Negro

There Are More Beautiful Things Than Beyoncé

Other People's Comfort Keeps Me Up at Night

WHO PUT THIS SONG ON?

MORGAN PARKER

EMBER

Text copyright © 2019 by Morgan Parker
Jacket art copyright © 2019 by Adriana Bellet

All rights reserved. Published in the United States by Ember, an imprint of Random House Children's Books, a division of Penguin Random House LLC, New York. Originally published in hardcover in the United States by Delacorte Press, an imprint of Random House Children's Books, a division of Penguin Random House LLC, New York, in 2019.

Ember and the E colophon are registered trademarks of Penguin Random House LLC.

Visit us on the Web! GetUnderlined.com

Educators and librarians, for a variety of teaching tools, visit us at RHTeachersLibrarians.com

The Library of Congress has cataloged the hardcover edition of this work as follows:
Library of Congress Cataloging-in-Publication Data
Names: Parker, Morgan, author.
Title: Who put this song on? / Morgan Parker.
Description: First edition. | New York : Delacorte Press, [2019] | Summary: "17-year-old Morgan is a black teen triumphantly figuring out her identity when her conservative town deems depression as a lack of faith, and blackness as something to be politely ignored" —Provided by publisher.
Identifiers: LCCN 2018051979 (print) | LCCN 2018056566 (ebook) | ISBN 978-0-525-70752-3 (ebook) | ISBN 978-0-525-70751-6 (hc) | ISBN 978-0-525-70753-0 (glb)
Subjects: | CYAC: Depression, Mental—Fiction. | Identity—Fiction. | African Americans—Fiction. | Community life—Fiction.
Classification: LCC PZ7.1.P365 (ebook) | LCC PZ7.1.P365 Who 2019 (print) | DDC [Fic]—dc23

ISBN 978-0-525-70754-7 (pbk.)

Printed in the United States of America

10 9 8 7 6 5 4 3 2 1

First Ember Edition 2021

for my brother

& for Nick

& for Actual Morgan Parker, age 15

& in memory of Aunt Teri after a Cadillac

margarita

"Being Emo: A Memoir

SUSAN

This is a story about Susan. Draped permanently on the back of Susan's chair is a sweater embroidered with birds—that type of lady. She has this thing I hate, where she's just always medium, room temperature. Susan looks like a preschool teacher with no emotions. She smiles, she nods, but she almost never laughs or speaks. That might be the number one thing I hate about coming here. She won't even laugh at my jokes! I know that life with me is a ridiculous hamster wheel of agony, but I'm kind of hilarious, and I'm just trying to make this whole situation less awkward.

I'm the one who begged for my first session, but I was desperate, and it was almost my only choice. Now that I'm actually doing this, I hate it. I just want Susan to buy my usual pitch: I am okay. I am smart and good. I am regular, and I believe in God, and that means I am happy.

By the way, of course my therapist's name is Susan. It

seems like everyone I meet, everyone telling me how to be, is a Susan.

I don't trust a Susan, and I don't think they trust me either.

I don't like Susan, but I want to impress her—I'm usually so good at it.

But this is what I mean about the bird sweater. I know the bird sweater is awful, and just uncool and unappealing in every way—it doesn't even look comfortable. But other Susans like it, and generally all Susans do. It is a sensible piece of clothing; it is normal, and it makes sense. Wouldn't it be so much easier if I liked the sweater, if I just wore the fucking sweater and didn't make such a big deal out of everything?

THIS IS A STORY ABOUT ME

This is a story about me, and I am the hero of it. It opens with a super-emo shot of a five-foot-nothing seventeen-year-old black girl—me—in the waiting room at my therapist's office, a place that I hate. It's so bright outside it's neon, and of course the soundtrack is *Yankee Hotel Foxtrot* by Wilco, because I have more feelings than anyone knows what to do with.

The smell in here is unlike any other smell in the world, some rare concoction of pumpkin pie–scented candles and every single perfume sample from the first floor of Macy's. I bet Susan Brady LCSW decorates her house with Thomas Kinkade paintings and those little figurines, cherubs dressed up for various occupations, I don't know. The other thing I hate about coming here is the random framed photo of, I believe, Bon Jovi on the coffee table, which also features a wide assortment of the corniest magazines of all time.

(White people love Bon Jovi. When Marissa and I went to Lake Havasu with Kelly Kline, because that's what white people do here in the summer, Bon Jovi was the only thing her family listened to—that freaking scratched-up CD was actually stuck inside the thing on their boat. I had a moderate time at "the Lake," except for when I had to explain my summer braids to Kelly and Marissa, for probably the eight hundredth time, to justify why I didn't have a hairbrush to sing into. They made me sing into a chicken leg because of course. I was also shamed for not knowing any Bon Jovi lyrics. That was around this time last summer, but it feels like a past life.)

(Another thing I hate about coming here is how I have to think about everything I've lost, everything I've done wrong, and everything I hate about being alive.)

The thing I like about it here is that there's Werther's.

Susan opens the door and spreads her arms to me in a weird Jesus way, the sleeves of her flowy paisley peasant top billowing at her sides. She has kind of a White Auntie thing going on, or a lady-who-sells-birdhouses-at-the-church-craft-fair thing: a sad squinty smile, a dull brown bob, a gentle cadence to her voice. I can tell she's used to talking to children—probably rich white children—and as I stiffly arrange myself on the couch in her office, I'm suddenly self-conscious about my largeness, my badness. I just feel so *obvious* all the time.

It's like that song "Too Alive" by the Breeders. I feel every little thing, way more than regular people do.

"So, how are you doing today?" Susan asks too cheerily, like a hostess at Olive Garden or something. "Where are you on the scale we've been using?"

(I feel so deeply it *agonizes* me.)

"I'm okay. I guess on the scale I'm probably 'pretty dang bad,' but better than yesterday and still not 'scary bad.'"

(Now, probably to the soundtrack of Belle and Sebastian's "Get Me Away from Here, I'm Dying," there's a longish montage of me zoning out, imagining the lives of everyone I know. Even in my dreams, it's so easy and fun for them to exist.)

"Are you still taking the art class?"

"Yeah. Every Tuesday."

"That's wonderful. And how are you liking it?"

"It's fine. Sort of boring, but . . . I guess it takes my mind off things."

"Do you want to talk about what's on your mind the other times?"

"Um, not really," I chuckle, in my best joking-with-adults voice. The AC churns menacingly, like it always does, taunting me. Susan, with her wrinkled white cleavage, unmoving and unrelenting. Susan doesn't play.

I think about grabbing a Werther's from the crystal bowl but don't, even though I want one. (Will Susan write *Loudly sucks on Werther's* in my file as soon as I leave, right next to *Is probably fine; just being dramatic*?)

"I guess just people at school. Why I'm so different."

"Can you say a little more about that? What are the things that make you feel so different?"

"I don't know." My chest is welling up with everything I've been trying to stuff into my mind's closet. "I can't get happy."

It happened only three weeks ago, but since my "episode," no one in my family has uttered the word *suicidal*. It's easier not to.

I glance down at my Chucks, trying to divert my eyes from Susan. Stare at a lamp, the books stacked on her shelves. I spot a spine that reads *Healing, Recovery, and Growth*, and immediately feel ridiculous. Sweat pools in my bra. This isn't gonna work.

"Morgan, why are you so angry with yourself?"

I clench my jaw. "I'm not!" This is a lie, but it hasn't always been. "I'm annoyed," I admit, sighing, "and embarrassed."

"Why are you embarrassed?"

"Just—I don't know . . . ," I whine. Words begin to spill and spew from my lungs like a power ballad. "Like, why am I the only one I know who has to go to a shrink? How did I become the crazy one? I have to be the first one in the history of our family and our school to go to therapy?" I bristle. "I'm pissed I can't just get over stuff the way everyone else seems to."

I purse my lips resolutely and fold my arms tight against my boobs. Your ball, Susan. She just nods and squints like she has no clue what to do with me.

I've asked God and Jesus and all their other relatives to "wash away my sins," but it doesn't feel like Jesus is living inside me—I can't even imagine what that would feel like. I'm so full up with me, me, stupid me.

"Mmm . . . ," she finally grunts. "I see."

Fighting the near-constant urge to roll my eyes all the way to the back of my skull, I snatch up and devour a Werther's.

A little buzzer goes off on Susan's desk, and she clears her throat. Time for her little closing statement, usually some sentimental crap that clears up nothing for me.

"I know you're worried about school"—I lean forward to disagree, but Susan puts up a stubby hand and continues—"but maybe you'll be surprised. In the next few weeks, I'd like you to write everything down, exactly as you see and experience it."

Only Susan could make writing in a journal sound so boring and corny. I roll my eyes on the inside, but I nod dutifully.

"Well, we have to stop," Susan sighs, and I feel every atom in my body exhale.

Before I leave, she gives me a book by someone named SARK on how to "free the creative spirit" and instructs me to practice my breathing and meditation every day. I am heavy with dread just hearing the words. I thank her (for what?) and shuffle to the parking lot of the office park, where my mom is waiting in her black Mercedes.

She grins theatrically when she sees me. Much too peppy for my mood, she tosses her James Patterson novel into the backseat and turns on the engine. "How was it?"

The afternoon sun is offensive. As usual. Too damn bright. I lean my forehead against the car window and survey the place where I live: tan stucco as far as the eye can see; dirty cars parked in front of a Denny's; a Stater Bros. parking lot bustling with Susans; a billboard asking *Where Will You Spend Eternity?* I don't know why, but it feels significant.

"It was okay," I say wearily.

And nothing else the entire ride home.

...

The Diaries of Morgan Parker

August 10, 2008

<u>I am in THERAPY.</u> And in honor of such an occasion, I am starting a new journal. And, yes, I am writing in crayon because I still like crayons, so there.

Summer is gone. I've spent it fighting with everyone around me and crying in bed all day. I'm so pathetic. I keep thinking, I wish I didn't do this. But it's like I can't help it. Because of my depression.

I have this same dream over and over, that I'm driving on the 10. I recognize landmarks: the theme park where I flipped out and ruined Marissa's birthday, the strip club billboard with that senior cheerleader who supposedly overdosed on pills in the girls' bathroom and then got kicked out right before graduation. I'm driving up on the side of a mountain, but I can't turn the wheel, I can't slow down, and I'm just about to crash, but instead, in the next dream, I'm in the orange groves. They're on fire. Suddenly a storm cloud covers everything. I hear thunder, but no rain ever comes.

As soon as I wake up I have a bad attitude. It's how I know I'm alive, again.

THE BLUE ALBUM

At an hour that is completely unholy, my mom bursts into my room—my precious hideaway—carrying the force of a hundred black moms, all armed with inexplicable Saturday-morning energy, gospel music, and cleaning supplies.

I'm barely awake and already steeping in despair. (There isn't anything worse than the moment, the *Ughhh*, shortly after waking up, when you realize everything is where you left it.) I roll over and groan.

"I know you don't want to go, Morgan," my mom speaks down to the me-shaped floral sheets. She clears yesterday's untouched coffee from my nightstand and replaces it with a hot one, then sets off scooting around in her UGGs, humming to Kirk Franklin and coating everything in Pledge or Windex.

"You need to get out of the house. I'm not doing this with you today, Morgan." She pauses at the foot of my bed and huffs loudly until I peel the sheet from my top half.

"Mom, I won't be any good out there. I just can't handle it."

My whole summer vacation has basically been a bad performance-art loop of me "causing a scene" or "having a fit" at barbecues all over town. Even my birthday dinner in June, at our family's favorite Newport Beach pizza place, ended in tears and screaming and folded arms: me in the backseat on the drive home, invisible to my parents and my brother, stewing in shame and *OK Computer*. Everywhere I go, I am an embarrassment.

Balancing the coffee cup and an empty ice cream pint in one arm, my mom raises the blinds, letting in the brightness. I squint and grimace; I hate how the sun exposes my darkness.

"I'm trying, Morgan." It always seems to be about someone else—what I'm doing to other people, instead of what's happening to me. "I'm trying!"

"Trying to do what?" I shriek.

"To deal with this." Because of an overactive thyroid, my mom's eyes bulge when she talks. It pisses me off.

"Then stop yelling at me! Mom, I can't control this."

I know that I can make it, Kirk Franklin and his gospel choir sing. *I know that I can stand.*

"I know," she relents, scripted. There's more frustration than sympathy in her voice. I hate that I'm the kind of person people have to "try" to be around.

It's a whole thing; we both start tearing up for no good reason.

She offers to flat-iron my hair for the party, a veiled bonding attempt and a backhanded remark about my "presentableness," so I begin the grueling mental process of preparing to drag myself out of bed and into the world.

"I'm just scared," I say too loudly as she's leaving the room. "It's scary for me."

She nods gravely with her lips closed. We're both very dramatic people.

Sitting at my mom's vanity, I stare brutally at my face in the mirror. I guess I'll always have this face, which is super annoying. The prospect of carrying this body around day after day makes me want to crawl right back into my little womb of woe and just shut everything out.

However, today I'm going to Meg's tea party because my therapist and my mom are making me. When Meg Sloane called to invite me, I was actually shocked—I haven't been to one of her birthdays since back when we had to include everyone from class.

My head jerks with each stroke of the hot comb as my mom brushes and flat-irons my hair into submission. Apparently, I am tender-headed, which is a black thing. My hair is such a *thing*. To distract myself, I pull up some videos of the Get Up Kids on my laptop. In the mirror I see my mom wince and suck her teeth.

"What are these white boys so upset about? This whining is . . . really extreme."

"It's called emo."

"It's sort of irritating, isn't it?" She laughs, and it's not a ha-ha laugh. It's some kind of mom code I can't understand.

"It's not just music, Mom. It's a style. It's a way of life."

I know it sounds dumb, but whatever, it's true.

"I guess I just don't understand what's so cool about being sad."

This is a very popular sentiment at home, at school, in my whole tiny world. Every bad mood is temporary, just waiting to be overcome. I've always been told that the solution to all problems is prayer and serving others. If you are holy, you are happy. I guess I'm just not good enough.

(Now that I know what depression is, it's glaringly obvious that I've been depressed for years, maybe since birth. I've always been wrong like this. For example, I've been banned from having a slumber party since I had my first and only birthday sleepover at age ten and was so aggravated that I screamed at everyone there and tried pulling my hair out. My parents always say I "threw a fit," but it sounds like the way Susan describes anxiety.)

(Later, when my friends made fun of me about it, I pretended to laugh it off with them. I did the same when it happened on a school trip to Six Flags. And there were all those times at the crowded mall in Riverside when I "had a fit" on the benches outside the Body Shop because I thought I couldn't breathe—panic attacks.)

Of course my mom doesn't understand being emo. She still asks me every year if I'm going to try out for cheer, and she's so unsubtly horrified by all my outfit choices. She can't hide anything in her face, her over-the-top expressions. Dad, Malcolm, and I have started to retort, "You didn't need to," when she cries, "I didn't say anything!" It's sort of funny because it's so blatant, but mostly it's frustrating. I wish she would just say how she feels about stuff, what she really thinks—otherwise, why do I have to?

In high school, she was a cheerleader when she met my dad, a football player at a rival school. In college she pledged a black sorority. She always had a boyfriend. She's trendy, at least in her mom way, wearing low Converses and Banana Republic sweater dusters over my brother's jersey for game days. She makes sure the house is always cute, spotless. The mainstream works for her. And then she gets a daughter like me.

The best way for me to describe our little Southern California town is "nothing surrounded by something." Mountains, Disneylands, Hollywoods, Laguna Beaches, casinos, Palm Springs hotels: we have it all. We have all of it only forty-five minutes away. Our town is known for its oranges; for 0.8 miles of Route 66; for its abundance of conservative churches and their simple, kind congregations. The houses line up in clean rows. Front yards are neat green squares, SUVs and raised trucks piously adorned with Jesus fish emblems and Republican party stickers. The sun is involved in every day, pressing on spotless sidewalks, the tops of shiny cars. Eyes glaze over with tracts of artificial grass. Shit is extremely pleasant.

I hate it here.

After only one and a half dreamy, grungy songs from Pavement's *Slanted and Enchanted*, I arrive at Meg's mom's address. As I park I have a faint sense of having been to the house before, but I could be wrong. (In our landscape, things are like sitcom reruns, people and events repeating, all more of the same.)

My outfit is: a striped polo shirt from the boys' section of Goodwill, cutoff jean shorts, and (just because) a pair of red kitten heels left over from my fifties housewife phase. (No "Is that what you're wearing?" from Mom—a distinct Bummer Summer perk.) Making my way up the driveway, I wipe nervous sweat from my neck and tug at my cutoffs.

A little blond girl with a large forehead, maybe seven, greets me at the door before I even knock. She wears only a one-piece swimsuit, her stringy hair dripping wet all over the entryway tile. I panic—I didn't know this was a pool thing.

"Who are *you*?" Her neck snaps back as if on a pulley.

"I'm here for the— I'm here for Meg." She stares blankly. "Morgan," I point to my chest like a caveperson.

If I have been here, it was years ago, before Meg's parents split up—this is my first encounter with the result of Liz Sloane's remarriage to a much younger, Scandinavian-looking guy.

"Okay," she says, smiling creepily with gummy cheeks. Disclaimer: I really do not like children. I'm a little bit afraid of them. Malcolm's only two years younger than me (sometimes we even say we're twins), so I can't imagine living with such a small, foreign thing. I don't even babysit—I wouldn't know what the hell to do.

The girl makes no attempt to hide her gaze, which starts at the top of my head and slowly moves down to my feet. Her verdict: "You're brown. I like your shoes."

I laugh, my first instinct. But I feel hella awkward. I mean, the kid is just stating the obvious. That I am brown and have awesome shoes on are two true things about me.

(So what's this feeling, like dark, inky water suddenly rising around me?)

My mouth hangs open and I finally blink, noticing that Meg has appeared in the doorway.

"Geez, let her get through the door first, girl," Meg says. She lifts up the little freak with one arm like a grocery bag and drags me by the other hand into the foyer. Muscles bulge like clementines under the pale skin of her sticklike arms.

"This is Jessie," she says offhandedly as the girl wriggles from her clutch and bounces away. Meg flings up her free hands flippantly. "So, welcome to the party and all that good stuff."

Every wall is adorned with yearly coordinated-outfit mall portraits of their entire blended family and school pictures of Meg, Jessie, and Meg's older brother, Ryan. A ceiling fan hums in the sunken family room. It smells like any other white person's house: a little musty maybe, like the past, and also like Sea Breeze Yankee Candles.

"Sorry I, uh, didn't know it was a pool thing."

"It isn't," Meg laughs. She's wearing baseball sleeves under faded overall shorts, and a White Stripes pin. It is a very good outfit. "Wanna come sit outside?"

"Sure." I present her gift. My mom bought it, as if I'm in first grade or something. It's some lotions from Bath & Body Works that Meg will almost certainly never use.

"Thanks," she says a little uneasily. "Listen, I'm sorry about what my sister said back there—"

"Oh! Don't worry about it!" Her "sorry" is my cue to immediately shake my head and wave it off. Knee-jerk polite black friend.

"She didn't mean anything by it. I just don't want you to be offended."

"Oh yeah, totally. No way."

"Cool." Meg nods, genuinely smiling. "Anyway, I'm glad you're here. James and I are trying to settle an argument."

Out on the patio, James is sitting with Kelly Kline, freshly initiated to varsity cheer, and eternal student council president since eighth grade. (Who could deny her the title? She seriously takes pleasure in planning stuff, in like a scary way. I did a group project with her on *The Outsiders* for eighth-grade English, and she made like a million useless spreadsheets for the whole team.) Kelly is everyone's friend. There's nothing to really hate on her about. She's careful like that.

James and Kelly are sipping from teacups, pinkies out. On the table is a full tea set, doilies and tiny sandwiches and a cupcake stand. Meg's chair is decorated with feather boas, like she's a bride-to-be. Someone's iPod Shuffle deejays; it sounds like the Mountain Goats are playing.

"Help yourself," Meg says, pointing to a pair of empty

16

plastic chairs. I weirdly panic, then sit next to Kelly, start to panic about—*chill*.

I ask about their summers, and they all say "boring" at the same time.

"Yeah, me too."

"Okay, so, Morgan"—James turns to me and returns his cup to its saucer—"yours will be the tie-breaking opinion."

Kelly throws back her dirty-blond curls. "Are we still talking about this? Morgan, ignore them. Did you hear the new Weezer?"

"Kelly, we heard the Weezer, we talked about the Weezer, the Weezer is bad. I'm sorry, but it is just no Green Album and doesn't even begin to touch the Blue Album. Anyway, the question of the day"—he narrows his eyes at Kelly—"which you very rudely did not answer, is: would you rather be raptured before losing your V-card, or do it with any musician living or dead BUT get left behind AND become Kirk Cameron from the *Left Behind* movie."

"Wait, why do I have to be Kirk Cameron? That's so random." I smirk at the absurdity.

"It is! It is ridiculously random, and that is why it is not a legitimate would-you-rather." Meg presses her palms to the table to restore order.

James slurps his tea and shrugs, self-satisfied. "Just to spice things up."

"You guys remind me of *Seinfeld*," Kelly blurts, a pitch too high.

"Which episode?" (I have legitimately seen all of them, so I could coast on this chatter for the entire afternoon if necessary.)

"Um, all of them, kind of."

I snicker because I cannot help myself, and Meg snorts too.

James stands up for no reason. "Guys, let's do something tonight."

"Only in Dreams" winds to its crescendo, the last song on Weezer's Blue Album. The best Weezer, obviously.

"I can't." Kelly is taking stock of some butterfly clips in her tote bag. "I'm going to youth group. You guys should come!"

"Why would we want to go to school when there's still a solid two weeks of summer left?" groans James. "Let's go to the movies."

"Yes!" Meg chirps. "And cheese fries at Denny's!"

I'm mostly quiet, studying them, letting the conversation swirl around me. I'm totally overcome with how difficult it is to just, like, be. In my first therapy session, Susan asked me, "What brings you pleasure?" and I was horrified that I couldn't answer. Writing in my journal? Screaming Bright Eyes lyrics in my bedroom? Bette Davis marathons on Turner Classic Movies? I don't think these are right, healthy answers. I'm too busy trying to level up to survival to even consider pleasure.

Anyway, they can't possibly want me to tag along on their weekend plans.

"Consider it while I visit the loo," James says with a bow, pushing in his chair.

"What are you doing tonight, Morgan?" Kelly scoots in. "Wanna come to youth group?"

18

"Oh, I'm not sure, I might have to go—"

"Oh my gosh, Morgan, I can't believe I've never asked this! Do you and your family have a home church?"

This has to be one of my favorite questions from youth pastor types and other people's moms. The simple script of my Personal Faith Narrative has been delicately crafted over the years to halt a lot of annoying conversations. *I was baptized Catholic as a baby. I accepted Jesus into my heart at the age of five.* And the magic line: *I go to a black church.* That one always shuts them up.

"Oh, awesome. That's great." Kelly doesn't ask for the name. No one ever asks for the name. It's not like they would know it, anyway.

(For as much as I'm made to feel like an outsider because of my race, sometimes I think this is my superpower: watching white people's comfort and cool slide off their faces when I mention anything black. How fast they go from peppy and smug to terrified. I don't know what they're so afraid of.)

I look over at Meg and smile, pressing End on this missionary interrogation. "What movie are you guys gonna see?"

"No clue. James just wants to flirt with this cute guy who works there."

"So," Kelly inches closer to Meg and lowers her voice, as if James will hear from the bathroom inside. "Is James, um, *seriously* gay, or does he just kind of act like it and go along with it?"

"He hasn't admitted to anything, so who knows. He's just an attention whore." She rolls her eyes lovingly.

Kelly laughs, so I chuckle too.

"He's funny," I say, and they nod. It's all very polite.

"I just thought I'd ask because . . . well, you know the Bible is very clear-cut on this issue. And even the law in some states."

As lifelong Christian-school kids, I know this is our party line, the approved and agreed-upon message. But it's Saturday, and I wish Kelly would just turn it off. I didn't grow up believing that gay people are sinners—we even have some in our family. (Of course, as is our way, we never talk about it. My cousin Richard's boyfriend is still referred to as his "friend," and he's been coming to Christmases for seven years.)

I genuinely like Kelly, but this sucks. Like, who put this song on?

"But isn't the Bible all about love?" I interject, startling myself. "You know, basically?"

We've all read the Bible several times during our years at school, memorized huge chunks of it, acted it out, analyzed it. And this is what I really believe about the best parts of that book: that it's a book about love.

(I'm such a nerd that once, sitting with my dad at a black barbershop filled with old black men, I corrected a "biblical scholar," who was getting a haircut, on a Scripture citation. I was like thirteen.)

"Yeah. She's right," Meg says evenly. "I mean, Jesus was friends with prostitutes." She smiles my way, and I get a jolt of confidence.

"Nowadays he would have been pretty radical, actually, if

you think about it," I blurt, sitting up. "He probably would have voted Democrat!"

"Um, I don't think so," Kelly shoots flatly, and purses her lips. Last year in history, I was outed as our class's only Democrat, because "most black people are," according to Mr. K. (Is that true? I have no freaking idea, but it sounds right.) Still, *why the hell did I even go there?*

James steps back onto the patio, humming "Eleanor Rigby."

"What are we talking about?"

Meg smirks. "Well, Morgan here was just providing the blasphemous but highly probable theory that—" (My heart stumbles around on its knees.)

"We were just changing the subject," Kelly says quickly. She turns to me, and her face softens. It looks like pity. Like Sarah McLachlan in those commercials about orphaned puppies.

"No offense, Morgan. I totally respect that your walk with the Lord is different from mine. Plus, I know you're just kidding."

"Totally."

Disappear, I think. Blend in, disappear, disappear, disappear.

Kelly goes on about youth group. Meg sings that Kelly only wants to go to see her *booooyfriend,* Adam. Kelly blushes and is like, "Nuh-uh!"

I check the time on my phone (as I have been doing every four minutes or so since I got here, waiting for a moment to easily exit), and I'm so relieved it's been over an hour.

I "suddenly remember dinner at my aunt's house" and

21

say a lightning round of goodbyes. It isn't smooth: I do that thing where you feel super awkward so you try to flee from the situation but that makes it more awkward. All I can do is fumble my way out of the house and across the lawn, speed-walk down the street to my car.

Driving home, listening to *Ella Fitzgerald & Billie Holiday at Newport,* I'm so enraged with myself that I'm beyond tears. Who can't even handle a simple tea party? What is my problem? (Why can't I blend in with the manicured bushes that line every sidewalk, the Susans grinning as they jog? Will it always feel like this—carrying a secret shame, leaving parties early to cry?)

Cell phone towers blur past my side-view mirrors, dressed up as pine trees among the palms. I grit my teeth listening to Billie's "Lady Sings the Blues." I think I feel my car's engine stall as I take the first left into our gated community.

Maybe I was always supposed to suffer my episodes and "fits." Maybe the heaviness is a test I'm meant to endure, like Job, the actual saddest character in the entire Bible. God just kept making things shitty for poor Job and telling him that it was worth it, that his suffering was good and holy, that it would bring him happiness in the end. As if a vague promise of future relief is any consolation for complete torment.

Then something mysterious happens.

After I pull into the driveway, I see what I've done. Feathers are backlit in the evening dark by headlights, casting shadows of fluttering brownish wisps. I shriek, leap out of the driver's seat, and peer around to the bumper. A carcass. Bloodied, smashed into the grille. Even in its disfigurement, how it's pasted to the front of the car like gum on the bottom of a shoe, I recognize what kind of bird it is.

In eighth-grade Creation Science, we spent an inordinate amount of time deeply studying seven species of birds common to our area. This is a mourning dove, a sad-looking species with a dull sandbox-brown color and a weirdly long neck. I've always been struck by the name.

What is it trying to tell me?

Maybe I'm being paranoid. Maybe Bible stories and chemical imbalance have finally rendered me unable to distinguish fiction from reality. But this pitiful, ruined thing is here for a reason. It reminds me of the white dove that God sent to Noah after the flood, to assure him that everything was okay, that hope and peace were on the horizon. Except, you know, the opposite.

BLACK EMO: HOW TO BE A WALKING SAD-WHITE-WOMAN-FOR-DUMMIES BY MORGAN PARKER

I don't fit. That's it, no big mystery, no trigger that flipped the depressive disorder switch. I'm one of a few token black kids at Vista Christian, another place I hate, because it's like going to high school inside a church inside a PacSun. I'm basically a loner with the wrong taste in everything, the wrong dreams and fears and wardrobe staples. I couldn't be more awkward and incorrect.

Is there a history of mental illness in your family? I mean, probably. We don't talk about it, at least not that way. There's the delusional cousin who brags about braiding Snoop Dogg's hair, the uncle with all the far-fetched government conspiracy theories. These people are referred to as "kinda different" or "crazy." No one has any kind of diagnosis.

Therapy definitely isn't a black thing. It's like emotional stability is the least of our worries. Part of why I'm so ashamed of my depression is that it feels bratty, uncalled-for, a privilege I haven't earned. ("What do you have to cry about?" my parents scream when we fight, 100 percent perplexed.) Being emo is not black. At least I'm pretty sure it's not. My parents call my music "white music." In sixth grade, some boys in my class told me that I "act white," and it stung more than I want to admit. (That was the last time I ate lunch with the black kids.)

I've lost track of how many times I've been told I'm not *really* black, how many times I've been the only black girl at the sleepover, the only black person in the mosh pit, the only black person in the theater for *The Squid and the Whale,* or the only person at all who listens to Sunny Day Real Estate. I get that I'm not like black people on TV, and I don't only listen to rap or dress like any of my cousins, but being unique and depressed doesn't change my skin color. (Why should Modest Mouse or Noah Baumbach films or John Steinbeck be white things, belonging only to white people? Is it wrong that I love them?)

Not that I really know many black people outside of my family. There's another black girl in my class, Stacy Johnson, but she calls herself "mixed." She won't even use the bulky "African American people" that our teachers gingerly pronounce. The same goes for most of the other splotches of color around school—like, if no one says "I'm black" outright, it won't be a thing. A version of passing for kids who grew up in the nineties.

Plus, one of the major tenets of Christian schools, right after gossip and abstinence, is "I don't see color." Everyone acts like there's nothing different about my race, but they're just going by the script. We say the words, but it doesn't really matter who they're for or if we believe them.

Anyway, I was never a very good token, like Lisa Turtle in *Saved by the Bell*, or Gabrielle Union in *10 Things I Hate About You*. I'm too weird. If I was white, I could come across as a knockoff ScarJo in *Ghost World*, or maybe the girl in *Girl, Interrupted*. I might even be cool or cool-adjacent, a manic pixie dream girl that guys go crazy for. But no one gives a shit about the black version of that.

STILL LIFE WITH ANXIETY ATTACK

At the suggestion of Susan and all the books (*Living with Your Depressed Teen*, or whatever), my parents have been aggressively trying to get me to *be active*, even though they learned long ago that I am not big into activities. (Here is a list of activities I endured as a child, my parents always offering a new idea, desperate for one to stick: soccer, softball, ballet, tap, gymnastics, swim team, diving, karate, voice lessons, acting classes, debate, cheerleading, modeling, volleyball. Shame after damn shame.)

The compromise this summer has been an introductory art class at a community college in Grand Terrace. Populated almost entirely by White Moms with gray hair and cargo shorts (two out of eight are named Susan), the class consists of painting freaking watercolor sunsets while Adult Christian Contemporary music bores you to death.

But there is a cute guy. David. He's the only other person in the class who's under forty and not white. And in the parking lot before our very last class, I *finally* talk to him. He comes up to me while I'm sneaking a cigarette and brooding next to my car.

"Hey."

Dark messy curls shape his brown face, almost olive in the sunlight. His hair is an awkward length and frizzy, like he can't decide how long he wants it to be. A worn-out Billabong T-shirt and navy church pants. Like he can't decide on anything.

"Hey."

"Whatcha listening to?"

"Sunny Day Real Estate."

"Oh. Never heard of them."

"Most people haven't."

"What kind of music is it?"

"Um . . . kinda indie emo."

"Oh."

The rest of the strip mall is mostly a ghost town, but I dart my eyes around anyway, as if even the storefront of the frozen-yogurt place is more interesting than talking to him.

He thrusts his hands into his pockets and scuffs his Vans on the pavement, carabiner jingling from his belt buckle.

"Should we go in?"

"K." I smile weakly.

As we walk the few strides to the studio, I try not to let him see me glance over at his jawline, his arm swinging so close to mine. Me interacting with boys is excruciating, just disgrace-ful. I'm always crossing and uncrossing my arms; trying to hide my boobs or tugging at my jeans; trying to simultaneously come off as the ideal girlfriend and one of the guys; forgetting and then remembering my face and the rolls of flesh that make up stumpy, unsexy me.

In class today we're doing still-life drawings with charcoal. The objects for everyone's still life, positioned hurriedly on a card table before us, stare into me, garish and weird. I have arranged a tableau of stuff from my purse: a bubblegum-pink lighter, a bruised apple, the stub of a green crayon, *Dress Your Family in Corduroy and Denim* by David Sedaris.

It's a weird day because it's raining, but it's that humid, almost-steamy summer rain. The dampness awakens something in the stale paints and dried brushes in the classroom. There's a musty fog over everything. A quiet smell. The stillness makes me nervous and self-conscious. The room is a cocoon around me, everything pointed at me. The nineties posters of the color wheel and Matisse cutouts are closing in.

Then this dumb rom-com thing happens: as I reach for an eraser, my shoulder brushes against David's. It's a brief moment, but he turns to me and smiles, the *teeniest* bit of flirtation.

I picture all the boys from my class in the locker rooms before PE, changing into their sweat-stained Vista Eagles T-shirts, naming all the girls they think are hot, then landing on me and: *She's weird.* The nice ones I grew up trading burned CDs with might be gentler: *I could only really see her as a friend* or *She's not really my type.* The message is the same: gross.

And here's the thing: I'm not even sure I think any of them

are cute, with their white-boy freckles and spindly arms. That bland, all-American flatness. But I know I'm supposed to want them, and so I do. Am I immediately out of the running simply because I'm not just like everybody else? (Isn't it weird what gets trapped in your head like a splinter? The little voice you hear so long it sounds like yours?)

In the parking lot, a Camry zooms by blasting Shania Twain's "Man! I Feel Like a Woman!" and a Susan giggles on cue. I can't even muster the fake smile she wants in return.

I try to focus all my attention on my drawing but struggle with the apple's contours. My wrist's movements are totally out of my control. Annoyed, I look at the clock: still fifty minutes left in class.

Slip in my earbuds, attempt to get into a zone. Kim Gordon sings *You can buy some more and more and more and more,* and I smudge and smudge my charcoal lines. Nothing is recognizable. I don't hear David or the White Moms, but I can see them laughing, breathing easily. Go for the book, a straight line, fail. Lick my finger and try to smudge more. Get embarrassed. Clench my chest. *What the fuck am I doing here.* Am maybe going to scream. Can't move. Inhale and gasp for air like I'm in a pool. Eyes pin prick at my body. Abruptly zoom to the door. So awkward. *Am I going to die. Will I pass out.* Crouch on sidewalk, wring hands together.

After a few minutes my mind stops racing, and I come into focus. I'm still breathing like someone in a movie who's going into labor. The rain has stopped, but the world is beginning-of-*Wizard-of-Oz* gray. My butt is wet.

"Heyyy." It's David, singsongy but tender, plopping himself next to me. "You okay?"

"I just need a minute," I manage, probably snapping at him, probably being rude. I'm just so totally unfit for social contact right now.

"You, my dear"—he rubs my back—"are having a panic attack."

"Huh?" I wriggle away, press my flat palm to my chest and neck and inhale deeply. "Yeah," I breathe, glancing at him. "How do you know?"

"My girlfriend gets them sometimes."

Dang. Typical.

I picture her like basically everyone at my school, with a breezy personality and simple needs. Or even like Meg, smart and quirky. Either way, white. Some damn messy bun.

I do the yoga breaths I practiced with Susan: slowly and thoughtfully in through the nose, then out through the mouth with my lips pursed like a whistle. (I can't whistle.) (Or is it in through the mouth and out through the nose? Ugh, I can't even relax right.)

"Er, ex-girlfriend, I guess. I'm still figuring out how to say that, four freaking months later. Ex ex ex ex ex . . ."

He talks to the air above us, head tilted up toward the rolling duvet of gray clouds. "Sorry. Anyway, it will pass. We'll just sit here quietly and wait it out."

"K. You can go back in if you want."

"No way, dude. Wanna talk about it?"

I don't know anything about this guy. How could I possibly know what to tell him, what words to even use? How would I tell anyone, for that matter?

I stare at the small pool of rainwater that swirls around our shoes. And for a second, I just sit and exist. He lets it happen. He seems totally chill.

"I think maybe God smited me." I don't know if I mean it as a joke or as a true confession. Maybe both.

"Oh noooo, dude! A curse upon your house for all generations? Or just a low-key plague of locusts or what?"

"Nice." Of course, it comes off snarkier than I want. What I wish I could do is giggle and tuck my hair behind my ear. "I'm sorry, I just . . ." The empty space between us is so uncomfortable, but I can't think of anything else to say.

I close my eyes. I imagine being anywhere else. I imagine David not seeing me this way, not now or ever. I'm almost mad at him for being here, his hand limply cupping my shoulder.

We sit like this on the curb for thirty minutes, not saying much, every now and then passing movie recommendations between us. He's never seen my favorite, *All About Eve,* and I've never seen his favorite, *Fight Club.*

"Man, you gotta let me know what you think of the ending," he basically squeals.

I know I should feel warmth with David in this moment, maybe even butterflies. I'm grateful for his kindness and I think he's awesome, but it's hard to feel excited about making a new friend, because I can't feel anything. I'm watching it happen, but it isn't happening to me. I'm disconnected from everything outside my head.

The rain starts up again for a minute; we watch it splash down from the awning. I hate this kind of rain, the slanty kind that comes in short, hard bursts. Finally David jumps up and scrunches his face, appraising the wet butt of his pants.

"We should get going before we have to answer to the Moms."

"Oh, you're right." I dart up, damp and light-headed.

"Let me put my number in your phone."

"Huh? Oh yeah, okay." I fish my phone out of the pocket of my *Pretty Girls Make Graves* hoodie (I always wear merch hoodies on rainy days) and hand it over.

"And . . . ," he mumbles as he types briskly. "I'm texting myself. . . ." He hands the phone back to me, grinning.

"Hey, um, thanks, for today, for this."

"Psh, ain't no thing, dude."

He marches off swinging his arms in wide, weightless half-moons.

Settling into my car, I take a deep breath and collect myself. Glance over my CDs and decide on silence. My phone dings as I plop it into the cup holder. Text message from David Santos. David.

<3

Huh.

I try not to smile, but I'm only human.

MARISSA

This is a story about Marissa. Marissa was a pretend friend before she was a real one, back when you were thirteen. It was
convenient—her mom didn't let her watch TV, but yours did;
you could walk to each other's houses; you sat together at your
brothers' Little League games and stayed after to watch the
boys from your class. You lusted over her entitled relationship
to fun. Marissa flirts with the boys and they flirt back. Even her
crush flirts back, which you didn't even know was possible. In
your universe, it isn't.

If you're mad at Marissa, she finds a reason to get mad
at you. She has a way of turning the tables. She commits the
crime, but somehow you end up apologizing, and maybe you
even owe her. The scales of the world tip in Marissa's direction.

Marissa isn't really emo. (She listens to Good Charlotte.)
She's a poser, but the boys don't care. Wanting her makes them
not care about anything else. Marissa tells you you're jealous
that boys like her and not you, and then goes back to painting

her nails silver and watching Mandy Moore in the movie. She tucks a piece of thin long hair behind her ear with a sense of satisfaction and ease that you have never experienced and probably never will. Not in this universe. Everyone you can't be is a Marissa, and you are surrounded by Marissas.

This is a story about you. The night you spill the bottle of Disco Fever polish on the carpet in your bedroom, you feel pitiful. Everything about the moment—those dumb songs in *A Walk to Remember* and Mandy Moore's horrible dumpy cardigans; Marissa's puka shells; the sting you feel and keep feeling—reminds you how pitiful you are. Reminds you of your place.

You're the Laney Boggs in *She's All That*. You spill the nail polish and ruin your carpet. You swallow the words down.

But this is not a story about you. This is a story about me, and I am the hero.

MORGAN PARKER

NOT OTHERWISE SPECIFIED

This morning I am a scientific curiosity on the examination table at Dr. Li's office, a place I've been coming to since I was a kid. Except this time, I'm not getting shots for the new school year. I'm getting pills. Dr. Li already spoke to Susan about my symptoms and official diagnosis: *DSM*-IV 311 Depressive Disorder Not Otherwise Specified. (Go figure, even the *Manual of Mental Disorders* doesn't have a name for me. What a life, defying classification.)

He talked to my parents, too, and they probably explained that they are at the "end of their rope" and "don't know what to do with me." ("Are we bad parents?" they probably asked him, just like they keep asking me. "Is it something we did?" "How can we fix this?" *This,* in case it's not clear, is me, the fucked-up firstborn.)

The nurse gives me a photocopied questionnaire and a golf pencil that's almost too small to use. "Take your time!" she chirps, then slips out of the room, her blond ponytail shimmying.

There are these truly awful illustrations of bunnies and flower gardens filling the white spaces between the text: *Over the past month, have you experienced any of the following problems?*, followed by a list of statements like *I have little interest in my activities* and *I believe other people are generally better than I am.* I know all the right answers because I've already been through this with Susan. I check the same pathetic boxes and wait, hunching and straightening my shoulders and swinging my Vans.

Dr. Li comes in and greets me like always, planting himself on the swivel chair and taking out his ear-inspector thing. He talks fast and moves quickly but nonchalantly. I am always a good kid, an excellent student. I usually breeze through appointments like small chats with distant relatives on Thanksgiving.

"Morgan! How are we doing?"

"Fine."

"That's good, that's good. Open for me?"

I do, and almost wonder if he'll find something in my throat, a depression hair ball or some marking never before seen in the history of medicine. Some proof.

"All right, everything's great. Let's have a look," he says, gesturing for my A+ quiz.

He looks at it on his clipboard sternly and silently for, like, a full minute. Then he flashes me a big, bright fake grin.

"So, Morgan, why don't you tell me what's been going on with you?"

"Um . . . um," I stutter aimlessly. "Well, nothing *happened*. I don't know why I'm . . . feeling kind of low lately."

Dr. Li smiles flatly. "Okay. We'll see if we can get you feeling more like yourself."

(But: *Myself* seems to be the problem.)

He writes me a prescription for a starter dose of Wellbutrin and breaks everything down. Some people, he says, are depressed only once in their lives. Others get depressed sometimes, when they're triggered. And some people just need to be treated for depression all the time. It's just a thing they have that doesn't go away. I'm obviously that one.

If the Wellbutrin doesn't work, we'll try Prozac next, or Lexapro, Dr. Li tells me. (I guess there are all these different types of antidepressants and inhibitors?) There will be months and months of trial and error and maybe some serious side effects. I'm told to watch for anxiety attacks, that if they become regular, I will also be prescribed Xanax. I'm told to look out for extreme fatigue, that if it persists, I'll be prescribed Adderall. I'm picturing myself morphing into a literal medicine cabinet, like the wardrobe from *Beauty and the Beast*.

"So, you're seventeen. Gonna be a junior?" he asks casually, shuffling some papers.

"Yup."

"Do you have a boyfriend?"

"Oh, I told the nurse before that I'm not *sexually active*." I use air quotes and make it a little comedy routine. Doctors never really laugh at your jokes.

"That's not what I asked. Do you have a boyfriend?"

"No." I fold my hands in my lap.

"Hmm." (Does he not believe me?) "Morgan, let me ask you something. You answered that you lost control one time—"

"I didn't plan it. I didn't really want to hurt myself. I just—"

He puts up his hand like a stop sign. I anxiously shift around on the crinkly paper underneath me.

"Was it about a boy?"

My eyes get wide with shock. "No! Nothing like that!"

"It's just that sometimes it's common with teenage girls, you know, to have feelings of rejection or low self-esteem. Maybe you're having trouble fitting in, or you aren't getting attention from boys. . . ."

I shake my head furiously. "No, I mean, it just sucks being alive sometimes. That's literally a fact!" (I seriously can't be the only human in the history of time who acknowledges that existence is not always magnificent.)

"I understand that, I do. Just as long as you know you are a bright and special young woman."

"Okay. No, I know, I do."

Jesus Christ. His whole thing is so corny.

(I don't know what's pissing me off more: how reductive and antifeminist it was to assume that some dumb boy is causing my depression, or how quickly Dr. Li concluded that I'm basically a boyfriend-less loser. If I didn't have low self-esteem before, he definitely made sure I wouldn't go home without it.)

"So, is your brother playing football again this year?"

"Uh, yeah, I think."

"Good, good. You tell him I say hi. And your parents."

I nod. "I will."

"What are you . . . was it the school newspaper you worked on last year?"

"Um, yearbook, yeah. I'm actually editor this year."

"Good to hear it. Well, keep up those grades. Still getting As?"

"Yep, all As."

He stands up to leave and slaps me on the back on his way to the door. "Good girl. See? Life's not so bad."

I forget to smile like I'm supposed to. The door slams shut.

You know those commercials for antidepressants with the little cartoon egg that has a gray cloud hanging over it? Or the ones where a lady gazes sadly through a window at all her friends laughing it up in a park?

The list of possible side effects is always so long that the commercials have to include a gratuitous montage of the formerly sad person grinning like crazy in various locations, finally laughing it up in a park.

This is what I mean—nothing is risk-free. No solution is quite perfect, not drugs or religion or even love. There's always the haunting threat of ending up right back in the dark pit where you started.

That's what I mean about the bird sweater, about all of it. I want be a formerly sad lady finally laughing it up in various locations, totally chill with wearing the bird sweater, delighted by parks and activities. I wish for it like a child makes a birthday wish—seriously, tightly. But what possible side effects am I risking?

Also, wait a minute, where the fuck is my sticker? Are doctors not doing that anymore?

ANOTHER SUNNY DAY I HATE

It's another beautiful day that I hate. Off to my certain hell of Rainbow flip-flops and bouncing messy buns, of flabby, sunburned teacher arms in flowered sundresses from 1995. The same cast of characters, shifted very slightly, like tectonic plates. I'm a different person too.

Malcolm rides icily in the passenger's seat this morning, looking through my CD case like it's a menu for his last meal on earth. When Malcolm and I are friends, we are best friends. Things are fun and spontaneous around the house; we're always joking, or sharing music, or watching a Disney Channel Original Movie we sickeningly know every word to. But I killed that entire vibe.

(One of the things I hated most about the night of my "episode" was the look on my brother's face as he peered from the next room at my breakdown. He looked like he was watching a bullfight. He looked at me like I was a monster, and he hasn't looked at me the same since.)

"What's this?" Malcolm finally holds up a burned CD labeled in fading black marker:

THIS   AL

BUM   IS

PERFECT

My handwriting. It's Neutral Milk Hotel, *In the Aeroplane over the Sea.*

"It's perfect." I grin cheesily. (I make a lot of jokes to myself.)

We don't say anything, just listen to the first song uninterrupted.

"Pretty good. What's the band again?"

"Neutral Milk Hotel. I know—the name makes no sense."

"Cool, maybe I'll check it out."

"Take the CD! I'll burn another copy. Besides," I kid, "you need my whole collection, anyway, before I go to college."

"Okay," he laughs. "I don't know about all that."

Banter! I turn to him and we bust up with the giggles; we temporarily laugh it up. I roll down the windows and turn up the music. A moment of escape. My eighties BMW, Rudy, putts along, boxy and stale-smelling and glorious.

The brisk morning all around you, the perfect soundtrack, a long road, and someone riding shotgun you trust more than yourself: it could be the way a movie starts.

We pull into the parking lot for Vista Christian School and Vista Christian Church, the singular buzzkill. "Alllll right," I exhale as I park between two identical Honda Civics. While Malcolm collects his stinky football pads and almost-empty backpack from the trunk, I glare at the giddy nerds scurrying around all enthused about their Christian education.

Malcolm gives me an ingrained hug goodbye when some buddies howl at him from the entrance, and before he jogs off, we dab each other with goofy smiles, like no one can see us.

"See ya."

"Have a good day, sis."

I made it. September. I know that sounds dramatic, but it's true. I have infiltrated high school once again, and triumphantly, kinda. I count to five and summon every grain of energy in my body, preparing myself for a day of normality. Normality, which I wear like a too-tight hoodie. Maybe I can make it work. All I have to do is pretend. Say my lines. Let the day blur around me.

But now I'm standing before the doors of my unfortunate, awkward reality. I'm not in the mood to pretend to care about God. I am totally not in the mood for all these awful smiles and idiotic people. Hordes of chipper white kids rush past me, reeking of Axe and sickly-sweet Victoria's Secret perfume. I'm flooded with dread at the thought of all the months ahead—all the weird dramas I won't see coming, all the possibility, the rumors and fights, the boys, the shame of PE, the pro-life, the African American History Month, the election stuff, the dances, so many freaking worship songs, not to mention keeping my antidepressants a secret. I won't see any of it coming, just like last year, and I won't be prepared.

"Excuse you!" someone says under their breath. A jab at my elbow sends all the noise of the hallway rushing back to me.

Some senior guys scowl as they push past. I mutter "Sorry" and a voice bellows, "What's up with her outfit? Hey! What are you supposed to be? Are you in a play or something? Hey, you!"

(It's like I'm freaking Ruby Bridges or something. Why is this my existence?)

(By the way, I'm wearing a very good outfit. I usually am. A vintage navy polka-dot shift dress and my high-top canvas Chucks. No one around here has style.)

And, of course, following behind their snickering is Marissa, my old best friend, and Jordan Jacobsen, a generally terrible person who was once a nice-enough kid. Marissa's just grinning at nothing in her little bubble, holding Jordan's stiff, bored arm, wearing some terrible tank top. We notice each other at the same time, and my eyes pretend to dart around.

"Hey," her voice squeaks haltingly.

I wave and grimace back. Suddenly a paw claps at my shoulder and I jump, startled. "Miss Morgan Parker!"

I spin around dramatically. "Hi, Mr. K."

As tall and gray and corny as ever.

"Can I look forward to you torturing me again in class this year? You're in the AP section, right?"

"Yeah . . . second period, I think."

"Bright and early, uh-oh!"

I side-eye back at him. I get the sense he thinks our little rivalry is cute; I do not find it cute. He's super annoying and obsessed with Reaganomics.

"Don't worry—they let me caffeinate in the teachers' lounge now." It's true: I'm terrible without coffee.

45

(All my teachers, so familiar with me and my whole thing, have no idea what to do with me. On the one hand, I'm consistently an excellent student. On the other hand, I'm a pain in the ass, I talk too much, I crack jokes freely and flippantly, I have one of the loudest laughs in America, and I blatantly disavow rules and decorum. The short, little black girl in the weird outfit, who you can hear cackling from all the way across the hall, who will never just do what she's told, will never just smooth down the edges, assimilate better.)

"Lucky me, and in an election year! You must be excited," he says with a Grinch smile. "You're probably loving all this Obama stuff."

"I mean, I can't vote yet." I shift my weight, consider screaming something about my time of the month and flying right back to my car. Instead I say my lines. "But, yes, for the record, I would be voting for the Democratic Party and the first black president of the United States. Like, duh!" Now I'm talking with my hands and everything, doing my shtick.

"Of course! I have to admit it's an interesting election cycle. So get ready!"

Maybe I'm hallucinating: he does some kind of shoulder shimmy, flicks his fingers at me like liver-spotted guns. Ugh.

Looking for my first-period classroom, I try to be anonymous, but it's impossible. There are sixty of us in our class, and we've been together since seventh grade, some of us since pre-K. I forgot how exhausting and repetitive this day would be, with all of the *How was your summer?!* and *Oh my gosh, hi!*

I'm not in the mood to catch up. It takes a lot of energy to fake-smile and lie through your teeth all day.

My first class is Honors American Lit with Mr. Howard, who I had last year for Creative Writing. I pretty much won his heart with all my writings in that class. He's the one who granted me teachers' lounge access—he usually asks me to re-fill his cup, too.

I'm a pain in the ass and all that, but I'm objectively a good student, and I mean well. I care about learning, I love reading, I'm passionate about writing, I don't mind helping explain things to other students, and I genuinely want to be good, de-spite all the ways I don't fit the usual profile. Something I've learned to do, at the very least, is be helpful. So my teachers en-list me for little tasks—grading, photocopying, note-taking—just to keep me busy. The school part of school is basically chill. The problem is that I'm here, and I'm me.

Hungrily, I scan the syllabus during introductions. We're doing poetry first, and I *hate poetry*. Mr. Howard hands out poems about cabins and farm animals by some old white men with beards, Robert Frost and Wally Longlegs or something.

"Twenty minutes of quiet reading while I have my coffee," he explains. "Sorry, did I say *quiet*? I mean completely and ut-terly silent." He laughs at himself, and no one else does.

I shoot up my hand. "Mr. Howard, this is gonna be a weird question."

Someone lets out a sinister snicker and says, "Of course." I don't even turn to look. Whatever—these people don't read.

"Yes, ma'am?" Mr. Howard takes a sip of his coffee from a mug that says *No thank you.* He has a squirrely face—if he were a cartoon, he might be a villain, but in person it kinda makes him look trustworthy.

"Can I sit on the floor while I'm reading? It helps me think."

"Whatever makes you happy."

After the summer I've been through, the least of my worries are the eye rolls spurred by my request, everyone laughing it up at me, the weirdo. Morgan, runner up for Class Clown, tied with the other black girl for Loudest, and sole original owner of the superlative Most Unique (not otherwise specified).

I don't care; now is about getting happy and comfortable, moving forward. I've looked into the face of the end of the world, and guess what? No one from school was there.

PART WHERE I DO NOTHING
SUGGESTED

Another thing that annoys me about this high school inside a PacSun inside a church: glorified Sunday school teachers posing as experts in the scientific method or British literature telling me it's time to "Get Serious," that I need to "Prepare for the Future." Meanwhile I'm like, *Um actually, what I need to do is stop wanting to die.*

Everyone in the junior class is required to meet with the college counselor, Mrs. Martinez. (Last year she was the school nurse. I need explanations.) My appointment Friday morning lasts basically ten minutes—she tells me I should "consider the Christian colleges right here in Southern California!"

Another thing I hate about it here is how almost every classroom is decorated with some version of that poster with the footprints on the beach, which I know is supposed to be inspiring but has always creeped me out. (What is the difference, seriously, between angels and ghosts? Why are we supposed to be afraid of one and cool with the other? And actually, same question goes for heaven and hell.) Mrs. Martinez has one of those posters right behind her desk, and I read the bad poem over and over while she talks.

"A degree from a Christian college isn't the Ivy League," she says like a freaking infomercial, "but it's nothing to sneeze at. You don't have to sacrifice your walk with God for a rigorous education."

I nod. I will be doing none of what she suggests.

When I am spit back into the empty hallways after her little brainwashing session, I take my time meandering to my locker. I *really* want to text David, but I don't know the rules about who's supposed to text who each day. Whatever. I go for it.

Hello please save me I hate it here

(His reply is instant!)

hey
DID
YOU
WATCH
FIGHT
CLUB
YET
????????
LOL
Ok so

I did, OMG! I will never hear the Pixies the same way again!

Was I supposed to understand the ending?

isn't it craaaaazy?!

I have some theories

Heading to bio

Oh cool

Talk later?

I type *Yeah!* Then *Yeah.* Then *Sure sounds good.* Then I just send a *K*.

Down the hall, James and Meg are parked on some benches outside the library. They wave, so I go over and plop myself next to them, as if I have nothing better to do. I sort of don't.

"What's up?"

"We're in 'study hall,'" Meg says, making air quotes and rolling her eyes.

"What are you guys up to for the rest of the day?"

James is picking all the chocolate chips out of a bag of a trail mix. "Isn't there a pep rally?"

I forgot about it because I was planning on faking debilitating menstrual cramps and hiding in the yearbook office. There's no way I can endure, like, three hours of pretending to laugh at our teachers throwing footballs or whatever. "But we should . . . not go to that, right?"

"You mean skip?" Meg looks skeptical. I raise my eyebrows at her, and James joins in with a devilish grin.

"Eh? Eh?" He pokes her shoulder like a little brother, incessant and playful.

She gives him a look, trying not to crack a smile, and sticks her finger in his face. "Okay, but you're driving."

I, straight-A student, well behaved and mostly afraid of hellfire, have never ditched school, so I never realized how easy it would be. There is literally no security at school, just some eternal angelic presence that's supposed to make us feel guilty enough not to do anything wrong.

When we get to the gravel parking lot, I take out a Parliament and light it, because why the hell not.

"Good idea," says James. Then, after selecting a baby-blue Nat Sherman from a silver cigarette case, he gestures at a dirty white truck with a ladder on its roof and some unidentifiable tarp-covered objects in the bed.

"By the way, you guys, I'm driving my dad's work truck. Hope you don't mind the absence of glamour."

"Oh jeez," says Meg. "I *suppose* we can do without glamour just this once."

But it does feel glamorous to escape, to be in charge of ourselves.

Up until now, everything has been commandments: *Don't* have a conniption. *Do* take the SAT practice test seriously. *Do not* question your faith. *Do not* ask questions about politics. *Do* vote Republican. *Do not* have sex before marriage. *Do* smile. *Do* pray.

Junior year feels different. I decided to keep being alive, so I have to decide how to do it.

Now *I'm* picking the music.

JESUS, ETC.

For the record, I don't *not* believe in something. I guess I'll just figure out later what "something" is. If you look at things from the other side, any option seems ludicrous. A magic surfer guy in Birkenstocks; the randomness of gas flickering in the sky; chimps becoming people. (I picture Eve the rapper as Eve from the Bible, holding an unidentifiable fruit in front of her paw-print-tattooed boobs. *Hilarious.* Sign me up for that religion.)

None of these dogmas provide a valid explanation for my life. Nothing can tell me how to just relax about everything.

What *would* happen if I died? What good would it be to know the answer?

(Still, in the middle of the night when I hear a noise that sounds like it could be a trumpet heralding the Rapture, I am terrified, ashamed that I straight-up am not sure what I believe or what I deserve. Where am I going?)

Marissa, my former BFF, was—*is*, I guess—*super* into Jesus.

God's Plan, Jesus-fish earrings, the whole nine. It's kind of beautiful, really, the way she walks a line between dark and light. She loves emo bands and guys who resemble the undead, but she still clutches her cross necklace and sings along in chapel. Kelly's like that too. She really believes.

(I don't sing in chapel.)

(Marissa doesn't really love emo bands. Once again: she likes Good Charlotte.)

Marissa and I used to listen to Christian rock and ska bands that played on Christian radio (between anti-gay and pro-life commercials sponsored by Focus on the Family), sometimes went to their concerts at megachurches. Some of the bands actually had really good music, but the lyrics were creepily passionate and uplifting, to the point where I could never all-the-way enjoy it. Like, Audio Adrenaline has a song that sounds like a Sublime song, or Elvis or something, but they're chanting *Do you know where you're gonna go?* and describing various unexpected ways you might die at any minute (run over by a Mack truck; or suddenly, while "nappin' in your easy chair"). *Do you know where you're gonna go? Straight to heaven,* the song asks, or *down the hole?* I get that dumb song stuck in my head all the time. It's weird that something that other people celebrate, find comfort in, can make me so traumatized and fearful.

I've been freaking out about sins and consequences since my very first day of pre-K at Vista Christian Elementary. School has always been a land of parables and warnings: felt boards depicting scenes of Jesus and his disciples. Moses and the Red Sea constructed with macaroni and painted lima beans. Always there is a snake. A staff becoming a snake, or a snake appearing in the trees, whispering temptation. I almost expected to find snakes slithering through lines of second graders at lunch, coiled under end tables in the church foyer, sticking their tongues out of my PE locker. Just waiting to catch me failing to be perfect.

If you didn't grow up in the American suburbs, or in any place that's designed to be a model of what is proper and wholesome and happy, then you might not understand what living here can do to a person like me, a person who doesn't want to go in the straight line of a paved and lighted path.

I could quote dozens of Bible verses about truth, about Christ as the Truth, the only Way, the Light. We nod and *Amen*. We say we love the truth. Maybe, sometimes, that's real.

But not everything true is good. So we keep it behind a wall, or covered with a table runner, or drenched in potpourri, or shelved away in an elaborate storage system from the Container Store. We pretend there's no elephant galloping around the room (or whatever elephants do), and we don't ask too many questions or cause any scenes.

It never really gets cold in Southern California, which makes our little corner of churches and expensive skate shoes feel like its own planet without seasons, where nothing ever dies and nothing ever gets dark. But if you start to see the suburbs differently, if you start to see the rules differently, you start to see yourself differently. You could be unborn again. You could start a new story.

Here is the church, here is the steeple, here is the church and the church and the church, all of these Good People. Imagine what living in a place like this could do to a person like me.

THE DIFFERENCE BETWEEN
ME AND THEM

Meg, James, and I are packed into the truck's bench seat, ladders clanging loudly on its roof. We drive aimlessly. Bicker about whether to listen to classic rock radio or the new Wolf Parade or the new Death Cab. Compare class schedules. Eventually we decide to go to a café downtown, on the ground floor of an abandoned theater. I order a black coffee, while James and Meg both get large teas. Meg takes two packs of Splenda in hers; James, milk, "like the English." I don't know where he gets this stuff.

James's family is notoriously kooky and blue collar—his dad is always covered in car grease; his mom always says way too much when anyone asks "how are you"—and it's kind of great. I know I'm supposed to find them weird, but they've always been nice and funny in our brief interactions over the years. Meanwhile, James loves to dress up for no reason, and at other times is completely unkempt. He describes himself as "socially liberal and fiscally conservative." (I want to say, *I'm*

not sure the conservatives really have your best interests in mind, bro.
But I just think conservatives are mean.) He's out of place but
perfectly easygoing and adaptable, kind of like his own vision
board. I get it.

Walking along Main Street, we wander in and out of comic
book shops, antique stores. Meg and I give bratty grins to
judgmental elderly people and giggle at James's theatrics. He's
such a great actor and, separately, a fantastically dramatic person. We both do the school play every year, but it's cool hanging out with him outside of rehearsals; we don't get to talk
much there because he's like, a lead, and I always play Rosa
Parks. (Not *literally*—I only played Actual Rosa Parks once—
but same sort of thing, just sit there quietly. Even my speaking
roles seem like nonspeaking roles. Somehow my costume is
always a woolen skirt suit.)

In the antiques store, poring over a stack of postcards with
Meg, I'm surprised how natural it is, even though we haven't
hung out since elementary school. It's like we're the same
shade of awkward.

"Ugh." I land on a portrait of Ronald Reagan. "We should
get this for Mr. K."

Meg titters, "Oh my gosh, he would probably frame it and
put it next to the one of Bushy."

"He would probably make us pledge allegiance!" I shiver,
tossing the cards down. "I am so glad we have that class together."

"Seriously." She squeezes my shoulder on our way out
of the store. A little bell jingles at the door. Meg and I raise

eyebrows at each other before sliding on our shades. Mine are big and round with white frames. Her lime Ray-Bans match the dinosaur on her shirt.

"How is this place still open?" I wonder out loud as we pass the scrapbook store, Hearts 'N' Crafts. "Jesus Christ. How many scrapbooks can people make?"

Meg snorts and joins me at the storefront window, where I'm gawking at rows and rows of stickers and puffy paint.

"Isn't that . . ." Meg squints at two blond women with short haircuts who are conferring about cardstock. "Kelly's mom?"

"Oh dang." I duck.

James wordlessly waves us over to a bookstore a few doors down, and Meg and I rush in, flustered, and collect ourselves. My heart pumps like I just ran laps in PE. (I could never be an effective outlaw—I'm way too anxious, out of shape, and perpetually spooked.)

We all float to different areas in the otherwise-empty store, which has some books but also CDs, fancy Bible covers, Precious Moments figurines. I glance over my shoulder at the dude behind the register, who's wearing a high-collared white shirt and too-long khaki shorts, and I'm disturbed to see him looking right back at me, not even trying to disguise his staring. Suddenly he abandons his post behind the counter to lurk at a display on my left. I feel his hovering like needle-pricks.

Meg and James are completely out of his view—they could be bolting out the door with armfuls of cross necklaces, for all he knows. I try to shake his suspicion, scrunch my eyebrows and begin purposefully flipping through books like I care. One spine in particular catches my eye: *The Negro and the Curse of Ham*.

Everything happens quickly: James shrieks, something topples to the ground; lurker guy darts over to them; Meg mumbling "accident" and "we'll fix it"; I get a rush of *screw it*, snatch up the book, and drop it into the abyss of my tote bag; I slyly exit the store. Truancy *and* theft. So punk.

Out on the sidewalk I sneak a look at the book's cover: in the background are a bunch of Noah-looking bearded dudes wearing robes and holding staffs, and in the foreground is a slave-looking guy in a loincloth and shackles. (Maybe this explains why I feel so doomed. Or at least why that dude was staring at me the way he was.)

Meg and James burst through the doorway, looking guilty and stifling laughs.

"Yo, what happened?"

James raises his hand as an admission of guilt. "I got a *little* too engrossed reading about Mormon underwear."

Meg doubles over cackling.

"Whoa, wait. What?" I ask, wide-eyed. "That was a Mormon bookstore?"

"Of course! You could tell because it was so creepy and clean," James explains, turning up his nose.

"What are they all about?"

"I think they're basically like Protestants but more racist?"

"Makes sense."

"I could be wrong, but who cares," trails James. He's already on the move, strides ahead of us, headed toward a wide alley. He makes a sudden turn into the little street, sidestepping a gutter.

Fatigue settles into my shoulders, and I start tallying up ideas for getting out of the situation, going home, shutting down, curling up. This is kind of a lot for me, the most socializing I've done in a while.

Meg halts. "Where are we going?"

"Don't worry about it. I know a place," James says coolly.

Sashaying is the only way to describe how he is moving. I've never seen him so comfortable. I feel special witnessing it.

"I just want to get an *horchata*." (Horrible accent.)

"You are ridiculous," Meg snorts matter-of-factly.

We follow, because what else can we do? He could be leading us into an underground cult situation, and we would go. Anything new is by default the most exciting thing that has ever happened to us.

"I'll wait outside while this whole situation plays out," I say, flicking my lighter to a cigarette.

"Me too," Meg says quickly, and James disappears into a taco shop. "I don't smoke, but I like the smell."

She squats, leaning back against the stucco, and I join her. What business do I have being pissed that someone wants to be near me?

"You know, I don't even really want this," I admit, and stomp out the cigarette after only two puffs.

We sit and exhale. She picks studiously at a fingernail bed. "Good call on skipping the pep rally. I'm so glad we didn't have to sit through one of Pastor Tyler's virginity lectures."

"Yes!" I gasp. "Some dumb sports metaphor about defending the goalposts or whatever. Thanks for being deviants with me. I know I could have just hung out in the yearbook room but . . ."

"Oh, this is way better."

"Yeah, I think I needed this." I squint up at the fluffy clouds and the relentlessly blue sky.

"I kinda thought you'd be into all that stuff because of Marissa. . . ." She sneaks a sideways glance at me; I shrug back knowingly.

"Psh," I say, like I'm totally over it. "Not since she ditched me for Jordan Jacobsen."

"Gross! When did that happen?"

"Oh, just on the very last day of school."

"Yikes. That really sucks. I'm sorry, dude." She presses her shoulder into mine, and I take a deep breath.

"You know, it does, but it's actually okay. I'm ready for something new, anyway. And I don't want a friend who's just gonna disappear over some douchebag."

"Yeah! Over some asshole! Who does that?"

I just shake my head. I can't look at her, because I'll fall apart, but I want to reach out and grab her hand and hang on. I want her quiet confidence, her self-determination. Like all other freaks, my mantra is *I don't care what people think.* But like most other freaks, I care desperately about what people think, how they see me, what makes my existence so different from theirs.

The restaurant door flings open with the sound of accordions and James bellowing "Gracias!"

"I have returned!" He poses, and we giggle despite rolling our eyes at him, pull ourselves up from the ground. "Ready?"

I give him a salute.

"Hey—" I'm suddenly enveloped in a loose, bony hug from Meg. It almost confuses me. "At least you have us now."

That's one thing I've always liked about Meg. She actually doesn't care what people think about her quirks or bluntness or ridiculousness. At least not enough to hide herself. You can't help but respect her.

What I decide to do next is get out of my own way. Hazy with exhaustion and hope, I link arms with them, James slurping loudly on his *horchata*.

"Yeah." I nod. "At least there's us."

THE PROMISE RING

Chapel is on Wednesday. That's the way it's been since kindergarten, and that's the way it will always be. It's part of the unspoken order of Christian schools. Without thinking we bow our heads. Without thinking we recite verses in weird dialects—*thou* and *whosoever* and *begotten*. We pledge allegiance to the Christian flag. And first thing on Wednesday mornings, we report dutifully to the auditorium, otherwise known as the gym.

I slide into a folding chair next to Meg in the back row and prepare to zone out. Later, during opening prayer, James takes the end seat next to me. Jenn Hanson leads worship today, like she has since freshman year, singing a version of Beyoncé's "Halo" with *Jesus* subbed in for *baby*. Adam accompanies her on the acoustic guitar as usual, his checkered Vans dangling as he perches on a stool, smiling with his eyes closed while he sings. Then Mr. K gives us a spiel about modesty, briefly citing something from Psalms but mostly making a long, involved case against short skirts.

(The Hot Girls uniform is short jean skirts, Abercrombie sweatshirts, and Rainbow flip-flops. Flip-flops even when it rains. After first period, they're always caught and given a lecture about Honoring God with Your Body, along with a pair of baggy gym shorts. If someone is wearing gym shorts, they are a Hot Girl, their thongs peeking out of the elastic waistband. It's almost better (hotter?), a badge of sexy badness. Marissa started wearing those ridiculous thongs last year, and I guess that's pretty much how I knew we were doomed.)

James is dozing; his hair falls down into his face, and he lurches his head up with a snoring noise. Meg is drawing pictures of dinosaurs in the margins of her Spanish homework, completed early and perfectly. I'm working on an assignment from Susan. *Make a list of things you like about yourself.*

1. *Good outfits!! Thrift store queen*
2. *Hilarious sometimes.*
3. *I get good grades.*

"I'd like to read from Deuteronomy," Pastor Tyler says soberly under a spotlight onstage, and hundreds of vellum Teen Bible pages flap their wings.

(I really don't like this guy. He says "rock on" all the time. Youth pastors have such a look. His hair annoys me.)

"However, if you do not obey the Lord your God and do not carefully follow all his commands and decrees I am

giving you today, all these curses will come on you and
overtake you:

You will be cursed in the city and cursed in the
country.

Your basket and your kneading trough will be cursed.

The fruit of your womb will be cursed, and the crops
of your land, and the calves of your herds and the lambs of
your flocks.

You will be cursed when you come in and cursed
when you go out.

The Lord will send on you curses, confusion, and
rebuke in everything you put your hand to, until you are
destroyed and come to sudden ruin because of the evil
you have done in forsaking him."

Damn. Whoa, what? (Also, what is a kneading trough?) The Lord is going in. This is why I haven't had the balls to read *The Negro and the Curse of Ham.* I already feel Pastor Tyler's words needling into me like a direct address. One word in particular: *overtake. All these curses will come on you and overtake you.* That's how my depression feels.

I get that this is supposed to be a back-to-school "make good choices" sermon, but it feels more aggressive than that. It's a reminder that some people are better—it is easy for them to walk in the light, follow the rules; it's their instinct to obey, to stay in line. The rest of us deserve every curse that falls on us, all the hardship we shovel through.

Suddenly something makes me jump in my seat, and I shiver. Turns out it's just my phone buzzing in my lap: a text. I don't recognize the number.

Two rows behind you.

Slowly I turn my head and scan the crowd. Immediately I spot annoying Tim McCloud, smirking in a too-big button down, and give him the evil eye. Ugh.

I text David instead. He says he's bored in English, talking about a David Foster Wallace story. Of course, I seethe with jealousy at his normal, real-world education.

We just watched the snl skit from this week.
Did you see it? With Tina Fay?
Oh awesome
*Fey
yeah, I CAN SEE RUSSIA FROM MY HOUSE!
So good! I can't believe Sarah Palin is real.
Yes!!!
I know she is truly unbelievable.

(Someone brought up Tina Fey's impression of Sarah Palin in AP Gov yesterday, and Mr. K literally put his hand over his heart. As we were leaving class, Jenn Hanson cornered me surreptitiously and whispered, "I think I might be a Democrat, can you help me?" as if it were a wasting disease or substance addiction.)

The spotlight on Pastor Tyler dims as he bows his head for closing prayer.

Father God these teens are in danger every day. They are fighting a war. Father I just pray that you give them the strength and courage and discipline to be your soldiers in the face of temptation. I pray they do not give in to earthly desires. Father God I pray this in your Son Jesus's precious name. Amen.

We repeat in unison, well rehearsed: *Amen.* The room comes to.

On my way to the yearbook room I run into Class President Kelly Kline at the center of a blindingly pink and bubbly cluster of girls from our class. I nod "Hey," and Jenn squeals, grabbing at me, and pulls reluctant, emo me into the fold.

"Look!" Her blue eyes pierce with delight. "Adam gave Kelly a promise ring!"

"What?"

"A promise ring."

Kelly extends her left hand and I see it, thin and gold on her ring finger.

"I don't get it. What does it mean?"

She lowers her voice, and seemingly her whole body. "You know," she whispers. "Don't have sex before marriage."

"What?" Stacy Johnson squeaks in her valley girl pitch.

Kelly spits when she repeats, exasperated, "Don't have sex before marriage!"

I cover my mouth as a laugh escapes. "Sorry." I bow.

(Everyone is so obsessed with virginity—the teachers bring it up multiple times a day. Sex, I mean. "Resisting urges." There's a whole lot of "saving yourself" and "save room for Jesus." What's wrong with having urges? You'd have to tighten all of your muscles and squeeze your eyes shut for the rest of your life to resist sinning. How can that be the good life?)

"So," I clear my throat, "does this mean you're supposed to get married? To each other?"

Kelly enacts the cartoon definition of swooning. Like, it's disgusting how stoked she is to leap gleefully into a sexless marriage with Adam; to give up on any life that isn't this one we're standing in right now.

"They don't always mean you're getting married," Jenn turns to me. "It's more of a promise to yourself. My dad gave mine to me, actually."

"Wow." I nod at the silver band on her hand, dotted with one ruby gemstone. I spread my hand out before me, too, inexplicably. Obviously, it is bare. "That's nice."

The Promise Ring is also the name of an American indie-rock band from the mid-nineties, whose iconic album *Nothing Feels Good* is one of *the* quintessential emo records, but I don't say anything about that stuff because no one cares.

At the end of the week, I'm exhausted. When I'm at school or in public, there's a little drill sergeant in my head asking, *What should you be doing?* I'm hyper-vigilant like a superspy, constantly nervous about whether or not I'm blending in, whether or not I'm being too me and not enough them.

At home, I wish I were invisible. I wish my family didn't see me as a massive cloud of gloom and difficulty hanging over every room, every daily routine. I wish I felt nothing, but I'm on fire with anger and discomfort and a whiny pitiful temper. I keep to myself, and I hope my family knows that my silence means *I'm sorry.* Means *Forgive me.*

This is my curse. (This, and Tim McCloud's creepy leers, and Marissa attached at the hip to Jordan Jacobsen, reveling in her dumb new life. This and the unrelenting sun.)

Over the weekend, waiting for a torrent of Interpol's *Turn On the Bright Lights* to download, I flip lazily around *The Negro and the Curse of Ham,* which is indeed an independently published text promoting the beliefs of the Church of Latter-Day Saints.

Could there really be a link between blackness and sin? The whole idea is offensive, but it still creeps me out, because as long as even one person believes it, there is a *sliver* of justification for how I feel. A reason for my pain, according to someone else.

One of my pet peeves is questions that aren't really questions, questions that inherently imply an answer. So, like, "Are black people cursed with dark skin and slavery?" It's a question that works kind of like a jingle; it gets stuck in your head until the only answer is yes. Apparently, according to this particular book, Noah's son Ham, whose name means "dark," was cursed by Noah to become "a servant of servants." The story goes that Ham's descendants became the "negro" race. Hence, slavery. Something like that.

Like we deserve whatever curses fall on our heads. Like we never stood a chance from the very beginning.

TIM

Tim is just a guy, basically. A stocky know-it-all from Mock Trial.

It was all planned out over instant messages, our "casual hookup" last spring. His idea.

I am a curious person and studious, and I approached giving him a blowjob as such. I let him put his pale hand under my Joy Division T-shirt. At first it was gross, then it was exciting, then it was boring.

I guess this is a story about how I ended up in the orange groves in the backseat of Tim McCloud's car in the first place.

He said I was the cutest black girl he's ever seen.

The rows and rows of orange groves, how you can almost taste the zest, how something so simply wonderful and bright can always be growing in spite of you—that's something I like about it here.

THE YELLOW NOTEBOOK

Kelly Kline may or may not have "kind of" had sex, promise ring be damned, and now she's convinced she's pregnant. She confesses her sin to Meg and me while we're standing casually by the lockers waiting for the bell before AP Biology, freshly paper bag–covered textbooks cradled close to our chests. "Last Thursday," she lowers her head in shame.

Meg gracelessly stuffs a fistful of blueberry muffin into her mouth. "Dude, it's only Tuesday."

"What about the promise ring?" I realize. "Didn't he *just* give that to you last week?" Maybe it had been like an invitation, a justification. A virginity loophole, like blowjobs.

"I know!" she shrieks, darting her eyes around. "And now my period is a day late!"

"Wait, hold on," I ask, certain that Sunday School has taught her nothing. "What do you mean, 'kind of'?"

What she describes is somewhere between second and third base. I roll my eyes.

"Well, first of all, I'm pretty sure that's not how pregnancy works. Or sex, even."

Kelly Kline is a sucker. She can be cool and fun, but she is also ridiculous. She's been talking about her wedding since middle school. While Meg, James, and I sit sulking and stage-whispering in the back of the auditorium during chapel, she's right up front singing all of the worship songs, gazing up at Adam spot-lit on stage singing with his eyes closed, like he's the Evangelical Dashboard Confessional.

I wish I could say I'm surprised. But I could definitely see her falling for the whole sensitive prayer-group-leader thing. Feeling the spirit.

"You know what to do," I say over the bell. "Talk later?"

She nods dutifully.

I reach into my locker and pull out a yellow spiral notebook. It's slim and bent. Spelled out in Sharpie on the cover, and positioned next to a smiley face sticker, is the title: *Love Lives, Rarr!* ☺ Names of approved authors are documented in a small column on the left-hand side of the cover: *Meg + Kelly*, and *+ James + Morgan*. I present it to Kelly in my open palms, an offering, an invitation for communion.

Like everyone else, we've been writing tons of notes since school started. For the most part, they're standard issue: Jordan looks cute today (James); I can't believe Mr. K told me to be quiet AGAIN in Government (me); I just discovered this band The Clash, they're so punk (Kelly); Where should we go for lunch (Meg)? Notes (and co-notes and group notes) can be literally anything—a list of Friday night ideas; someone's weekend summary; a few random pleasantries on a page Meg used to practice drawing hearts; *Are you mad at me?* on the back of a someone's Bible homework.

The Yellow Notebook is in a league completely apart from that stuff—it is absolutely reserved for discussion of honest-to-god crushes and significant romantic developments related to said crushes. The Yellow Notebook was founded with a mission statement. It's a piece of literature, a living archive, in the spirit of all the rom-coms we say we hate, the spirit of a Jane Austen novel. It exists to celebrate the unfolding of the story of love. Sagas. Confessions. Wishes. Questions.

Kelly's been dating Adam since their youth group went on a mission trip to Mexico the summer after freshman year, and he's super boring, so she doesn't have a lot to say. What with the promise ring and all. But that's just too bad for her.

(Last week, when she tried to slip in some comments about a *Gilmore Girls* episode, I immediately wrote, in the margins, "The Yellow Notebook is not the place for *Gilmore Girls* gossip. Write a separate note for that crap." She wrote, *I'm sorry! I promise not to do it again, Morgan.* Then she proceeded to write a separate note for the *Gilmore Girls* gossip. I don't watch the show.)

The Yellow Notebook—and romance—is strictly business, and serious.

Kelly basically kidnaps Meg and me from the yearbook room at lunchtime, forehead dotted with sweat, backpack sagging off her tiny frame. She's, like, waiting at the door.

"Lunch?" she begs.

I sigh and nod. "Yeah, okay."

Meg blurts out a condition. "We're getting Del Taco."

Kelly has clearly committed to this whole drama. Instead of asking us to lend her money, like she often does, she demands we pay for her lunch because she's "eating for two." I'm not letting this go any further.

The whole drive to Del Taco, Kelly worries out loud. I put on MGMT.

Meg groans. "Oh my Lord, you are not pregnant, Kelly! There's nothing to freak out about."

"My period was supposed to come two whole days ago, and it's pretty much always on time I think."

"Just chill," Meg replies. "Tacos will cure all."

"Seriously, Kelly," I say casually. "Sometimes my period is five days early. Sometimes it's a full week late. I don't know. Periods are weird! I used to throw up every month when I got mine."

Kelly shoots me a quizzical look and laughs, like she's not sure why she's laughing.

Meg yawns, puts on her knockoff Ray-Bans. "Great. Let's drop it and have fun being fatties. I'm having a chicken burrito."

"Hello ma'am welcome to Del Taco can I take your order?"

I have to maneuver my torso halfway out of Rudy to get close enough to the little drive-thru speaker because I'm so low to the ground, and top-heavy. It is no easy feat to get my boobs over the car window.

(By the way, that's yet another insecurity: my boobs came

way too soon. In fourth grade, just a year before my period. I leveled up from a training bra with lightning speed, traded it in for a wide-strapped monstrosity that was impossible to hide under spaghetti straps, which was what all the cool girls wore, with Limited Too roll-on glitter applied to their flat chests. Nothing has ever been easy for me.)

(My period also had impeccable timing, announcing itself on white board shorts during a class field trip to the water park.)

"Anyway, you're not pregnant. Just take a test if you're worried," I say, grabbing our bag of deluxe chili cheese fries, chicken burritos, and a bunch of tacos from a pimply middle-aged man.

Meg squeals a little. "I cannot believe you actually had sex! What about your chastity ring?"

"Yeah!" I gasp. "Didn't you just get it?"

I'm trying my best not to laugh because I know it's not funny that Kelly is completely riddled with guilt and despair. I get it, but also, I don't. What's the big deal?

"We were—we still are—saving ourselves for each other. But then he came over after church, and my mom wasn't home, and we just got caught up in the heat of the moment. It didn't feel wrong. We're in love."

I just shake my head noiselessly as we head back to school. Meg sings "Mr. Roboto" to herself.

"Hey you guys? No one can know about this. And not just the pregnancy scare. No one can know that I'm immoral."

"Oh, come on! You are super good at following the Bible. You just have a boyfriend you *looooove*!" I tease, trying to lighten the mood before she starts throwing verses at us.

"Yeah we need to know more," Meg raises her eyebrows. "You better be writing details in the Notebook."

"Do you really think I should take a pregnancy test?"

"Yes, absolutely, without a doubt. Then you can just move on."

"Will you go with me? After school? Please?" That baby voice she uses for casual manipulation.

I look into the rearview at Meg—we had plans to do homework at my house—and she rolls her eyes, giving the go ahead.

"Sure, okay."

Meg and I are anxious to get out of the car as soon as we park. There's just enough time before lunch is over to eat our Del Taco in peace on the benches by Mr. Howard's room.

"Okay, meet us here after your last class," Meg commands.

"Got it. One more thing, guys?"

"What." We don't even turn around.

"I still don't have any cash. You know, for the thing?"

"I know," I shout back. Obviously, what I'm doing today is paying for a virgin's pregnancy test, because this is my life.

"Oh, this is fan-*tastic*," Meg says to me, giddy under her breath. "Did she really use the phrase 'eating for two'?"

I didn't want to say anything because I didn't want you guys to think I'm a whore. He didn't cum, he just put it in for a minute. But we didn't use a condom. Anyway, I'm pretty much still a virgin under <u>*technicalities.*</u> *And yes, we're getting married and we're madly in love.*

78

Somehow after school we—rather, I—manage to scrape money together to buy a home pregnancy test. The plan is to pile into my car and head to my house where we can put the invented crisis to rest over a couple of iced teas.

We go to the Thrifty's between Waldenbooks and Honey Baked Ham. Since I'm still a virgin (not counting blowjobs) and stranded at Vista without Sex Ed, I know nothing about pregnancy tests—which one is best, or whatever. Meg and I linger dumbfounded in the aisle full of brand labels. Kelly waits at a counter for ice cream. (In her defense, they do have amazingly good mint chip, but I'm still baffled at the distribution of efforts among us.)

I text David.

Today is out of control.
What's up?
Just cursed. I can't believe my life. You?
Eating chips.
Amazing.
Sorry ur smited. Will new music help?
YES
Check ur email girlie. And clear your calendar on Saturday. We have a mission.

"Well," I hang an arm around Meg and hold up the first box I see. "Should we just get this one? I think I've seen it on a commercial."

...

My parents aren't home, and Malcolm is still at JV football practice, but for whatever reason the three of us still guiltily dart up the stairs to my room when we get to my house. When she isn't mouthing "oh my god" and "WTF" to me, Meg's being extra motherly with Kelly, super responsible, which is great because I can't stop thinking about David, and I really just want to gush and wonder about him.

Meg slowly reads every instruction on the pink and white package before handing it over to Kelly and sending her to the bathroom. She walks out silently, eyes focused soberly on the carpet, and closes the door to my room behind her.

"This is completely ridiculous," I say to Meg, and she laughs, taking a glug of her Arizona Iced Tea. Kelly is an absolute wreck a few feet away, but it's hard to be sympathetic when I know that no real crises exist in her world—her world makes sure of it. Also, I know what sex is.

Kelly isn't like me. I want the truth, even at my own risk. The coals of hatred I harbor for my town, my school—ugh, even the very ideas of babies and marriage and church and sidewalks—are really simmering, turning golden brown on each side like chicken skin, but I still live here. I don't know why I humor Kelly, but it feels important. She needs rules, and right and wrong, and guilt. Who am I to pull the comfortable rug from under Kelly's feet, or anyone's? She's happy, and that's more than I can say for myself.

Because this is not a Bible story, Kelly's test is negative. We allow her to put on a show of relief before Meg moves our lives along: "Now can we talk about boys?"

"Ooh!" I jump up, remembering. "Let's see what music David sent."

"Da-vid," Meg teases, and I feel myself blush brown.

"It's not like that!" I connect my laptop to my little portable speakers and pull up David's email. Kelly and Meg giggle and make faces behind my back. The subject line is *love lockdown.* "Oh, it's the new Kanye West. I haven't heard it."

"Put it on," says Meg. "Kelly?"

"Kelly doesn't really like rap, right? We don't have to if you don't wanna."

"No, I'm, uh, down! I like Kanye West I think."

Kelly is hilarious. "K."

I join them back on the floor, knee to knee on our little island of school supplies and massive cans of tea, cell phones and ponytail holders. Meg starts pulling books and binders out of her bag and we all strategize our various homework assignments or whatever, a little getting-stuff-done montage, scored by David Santos and Kanye West.

After a while I blurt, "We don't have to keep listening to this," because I am not enjoying this album at all.

···

KELLY ISN'T PREGNANT so I'm gonna talk about David and his stubble

You guys, our lives are so ironic! When I talked to Adam he was happy and relieved. But he felt embarrassed that I told you guys that his penis was big and that doing it was difficult.

I still haven't thrown away the test. It's in my car, and I don't know what to do with it!

James writes:

Congrats Kelly. Use condoms!!!! :)

Meg writes:

UM, THROW AWAY YOUR TRASH

This is the beginning of the end with Kelly, as far as I'm concerned. The thing about a Kelly is they will always be fine. They want whatever they already have. I want that other thing, whatever it is.

MAKE A LIST OF THINGS
YOU HATE ABOUT YOURSELF

It's getting a little bit better. Like I'm not bursting into tears every day, but every once in a while, something totally random—forgetting to roll up my car window, the question *How are you*—sends me into a whole spiral thing, like: *I'm worthless, I'm ugly, I'm weird, no one likes me, no one understands me, what is the point of all this.*

At therapy this week, I told Susan I wish I could be more like other girls. Marissas and Kellys and Jennifers and Ashleys. They never seem to worry about more than the usual high school stuff. Surface-level stuff, worries that will eventually go away. They've always been like that; their mothers are like that. They won't change. They could never carry what I do.

I really just want to be one of those wispy-haired, flat-chested girls from the dELiA*s catalogue who probably never poops or aches, doesn't have to tug and twist at clothes to fit right. (Having my boobs just means I can't wear basically any dress from

Urban Outfitters. It's all T-shirts from Goodwill for me, my too-heavy, too-adult boobs stretching out the cotton in front.)

"What do you think is the difference between you and them?" Susan asked. (Being a psychiatrist looks pretty easy to me; it's just asking hella trick questions.) "How are your struggles different?"

"Well, I guess I think I must deserve it."

It wasn't the right answer, I could tell.

STRANGE, FRUIT

Saturday begins like a Rilo Kiley song, twinkling and sun-bathed. The world around me is full of promise and faith. When I wake up to the sound of a lawn mower and feel my body, I'm an interruption, a pock ruining the whole scene. Out in the perfectly content cul-de-sac, my dad is cutting the grass at the same time as the neighbor dad. My dad and the Smith dad discuss types of fences and gossip about other people on the block. Boring stuff. The neighbor dad gives my dad advice on how to trim the ivy around our doorway. I rub my eyes and breathe before swinging myself from the bed. I can do this.

I really hope my dad doesn't trim the ivy, no matter how good it is for the house or the plant. I want to keep something growing wild around my window, almost creeping in through the sill to choke me. Or rescue me.

Downstairs, I go straight for the coffee pot. Dad's now on the couch slurping cut fruit from a paper plate, Nike T-shirt soaked with sweat, socks and tennis shoes in a little pile on the carpet next to him. I wonder if he went to an early morning spin class on his way home from the fire station.

"Hey," I mutter sleepily, feeling awkward for no reason. I try to be careful with my family. I understand that over the past few months, I have inadvertently put them through hell.

"Hey, Morgan, have some of that fruit salad. The honeydew is bitchin'. Super sweet."

"Oh, nice. I'm fine for now. I'll have some later, though."

I take my mug into the family room and fold my legs underneath me on the other side of the sectional. He smiles at me with his mouth closed, jiggling one of his legs, an annoying habit. When I make a face at them he says, "Sorry." We don't know how to be, with each other.

(My dad and I could not be more different. When he's at home, and not at the fire station, we don't talk much. He used to be home more, when Malcolm and I were little, and Mom worked full time. He drove on all our field trips, the lone dad among all the moms. He took us to Baskin-Robbins after school, our little routine—Gold Medal Ribbon for Dad, Rainbow Sherbet for Malcolm, Mint Chocolate Chip for me. Now Mom stays home, and Dad takes all the overtime he can. Last year he worked on Thanksgiving, and we went to the fire station to eat store-bought pumpkin pie with all the other guys on duty and their families.)

(I'm pretty sure my dad hoped his first child would be a boy, or at least a different kind of girl. *Kelsey* was the other frontrunner for my name. I can't imagine being that girl.)

"How'd you sleep?" He sucks at his teeth, some lingering piece of citrus or pineapple.

"Pretty good I guess. You? Were you on calls all night?"

"It was up and down. I got a few hours here and there. Wasn't too bad."

"That's good."

Between our silence, a grid of talking heads blares from the TV. First, it's *SportsCenter* or something, then there's some election coverage.

"What're you watching?"

"Nothing. You can change it." He sends the remote gliding over the couch's leather.

"I just really hate Sarah Palin," I announce, my voice too defiant.

"I'm so sick of her, man." He shakes his head. "Guys at work, you know, they're all about the guns, they love the whole 'maverick' thing. They're just scared to have a brother in the White House."

"I know. Racist white people are always so scared," I sigh, going to GUIDE. "There's probably a *Law & Order* on."

"You know there is!" (There always is.)

Munch has just made a one-line quip about murder, and the iconic song begins. We both bob our heads to it instinctually. (Our family kinda loves this song. Malcolm and I sometimes play the air flute during the bridge.)

Our relationship isn't one of contempt or anything; it's more like my dad looks at me with total confusion. As I get more and more depressed, as I move further and further inward, toward books and punk politics and thick black eyeliner, I think he's less and less able to understand me. It's not my fault or his—to him, I just do not compute.

("The only thing I know about is sports and hard work," my dad likes to say. "That's my thing." And even though I've told him—almost accusingly—I know that's not the whole truth, it's another reason I just wish I were regular, easier to understand. Another thing I hate about myself.)

"I better go get showered." I stand up and stretch as the show ends on a super-long close-up of Olivia Benson's steely, out-of-breath countenance.

"Hey, what are you doin' today? I gotta drop Malcolm off at the skate park later, thought we could go get some mochas at Starbucks."

It's totally random, but then again so is everything about how my family treats me since the incident.

"Oh. I'm actually hanging out with my friend from art class in a little bit."

"Oh good, good. That's cool. Maybe we can go tomorrow then."

"Sure, yeah." I nod too many times. "Okay."

He pops a watermelon square into his mouth, slurps mercilessly. It makes me giggle to myself all the way upstairs.

I still have a couple of hours before David picks me up. I should do homework, but instead I'm listening to Cat Power and researching curses, fingers crossed the internet will be like *You're totally crazy everything's fine high school just sucks.* I search "types of curses" and click the second result, because I irrationally believe that the second result is always more credible than the first. It looks academic enough.

There are three types of curses: (1) Biblical curses (2) Witchcraft curses (3) Curses by people.

Ugh, I don't know what's going on with me. I read the site until I can't stand the terrible grammar anymore, click around for a while, somehow end up at "see also: if the world hates you." Slam my laptop shut.

Meg texts a single link to a five-minute video of hippos eating watermelons.

I hope you have fun today dude, she follows up. *Wear the good bra.* I grin idiotically, with my whole heart. (Maybe this year will be okay?)

I am just friends with David Santos and so I am really trying very hard not to completely flip out about hanging out with David Santos. I keep reminding myself about his ex, how she's probably quiet and uncomplicated, with long white-girl hair and lip gloss. Still, he's so cute and cool, I know that hanging out with him will give me big fat restless butterflies.

The story about David Santos has a pop-punk soundtrack: moody, earnest, energizing, fun. He's a junior at Highland Valley, a public school and a completely different world, but our tectonic plates click together with snarky texts about Wes Anderson movies and guacamole recipes (which is a very intimate and important topic for Southern California natives).

Sometimes we chat all day, about nothing special. It's like we're always hanging out.

I wear: my Smith's T-shirt from Hot Topic, with the green lettering; camel-colored wool pencil skirt from the vintage store in Riverside; black Dr. Marten's Mary Janes that barely pinch my feet (but they were seven dollars!). I flip my hair with my mom's biggest curling iron. Put on purple eyeliner. Say my affirmations. I am in control. I am not crazy. I am cute. I feel good. Take my medicine. Slip my bottle of Xanax into my tote bag just in case.

I go downstairs to look out for David from the living room window. I don't want him to ring the doorbell and have to do A Whole Thing. My dad's wiping the kitchen counters and half-ignoring the *Law & Order* marathon. When I hear a car parking, I rush a goodbye hug and run out of the house.

David's walking up the driveway when I intercept him. "Hi!" I squeak. (So awkward.)

"Hello, madam. You ready?" He is wearing black jeans and a black T-shirt and is adorable.

I give a thumbs-up and my signature exaggerated smile.

"Nice shirt." He nods, and I'm too liquid to respond.

David Santos is driving his mom's old station wagon, un-ironically. With his Ramones bumper sticker and the yellowed paperbacks strewn in the backseat, it actually looks cool.

After he opens the passenger-seat door for me (!) and we both buckle our seat belts, I sit quietly, buzzing with nerves and trying desperately not to move. My goal is to be stone.

He whistles something while he fusses with the knobs for the AC, the CD player, the side-view mirrors, the seat back. And finally, he starts the car.

"This is an excellent song," he says as we pull away from the curb. He fist-pumps the air.

It's the White Stripes. "You're Pretty Good Looking (For a Girl)" from *De Stijl*.

"Ugh, I know, this whole album is so good!" (*Dude, relax,* I chant to myself.)

David drums the steering wheel. His energy is like a fourteen. I don't know where we're going or what we're about to do, and that is totally freaking killing me, but I'm way too nervous to ask anything.

"So. Morgan. Are you ready for the mission?"

He smiles as we slow to a stop sign. He looks over at me, and I make it a point to look back at him. His eyes are an annoyingly calm blue, crystal and sort of gray, the foggy waters of another world. I fall in.

"Let's break this curse."

THE EXORCISM OF MORGAN PARKER

My good old panic, this familiar terror. I wish I could explain, but it's like there are no exact words. Every single interaction is potentially hazardous. Medicated, unmedicated, important, frivolous—everything could be a second away from destroying me. I swear we can both totally hear my heart pounding with nerves.

But the day has decided to be epic.

"Okay, first thing's first," David takes a deep breath, flings a hand off the wheel into the middle console, and starts rummaging. It's full of all kinds of random stuff. Candy wrappers, supermarket discount cards, sticky pennies. The car is brimming with stuff, evidence of aliveness.

David finally fishes out a jewel case and solemnly presents it to me. "I made you a mix."

(I am *dying*! But I try to hide it. This is unquestionably the first time a guy has ever made me a mix, and it is, in my book, significant. Above making out on the romance scale. Like, John Cusack in *Say Anything* level.)

Scrawled on the notebook paper insert in he-did-his-best handwriting is: *The Exorcism of Morgan Parker*. David catches my eyebrows leap up at the title.

"Not that you're like, possessed," he rushes. "Just like, you know, that movie. Maybe it was a bad joke. It's just a weird thing I do."

I laugh; his tension escapes through the car windows.

"No, it's rad!" I flip over the case but it's blank. "No track list?"

"Well this is Wolf Parade, 'It's a Curse.' Another stupid joke. Anyway, and I'll write it down for you later, but every single moment starting now will be a surprise."

The sentence resonates in a super-deep way, like he's not just talking about the CD, he's talking about life. Our life, together. It occurs to me that he put a lot of thought into this, into today. Does he think *I* am "pretty good looking (for a girl)"?

(Now playing: my spiral of self-doubt. Why would anyone want me when simple-minded, skinny blonds in flip-flops and jean skirts are running around everywhere like extras from *The O.C.*?)

"Thanks so much." I peel my hand from my lap and reach toward his arm but then chicken out. (How do you flutter your eyelids, by the way? Are we sure it looks cool?) Leaning into the headrest, I try to look softly at him—just smiling creepily.

His warm tan complexion, that curly hair, how his eyes are always smiling. I watch the muscles in his arms as he steers.

"You are super welcome! So, here's my proposition," he claps. "Soul Searching."

I nod. "Okay. Yeah, this sounds right. Where do I start? And also, where are we going?"

"Two, I have no idea and I am literally just driving around until we get to the bottom of this. And one, well, if you feel like the universe has cursed you, you for sure need some kind of come-to-Jesus moment. Like maybe a baptism? Or a re-baptism or something, I don't know your life."

I reply almost reflexively, practiced from years of probing from teachers, moms, youth group leaders: "I was baptized Catholic as a baby."

"So?"

"Yeah, I don't really know what that does. I didn't do communion. We don't really go to Catholic church anymore."

Services at the Catholic church across town (closer to where we used to live, and closer to "the hood" as my parents say), where I was baptized, are extremely and intentionally boring, and no one can really understand what the priest is saying because he's like two hundred years old. When our family went, mostly on holidays, Malcolm and I always fell asleep or played games too loudly in the pews. The congregation is mostly black and Mexican, people with major troubles asking for prayer. It's real to them. When they say *suffering*, I understand. It isn't about restriction, and it isn't about threat. Everything's not some episode of *7th Heaven*. It's life and death. It's survival.

I actually did go to one communion class but was disappointed in the lack of discipline among the other students, and plus, I didn't know any Spanish. I was even in the choir, which I quit because I am a horrible singer, and also because the rest of the choir were senior citizens. I've given a lot of things a try.

"I mean, it wasn't bad, I guess," I add, catching some breeze on my cheek from the open window. "It was just *sooo* boring. I didn't really feel it, you know?"

David laughs. "Jeez, yeah, I do know what you mean. It wasn't for you."

"Nothing's for me," I mutter before I have time to censor myself. "Or maybe I just haven't found my thing. Whatever it is doesn't grow in this town."

I suck in a big, meditative breath, choosing my words. David stays quiet, nods.

"But I need to believe in something. I have to believe something's on my side. That's how people do this life thing, right? At least I think so."

"Yes! Now we're talking. Optimism looks good on you. I've never seen it before."

I laugh and kick my feet up on the dusty dash. He's right. A teeny bolt of hopefulness darts up my spine.

"So let's expand that worldview, kid," he says, business-like. "Find you some salvation."

"I don't even know where to look. I mean, this is what we're working with," I wave my hand at the intersection: two churches, a bakery that's always closed, a store called Tuesday

Morning that sells who knows what if not orthodontist appointments.

"Wait a minute, this is coming from the self-proclaimed nerdiest teenager in America?"

"You're so right, I did proclaim that."

"Yep. You're gonna love this place." He whips out of a cul-de-sac and heads to the freeway.

David knows a bookstore that is neither Mormon nor a Barnes & Noble. (Do I mind taking a little ride? Abso-freaking-lutely not!)

In traffic on the 91, I'm chastising myself for not preparing conversation topics when David turns down the music and blurts, "So—" He says it so loud we both laugh uncomfortably. "Uh, so, we go to a Catholic church once a year, when my grandma makes us. It's definitely pretty boring."

"That sucks." I cross and uncross my legs. "Is she super religious?"

"Kind of, yeah. Well, no—" He flip-flops his hand, thinking aloud to himself. "She likes tradition. Saying the rosary, Ash Wednesday, stuff like that."

"Yeah . . . like the rituals?" He nods empathically and in spite of myself I keep talking. "I was really into the holy water. I liked feeling special; I always liked the idea of communion. The symbolism, I guess. I don't know if that makes sense."

I badly wanted to drink the sip of juice and eat the wafer. I wanted in on the whole ceremony. My favorite part of Catholic church was always leaving—crossing ourselves with holy water and shaking the hand of the sweet old priest before being let out into the warm sun, a procession of the blessed.

"Yeah, exactly. The symbols, the rituals. My grandma's really spiritual about that stuff, which I think is cool. She's not like *You're gonna burn in hell* or anything like that." He snorts. "She's, like, a grandma."

"Ha," I laugh softly. "No, that would be everyone at my school."

"Dang." His dark brow furrows; those eyes have the nerve to look silently into my hurt. "That's wild."

"It's . . . yeah, it's something. It's like everything is about judgment. Or about being 'pure.' I don't . . . feel like that." (Maybe I don't even want to.)

"Have you ever thought about Buddhism?"

"Hm. I mean I know Allen Ginsberg was into it, and I did get really into *Siddhartha,*" I remember, then roll my eyes. "But I don't want to be like one of those white girls at Coachella who wears . . ." I gesture to my forehead.

(I don't want to say the wrong thing. I hate how little I know about the world. How few histories and cultures I get to learn about, too bombarded with all the missionary narratives at school. How little I'm allowed to know.)

"A bindi?"

"Yes, that's it! I'm sorry, they don't teach us much in White People Studies."

He laughs; it's throaty and exhaustive.

"Sorry, that was messed up. I actually love white people."

(If I had a dollar for every time I've said *I love white people* in my seventeen years of life, I would be able to buy an original press edition of Sonic Youth's double LP *Dirty* on eBay.)

"I mean, I'm not white"—he grins in my direction—"so we can keep it between us."

I don't know what to do with the beat in the conversation, so I just sit there and wait for him to speak. Susan has me trying "stillness" and "mindfulness," even though I told her I'm not built for it, that it actually *increases* my anxiety.

"My mom's Mexican and white, and my dad's black. He's light-skinned, though," he says, by way of explanation for his own particular shade, hints of butterscotch in coffee ice cream.

"Oh, cool."

"Yeah, I like them all right."

"Are they religious?"

"Not really. My mom grew up Catholic, but my dad's an atheist."

"What about you?"

"I'm nothing. Maybe I'm somewhere in between. But I mostly think . . . we're alive, and then we're dead."

His phone buzzes loudly in the cup holder, clinks against some loose change.

"Oh, it's just my cousin. Do you mind?" He puts it on speaker. They have a little choreographed greeting, where one goes *Wasssuppp* and the other goes *YoYoYoYoYo,* like in a buddy comedy.

"Before you say anything," David shouts into the phone,

"you are on speakerphone right now, and I have a friend in the car and yes that friend is a girl, so just—"

"Oh-ho! Well, hi, David's friend."

"Hi," I squeak, tilting my head as if it would have any bearing on the quality of the phone call.

"That's my friend Morgan," David establishes. "So what's up, buddy?"

"K, real quick, are you coming over for Rosh Hashanah?"

"Oh, I totally forgot about it." We hit another stretch of traffic, ending our six minutes of smooth sailing. David's head flings back like the top of a Pez dispenser and he emits a quiet groan. "When is it?"

"Saturday the eighth. Just write that down. Actually, I'll just text it to you. Will you remember to bring those Vonnegut novels?"

"Already in the glove box."

"And my *Freaks and Geeks* DVDs, and my Joy Division T-shirt?"

"All right, all right, I get it."

"Sorry, I'm going. Nice to meet you, Morgan!" Not gonna lie, his voice sounds pretty hot.

"Love you bye," David says, ending the call, which is adorable. He smiles apologetically at me across the sticky console. "So, sorry about that."

"No, don't worry about it!" *Too eager, always so eager.* I try to lean back in my seat coolly, but you can imagine how that went. David's not paying attention anyway—he's pumping his fist because traffic is moving, finally.

"So that's my cousin, he's cool. Also, he's Jewish. Hence, Rosh Hashanah. We always have dinner at his house for Jewish holidays."

"That's cool. I actually just realized—I don't know any Jewish people."

"Seriously? How is that possible?"

"Where would I meet them? Not at a school thing. There are no Jewish people at my school—zero, even less than black people."

"I thought it was 'nondenominational.'"

"Oh, they just say that."

"So, you really don't believe any of it?"

"I don't think I believe in sins, or at least not the sins in the Bible. Sins sending you to hell." (Or maybe I do. I just want to find out for myself.) "Who is this?"

"The Microphones." He keeps quickly turning his face to mine, and I do not think I am imagining how it keeps softening, becoming more . . . something. More knowable. He does this squinty smile thing that I am obsessed with; it makes me want to know everything about him.

"This mix is really, really good, David, I love it!"

"Yes! I'm so happy. I hope you like this bookstore too, I think you're gonna. Wanna get some coffee after?"

"Totally."

The next song is one of my favorites, "KC Accidental," from Broken Social Scene's *You Forgot It in People,* which is another album I think is pretty perfect. I feel special. (And this is what I mean—the part of me that makes it impossible to enjoy this feeling, to live this feeling without ruining it with the terror part of my brain—that's the curse I need to lift.)

"Hey." He nods toward the glove compartment. "Open it. Check it out."

Shoved in there with a broken pair of aviator sunglasses and an empty Milk Duds box are two paperbacks. "Oh cool. I've actually never read any Kurt Vonnegut."

"He's so great! In that one, *Cat's Cradle,* he actually invents his own religion. It's bonkers."

"Really?"

"Yeah, it's called bokononism. It's a whole thing; there's something about feet? It's hilarious, and it kinda points out how, you know, all religions are random, anyway. It's just people believing whatever lies they need to in order to deal. Basically 'ignorance is bliss' or whatever."

"Whoa." I squint. "Not the worst idea. Maybe I'll invent my own religion. I didn't think you could just do that but, why not, I guess."

David slaps the dashboard in exclamation. "Genius!"

He lightly jabs my arm and steers us toward the exit lane.

"This really is the beginning of something," he says, and I laugh a little bit, because I don't want to say anything to ruin the perfection of the moment, the airiness, the comfort I completely forgot is even possible.

On *You Forgot It in People,* there is the incredibly satisfying sequence of songs following "KC Accidental," so unstoppably beautiful that by the time you get to "Looks Just Like the Sun," you believe it.

This is a story about my day with David. He is <u>amazing</u> and we hung out for like 6 hours. We went to a cool bookstore in downtown Riverside and sat on the floor and read and laughed really loud, then we went to Coffee Bean. I got iced green tea and he got some kind of frozen chocolate thing and I told him he messed up. (But later he was like: next time I'll get tea, so I was like hmmm next time?) So anyway, we just walked around there for 2 hours talking. We talked about everything and I'll fill you guys in more later but he doesn't like eggs! Isn't that weird. It wasn't mega awkward, but it was a little bit. I don't know! AHHH! Could I fall in like? I don't think he really likes me like that. When he dropped me off at home, he was like "You're not so bad, Miss Morgan. This was fun." And then . . . he shook my fucking hand. Sadface.

HOW TO BE BLACK AND MILD

"I know, right?" says one pretty-much-my-age white girl on TV to another, looking over the middle console of a convertible. They are discussing sunglasses. For at least seven minutes. A gust of night breeze whooshes and puffs at my open window.

I am at my desk starting a fresh new notebook. The Black Notebook. I cut out a story title from *NYLON* that says "Black Magic Woman" and collaged it on the front with photos of Langston Hughes (basically one of the only poets I like) and Zora Neale Hurston. I don't know what to write on the first page, so I've mindlessly been doodling patterns of lines and circles. A new notebook is always so much pressure, and I want this one to be special. I want it to be dedicated to truth and discovery.

I wonder if I need organized religion at all. Like, if it were up to me to choose, not my parents or my school. I don't want to send myself to hell or anything, but Christianity hasn't made me feel at home, only guilty and afraid. There must be some other way to be saved, protected, forgiven. To eliminate the constant threat of hell.

Notes for the Beliefs of Morgan Parker:
Religious & Otherwise

—*Darkness isn't a bad thing.*
—*Don't follow rules you don't understand.*
—*You can escape.*
—*There is a lot of stuff that no one knows. (Like what*
happens when you die.) Don't trust know-it-alls.

David texts just then: Yo what's up?
I lunge for the Yellow Notebook and scribble: *ADDEN-DUM: HE JUST TEXTED.* I go back to the Black Notebook and write

—*Anything can happen.*

I'm about to craft my witty, chill response back to David, something like "everything and nothing" or "will you marry me," when I'm startled by a loud rapping at the front door. It's a little weird for the time of night, but our neighbors are always coming over unexpectedly to "gently" complain about where we park our cars or sell wrapping paper for their kid's whiffle ball team, or whatever other boring thing. My mom's already asleep, but my dad's downstairs watching *Sunday Night Football*, so I am off the hook for getting the door.

The knocking gets harder and louder. Which means it can't be Linda from down the street, no way. I peek through my dusty blinds, careful to keep my face hidden. Is that a cop car? Either something isn't right, or something exciting is happening. Butterflies swim laps in my belly, and I rush to the top of the banister as my dad answers the door.

Facing him is Malcolm, his Abercrombie polo shirt collar in the hands of a uniformed policeman. The man has a round face and a red mustache. His eyes are slits, obscuring any emotion. He and Malcolm have almost the exact same height and shape (tall, lean, and strong), but one's figure exudes threat, and the other, submission.

"Is this the Parker residence," the guy bellows.

"Yes, sir. What's the problem?"

My dad, usually so affable and casual, looks robotic and dimmed, like a video game character losing one of its lives.

"This your son?" the cop grunts. Malcolm peers upward, likely searching for me. (I am a known busybody in the family, but this time I'm trying to spy and remain unseen.)

My brother's arms are stiff at his side, his eyes glossy with tears. He sniffles.

My dad is saying *yes* and *okay* and the cop is gesturing with his free hand and saying something I can't quite make out, and the cop is still clenching Malcolm's collar. His grip looks uncomfortable, even painful, and I get mother-hen protective.

I think about shouting down to the entryway asking if my brother's under arrest, but I stay quiet and let my dad say whatever he says to get the cop to finally release my brother into the house with a little shove.

"Thank you, Officer," my dad says, closing the door. He locks it, which is rare. (Why do we always thank people for no reason?)

The patrol car peels away and I dart down the stairs in my socks, gasping.

"What *happened*?! Malcolm, are you okay? What's going on?"

"He's okay," my dad says. "It was a misunderstanding. Let's give him a minute."

Malcolm is completely shaken, stunned even, and my dad's leading him calmly to the dining table. I pour a glass of water in the kitchen and place it in front of my brother. I sit. I'm quiet, but anxious. I consider taking a Xanax but snap my attention back to Malcolm. He gulps the water and presses his palm to his chest, still trying to stop crying.

After a few minutes, I try my calmest concerned voice. "Did you get hurt?"

"No."

Malcolm takes a deep breath.

My dad turns to me, jaw clenched, whole body clenched.

"The officer said he saw him 'looking suspicious.'" He sucks his teeth. Now I can see that behind his composure, he's pissed. "Bullshit. They saw a young brother outside of the hood and assumed he didn't belong."

I hold my mouth agape. "Where was this?"

106

I scoot my chair closer to my brother's. I can't believe he's been through a whole drama, just like that, just tonight while I was watching *The Hills* or whatever, Malcolm was experiencing the real horrible world. I'm his big sister. I'm supposed to be the sad one. I'm supposed to feel all the awful things so he doesn't need to.

"I was walking home from Tony's." Marissa's brother. They live a few blocks away, a five-minute walk.

"I thought you were supposed to spend the night there. You and what's-his-name. The silly dude with the little pin head." One of my dad's charms is how he never remembers anyone's names, even kids we've gone to school with since kindergarten. Instead, he qualifies everyone with some distinctive quality or feature; most frequently someone is referred to as "that dude with the big ol' head" or "that guy with the little pinhead," respectively.

"Yeah, but they were bugging me!"

"Like how?"

"First, Tony said the n-word. He said he was just kidding, cause it was in the song we were listening to, and I asked him not to say it. I asked him nicely. I said 'Hey, that's racist if you say it.' But he kept saying it. Like over and over. And he kept saying it was okay because it was in the song. But then later he told this joke, he said it was this messed up joke his grandpa said, and he used the n-word again. It wasn't funny at all. After that I just had to get out of there."

I know lots of people like Tony, who can't stand that they're not allowed to say the n-word, so they keep trying to find loopholes, any excuse to trespass. They repeat racist things they hear and ask, "Isn't that bad?" when really, they're excited for the chance to say it. And us, the black kids, we're supposed to be like, *Yeah, that's crazy* (as if we're surprised), or *Oh yeah, I know you don't mean it that way.* We're not supposed to say how it makes us feel.

Once, when I was maybe five or six, I was at Albertson's with my mom. I sauntered through the aisles trying to be helpful, grabbing cans of green beans or sleeves of crackers and holding them up to her face asking, "Do we need this?" "Should we get this?" "Did I pick right?" We creeped down the cereal aisle, where a young white mother in a Ralph Lauren polo was taking in the way-too-many options. Her toddler snacked on grapes in the cart's child seat. And as we got closer, I realized he was staring at me. Wide-eyed. It wasn't a glance, it was a leer. As our cart passed theirs it was like slow motion—the baby pointing his chubby white finger at me and screaming some gurgled syllables in terror; the young mother giving me the stink eye and hurrying their shopping cart away. My mom pulled me in close to hip, kept pushing down the aisle. Under her breath she said "bitch."

"Mom, what did I do?" I asked with my outside voice when we rounded the corner to the meat aisle, rows of red beef nestled in shrink-wrap-and-Styrofoam sleeping bags. "Why did they look at me like that?"

She shushed me, bent down to look me in the eyes. "I think maybe they were prejudiced. You didn't do anything at all. Some people are just prejudiced."

"Oh."

The code word—*prejudiced,* not *racist,* or *bigots*—conjured images of rich, unsmiling white people, and my developing understanding of civil rights, of injustice and fairness. They were large, serious ideas that didn't make any sense to me.

"But why did the baby yell at me?"

"Maybe he's never seen a black person before."

That was the first time I felt like an animal.

Across from Malcolm in the dining room, Sunday night's usual quiet completely disturbed, I am fucking *seething.* "What was the joke?"

Probing Malcolm to relive a traumatic incident is not the right move, but I'm relentlessly nosy, and for some reason, I'm morbidly interested in outright racist statements. Maybe because it feels strangely like validation, proof of what I suspect many people are thinking, but don't say in front of me. Hearing people, even people in movies, say blatantly racist things always meets me with a kind of awe. I can't wrap my head around how much hate it would take, how many pent-up vile feelings, to be racist.

"I don't want to say."

"Okay."

"Son, why didn't you call me to pick you up?"

"I thought the walk would help me clear my head. It's a nice night out."

I love sensitive Malcolm. It's rare, but it reminds me of when he was a baby, when he needed me, when he was gentle and goofy.

"But what happened? Why did the cop bring you home?"

"I said I lived in the neighborhood and was walking home, but he didn't believe me."

My dad and I shake our heads in a huff. But we both know instinctively there's nothing to say or do, except listen to Malcolm and try to comfort him. (Try to comfort ourselves?)

"I'm sorry, Dad. I was scared. I didn't know what to do."

Don't follow rules you don't understand.

I reach for Malcolm's hand and hold it in mine. Dad stands up and walks to the bar, uncorks a bottle of Kentucky bourbon.

"You did everything right, son."

MAKE A LIST OF ALL YOUR SINS

In third grade, I lied. I faked a stomachache, a horribly executed ruse to get out of my suffocating classroom, the stress of my classmates fumbling through multiplication tables cutting through the air like a scent. I wanted to be rescued into the sunlit day, cared for, shown mercy.

Later, some snitch reported me strutting to the lunch tables from the vending machine with a lollipop in my mouth, and in one abrupt and belly-sinking moment I was called to the teacher's lounge. I was still berating myself when I walked in to the sound of someone's Cup Noodles microwaving. Miss Gloria snatched the sucker right out of my mouth.

"I thought you had a stomachache," she accused. I licked my blue lips. The other teachers looked on, noiselessly swallowing their sandwiches. I kept thinking, *Why?* Why did this lady make me feel so small?

I knew then that I was not good. The thing was, I *had* felt sick. I always do.

...

I guess this isn't a sin, but I don't know what it was—I felt like I was possessed. I was ten, and it was right after we moved into our gated community, near Marissa and all the other portrait-ready white families. It was almost a dare to fit in, to look as wholesome and generic as the other families on the block, rendering our African Americanness merely incidental. It was hard work.

At Christmas, my mom was anxious about decorations. Which tinsel should wrap around the banister, which doorways should be adorned with synthetic wreaths. Dad spent hours out front on a ladder fussing with the lights, took a two-hour trip to Home Depot, and came home to start all over. I sat in the living room with Mom as she went through boxes of our old decorations, frustrated with how they weren't living up to our bigger and glossier home. I was in a good mood that day, I remember, humming along to *A Charlie Brown Christmas* and making myself useful by untangling a string of little white lights.

I have no idea what inspired me—years of overthinking the moral consequences of every small deed, suddenly gone—to wield an ornament hook and set out defacing a brand-new dining chair. In our first-ever dining room. Pristine wood, still wafting new-furniture smell. And there I was, tattooing it discretely. A sleeve of tattoos: a tiny crescent moon, my initials, a shooting star, a daisy, a heart. When my mother saw what I did, I realized it too. We both screamed, and I began to wail with regret, looking down at my hands in horror.

"You didn't know what you were doing," my mom said when she found me sobbing in a roly-poly ball on my bed, slapping myself on the cheek. She rubbed my back with closed eyes and whispered *shhhh,* the way she used to when I had insomnia as a kid. "You're not in trouble. You didn't know what you were doing."

The messed-up thing is, I really didn't. Being bad, doing wrong, it's just my impulse. That's how the depression feels, too. I'm not in control of myself.

It takes me forever to fall asleep, even after I finally hear Malcolm snoring safely in his room. I lie awake with my duvet pulled up to my chin and my eyes darting around in the dark.

Insomnia, like depression, is a unique blend of loneliness and fear. After years of being awake when everyone else is asleep, the loneliness is as at-home to me as the birthmark on my thigh, the way I hear my voice.

At school the next morning, I see the taco-truck-looking Bloodmobile and roll my eyes. Every year the school sends home a flyer about the American Red Cross blood drive, and every year I manage to forget, mustering last-minute courage to watch part of myself drain into a bag between classes. Today, feeling resolute and wanting an excuse to be late to class, I decide to get the whole gory scene out of the way. As always, I try not to look as the nurse pierces my skin, but of course I look. For a moment, as she presses the needle into my forearm, I feel a shower of calm and consider getting a tattoo, a small one that my mom couldn't find. Then I remember summer, how I wanted so badly to escape, but even then, couldn't commit to coaxing my own blood out of my body. *I guess that's the reason I'm still here,* I think. *Cowardice.* But maybe there are other reasons I don't know about.

"IS AMERICA REALLY READY FOR AN AFRICAN AMERICAN PRESIDENT?"

The question screams at me from the whiteboard when I rush in, sweaty, to AP Government. I toss the Notebook onto Meg's desk and slide into the last empty chair, right up front, of course. Mr. K gives me a look; I give him a thumbs-up.

Since it's an election year, Mr. K explains, we'll have in-class debates every quarter, so we can discover our own political opinions and prepare to be voters. What I hear is *So we can confirm the beliefs and opinions we've always been taught and prepare to vote Republican or else.* Today the topic of conversation is Barack Obama, the youthful, handsome black guy who has recently secured the presidential nomination for the Democratic Party (or as Mr. K refers to the party, "Morgan's people"). I am not in the mood or condition to perform as the "African American perspective." I can't be the entire black student body; I'm not even sure what my individual stance is. I'm light-headed and I just want class to end so I can get a burrito for lunch.

I hate the way all our teachers say *African American* instead of *black*. I want to tell them that it's fine to say *black,* that it's not like the n-word, but clearly, they have their own ideas about how to label and categorize us. Sometimes, in our white oasis, it's hard to tell what year it is, exactly how far America has come or not come.

The class is split into two groups, tasked with arguing FOR or AGAINST. Conveniently, I "end up" on the FOR half of the room. Mr. K knows that if I had to argue AGAINST, I'd probably launch into my own mini Democratic National Convention. This is a dude with a collection of Ronald Reagan beanie babies. He basically relies on me to teach half of the class, unable to bring himself to objectively explain liberal viewpoints. I mean, we're only a few weeks into school, and already I have a routine of holding informal office hours after class, filling in my classmates with what little information I can Google on Ruth Bader Ginsburg or the right to choose. It's pretty much a complete mockery of a "Government" class, and we are all hopelessly doomed to fail the AP test.

The two groups scatter to different parts of the room to compile talking points. Most of the know-it-alls and big-mouths (myself excluded) are part of the AGAINST team. I bristle thinking about what they might blabber under the guise of "devil's advocate." I picture Tony spitting the n-word into Malcolm's face with a nauseating grin.

Our group is me, Meg, Kelly, a kid in an oversized Korn T-shirt who never speaks, and two bland "hot girls" from the soccer team. The other side is Tim (to whom I have not actually spoken since we hooked up last year in the orange groves); chapel's American Idols, Jenn and Adam; a trio of Dungeons and Dragons "well, technically" guys who play hacky sack between classes; and Stacy Johnson, the other black girl (who's "mixed"). It's a legendary match of all-star idiots.

Kelly unclips a clean sheet of three-holed paper from her binder and assigns herself as stenographer.

"Okay, this is easy," says a soccer girl, scooting her desk closer to our circle. "I know exactly what to say. We just say everyone was created in God's image."

Oh *God*. I wince and tilt my head, but the others slowly begin to nod. *Don't follow rules you don't understand.*

"Okay . . . ," Meg starts, "like no one should be judged by the color of their skin? That kind of thing?"

"Let's use the Constitution. 'All men have been created equal in the eyes of America,'" Kelly offers.

"That's the Declaration of Independence," silent guy says flatly, "almost."

"Ooh, I know! Let's say Martin Luther King! Like, duh, am I right?" Soccer girl #2.

"Well, what do you think, Morgan?" Kelly's lips are the only ones moving, but I hear the question as a chorus, everyone's head creaking to my direction.

"I think he's cool," I say, and close my lips decisively. When the circle of faces doesn't change, I add, "Not because he's black. I mean, it's cool that he's black. But I just like him. He's smart." Also, just saying "Martin Luther King Jr." doesn't wash all racism away.

"Rousing argument," says The Hermit, and my face gets hot. *There is a lot of stuff that no one knows.*

"Okay, whatever, I don't know what to say. But I don't think we can just be like 'Martin Luther King.' That's dumb. That's not an argument either."

I side-eye the soccer girls so hard my eyes are basically closed.

How can I take on the responsibility to represent an entire population of people that, frankly, I don't know so well myself? Having a black president seems simultaneously totally reasonable and insane. Either way, remarkable. When my parents were growing up, black people were still getting sprayed with firehoses.

"He is very smart," Meg affirms, filling in the silence. "At least he uses proper grammar, and that's more than we can say for Bush."

Kelly nods and jots bullet points. "So, we'll say the color of his skin doesn't matter because he's smart and qualified."

The first soccer girl is obnoxiously chipper, eager to apply her optimistic, "godly" attitude to the cause. Mostly, it's distracting.

"And you know what!" she offers, completely unprompted and uselessly, "The question is like 'Is America ready,' so if we have an African American person as president, that's like, America is totally over racism."

"Oh, come on, racism is *not* 'over,'" I snap.

"Is it? In a way?" Meg turns to me; I squint back. "I just mean, we're friends and I love you the same as anyone else."

"Two minutes!" Mr. K shouts. "Finalize your arguments!" The room buzzes urgently.

Saved by the asshole. "Never mind," I huff.

The Hermit says, "Let's just say that change is good, okay?"

"Right," says Kelly, writing furiously. "Progress!"

The second soccer girl, who's been texting most of the time, says, "I think we have a solid argument."

"I mean, I don't really think we have a stance . . . ," I mutter, "but whatever."

"Time's up!" Mr. K chips. I can hear the grin in his voice.

Um, am I crazy (rhetorical question), or did no one say anything? No one's being convincing or passionate, not even me. And I had one job. In the history of my high school career there has never been a more me-shaped situation (usually they look at me like some extra puzzle piece), but it's like I just forgot my lines.

We scoot our desks to face the other team—actually the worst sound ever, since chalkboards are obsolete—and Meg turns her notebook to me. It says, "U ok?"

I wave it away.

The "Well, actually" and "To play devil's advocate" guys are so firm in their argument and conviction that I wonder if they really *do* think white people are better than black people. As if it's simple biology. First, they start with a bunch of articles and documents, all basically pointing to the suspicion of black people, and their threat to the "tradition" that makes America,

America. The tradition is white people are in charge. Their stance is sameness. Their answer to the debate question is basically "maybe," because that's the only argument for their side that doesn't sound outright racist. But instead of going deep into the inferiority of black people, they hone in on the inferiority of Barack Obama, which, basically, has the same effect.

Unsurprisingly, Stacy presents their opening statement. It's very clear she's not the team leader (this bitch is like, allergic to opinions), but as the only sort-of "African American" member of their team, it's an understandable strategy. Since she only brings up her race if pressed (by a white person), everyone knows I'm the better Afro-American Spokesperson in the class, but today, she will do. She can play a mild, palpable blackness.

Stacy folds her hands on her desk and leans forward before launching into the team's stance. She tucks a piece of stiff, hot-combed hair behind her ear, and twitches her face when it doesn't lay down whitely. She clears her throat, and I cringe preparing for her squeaky pitch.

"Perhaps," she over-annunciates, "America *is* ready for an African American president, but, that doesn't mean we need one. Like, African Americans in America are still making progress. Maybe we shouldn't rush things."

If centuries of literal enslavement—plus a hundred more years of figurative enslavement, and then decades of discrimination—is the definition of "rushing" progress, well, damn.

Nodding smugly, Stacy then gestures at Tim, who for no freaking reason at all, stands up from his desk. He folds his hands behind his back and begins to pace like an ADA on *Law & Order.* Stacy was merely the hype-woman—Tim is the real show.

He bellows, "And especially not with someone inexperienced. Sure, Mr. Obama is charming, but how much do we really know about him?"

I roll my eyes and remember a movie I saw on Disney Channel about a teen who leaves her body at will. Alas, there I remain, and Tim—(I have seen his penis! Clear and weird! I put it in my mouth! He made that groaning sound!)—asks Adam to introduce "Exhibit A," some odd, Comic-Sans-on-black-background blog post comparing Obama's proposed policies to Marxism. Not that we have ever studied Marxism. Much like sex, we're instructed only to fear it.

Tim emerges from behind his desk and moseys the tile between our rows.

"Now, I direct your attention to a particular passage in the Book of Revelation," he says. "Which warns that the Antichrist will be of Middle Eastern descent, and a very persuasive orator. Think about it."

A soccer girl gasps and whimpers a little. Even people on my team are getting got, and my blood is boiling.

"Oh my god, I'd never thought of that! And remember that sermon during chapel about how Hurricane Katrina was a sign of the times?!"

"He was born in Hawaii," I spit, and Mr. K reflexively shushes me.

And here we are: same shit, exciting new package. I feel like a novelty. I feel like an animal, some unidentifiable species under glass in the science lab. I try to remind myself what Meg said: I'm just like everyone else.

No—I know better.

"That may be, opponent." Tim looks directly into my eyes, and I squint back in derision. With where my mouth has been, the least he can do is call me by name. Asshole.

"But it *is* undeniable that *Obama* and *Osama* are homonyms. And anyway, why should we trust him? Just because he's black? I mean, I'm not a racist"—and here he turns his back to us, eliciting murmurs of support from his team—"but this is affirmative action all over again. It's the welfare debate. It's O. J. Simpson. I beg of you, esteemed opponents, is this real progress?"

This is the most I've ever seen Tim speak, and it is horrendous, vile. I'm disgusted. With myself. With everyone.

Next, my team presents our wack-ass rebuttal, and all I can offer is a few nods in black confirmation of Kelly's enthusiastic talking points. Really, I'm studying Tim—the arch of his thin reddish eyebrows, his self-satisfied upper lip, his nasal voice, every dumb, rude thing coming out of his mouth. He repulses me. What was so exciting about hooking up with someone that I don't even like? Was I just testing out how far I'll go to quench my boredom? I wish I could take it back. Cover it up with a new feeling.

■ ■ ■

As soon as class is over (report: no one learned a freaking thing), I rush dizzily to my locker, out-of-sorts, starving and irritable. Why is everything the worst?

I dodge and weave through the main hallway and its conservative zombies, pretending shouts and giggles around me are just white noise. I desperately need food and some air-drumming to Fugazi songs to find my center again. I need me time.

You can always escape.

I open my texts and scroll through the last few messages between me and David. I didn't text him back last night, and apparently sometime as I was driving to school this morning, he texted, *hi did you get raptured.*

I grin and type, *Long story.* Then: *When will I see you again?* Part of me immediately regrets the text, but not the part I like.

Meg catches up to me at my locker, cheerier than I've ever seen her. She was eying me all throughout class, trying to get my attention. I don't want to talk about it. Definitely not now.

"Wanna go give blood and then get lunch?" She adjusts the straps on her yellow JanSport.

"I already did it. Even ate the cookie. I think I'm just gonna drive thru somewhere and read in my car. Today sucks." I toss my government textbook haphazardly into my locker. We didn't even open it in class.

"Are you upset about class? Tim is such a dumbass. And Mr. K is like, stuck in the eighties. Don't listen to them."

"Yeah, I know. It's not really that. I'm just tired."

James clomps up to us and leans his shoulder into Meg's as a greeting. "What are we talking about?"

I sigh theatrically, "Oh, just how Barack Obama is very likely the Antichrist, according to many of our peers."

"Do *you* wanna go get blood cookies with me? Morgan already went."

"Pardon me?"

"It's the blood drive today. Wanna go? By the way, you're up." (James accepts the notebook graciously.)

"Oh right. Yeah, I went earlier too. Gross."

When? I wonder idly. James has English first period, and he never skips it; his papers are a hot mess, so he lives and dies by participation points. Whatever.

I turn to Meg. "Sorry, dude. See you in the yearbook room after school?"

"Okaaaaay." She frowns. The three of us scatter in different directions, like atoms splitting and becoming new, lonely units.

Darkness isn't a bad thing.

You can escape.

I drive through Del Taco and sit in the parking lot listlessly, kicking my feet up over my steering wheel. I find Bright Eyes on my iPod. Everyone else is into "First Day of My Life," but my favorite album is still *Fevers and Mirrors*. I don't think their music is about love. It sounds more like mania, but a wild, celebratory madness. The way Conor Oberst slurs and screams and doesn't hold back. Even though we aren't screaming about the same things, I feel like he understands.

I take two bites of my disappointing Del Beef and feel gross, so I wrap it back in its waxy paper. I am a miserable combination of the following: annoyed, woozy, sad. I don't want to go back to school. I don't feel like talking or smiling. I need an outlet.

I sort of think I've felt this way for longer than I can remember.

David texts back: *how about Friday night, my dear?*

Butterflies. It's so dumb, I know, but it's the kind of dumb I need to hold onto right now. A distraction. A harmless surface delusion. Some *Seventeen* magazine fluff that has nothing to do with politics, or curses, or rules, or chemical imbalances.

It's a date, I reply, and it's enough to get me to turn my engine, blast No Doubt's seminal *Tragic Kingdom*, and return, armored, to the united states of my stupid fucking school. I have time to go to Jamba Juice before English.

PART WHERE I AM
TOTALLY CASUAL, I SWEAR

Whatever, sometimes you just need to cry for no reason. Not because you have depressive disorder not otherwise specified, or because you're lonely even with your friends, or because of the Bible or David Santos, or because you gave a blow job to Tim McCloud. You cry instead of thinking about the reason. A Tilly and the Wall song fills you with feels. Whatever. They sing, *It all went to my heart*. It feels good.

I let the tears come. Then, neatly and calmly, I flush the evidence in the farthest stall of the girl's bathroom.

When I step out of the stall, Marissa and Jenn Hanson are at the other side of the sink, outfitted for soccer practice and acrobatically pulling their hair into messy buns. I smile at them in the mirror while I'm washing my hands, but I don't know if they see me.

...

I have the yearbook room all to myself tonight. The newbies are out getting quotes about the upcoming homecoming game. (A bullshit assignment. They'll come back with stuff like " 'Go Eagles!' said front office assistant Ms. Fischer," or " 'I'm excited,' said freshman Jill Matthews.' " I'll have to rewrite the entire article myself right before deadline, but it's worth it for the peace and quiet now.)

I'm brainstorming story ideas for my editorial features. (Ostensibly I am. I know all the best ideas will come to me at the last minute, so I'm mostly just hanging out. It's my process.)

The empty yearbook room is a rare and heavenly gift. I put on some music and start the electric kettle, which will take approximately four whole songs to heat water for tea, and I settle in at my desk to catch up on the latest episodes of The Notebook. No one really has assigned computers, but I'm the editor, and mine is mine because it's tagged with the sticker from a pink lady apple and an orange Post-it that says *TL, DR*. Above the screen, there's a sign handwritten on computer paper: *Please do not hover. It makes Morgan very uncomfortable.* Ha! I don't know what I would do without this place, a little sanctuary in the middle of a battlefield.

The Yellow Notebook has traveled from Meg to James to Kelly and is now back to me.

Ok so you guys know that cute sophomore with all the hemp bracelets and the hair who also works at Coco's? He's in my Spanish 3 class AND TODAY HE

SAT NEXT TO ME. James knows him from Computer class and says he is single . . . And, um, he asked me if I want to come over sometime and play Halo with him. I said you're on. And you know what? I know how to play Halo. Dang, we are HOTT. We are so good at boys!

Doesn't it suck when the person you <3 doesn't appreciate you AT ALL!!!
    Anyway, that's why I'm sad face . . .

So exciting, Morgan! I'm so happy for you, Meg! James, I totally get how you feel! Ugh! What are you guys wearing to the homecoming dance? I'm going with girls from cheer, and they're making us all wear matching shirts. Ew!

You guys are all doing awesome!!!! Meg, teach me how to be good at boys!!! Every time I talk to David I feel like I'm gonna say something stupid and he'll snap out of it like, whoa this girl is a freak, and go back to his adorable funny weird-in-a-charming-way life where he could date any Abercrombie model he wanted. Him being my boyfriend would be like Seth Cohen from The O.C. going out with a sad Muppet. So, James, I feel you. Maybe that person just isn't the one. Maybe the one could be waiting for you at Coco's. I'm hungry.

. . .

Meg slinks in right as I'm really going for a pitch I cannot reach, singing "Maps" by the Yeah Yeah Yeahs. She smirks and takes a seat next to my computer. "Hey girl."

I try to laugh myself away. "Hey. I can't sing. What's up?"

She lets out one of those what-a-day sighs. "Oh, just wasting time. Today is weird."

"Yeah," I agree. I skip to the next song, trying to shift the vibe. "You don't have copyediting to do, right?"

"No, none of the children have turned in their stories yet."

"Good, me neither. I was thinking of reading for English, but I don't feel like doing anything."

"So are you okay, dude?" she asks, and the kettle finally steams.

"For sure. Yeah, I'm fine." I pour a cup of Constant Comment, which is an orange-flavored black tea with the name of an indie pop band. I keep a stash of the stuff in my purse, in my car, and in the yearbook room. "Did you get your blood cookie?"

"Oh, um, I didn't, actually. I mean, I didn't give blood. They said I couldn't."

"Huh? Is that a thing? I didn't know those vampires turned anyone away. What happened?"

"I guess they said I didn't weigh enough?"

Caught off guard, I subtly scan her body. She's just as skinny as she's always been, thin wrists and ankles, T-shirt billowing out at her hip bones. I think back—yes, she always eats lunch, and never significantly less than the rest of us. She doesn't talk about her body like all the vapid girls do. Then again, she's tight-lipped about her insecurities, if she even has any. Only her face looks a little different. Grayer, maybe, and the valleys beneath her eyes sunken, like she hasn't slept in days. Still, most of us look like that right about now—the PSATs are only a few weeks away.

"Are *you* okay?" (Sometimes it's like that's all we can say to each other, without saying too much.)

"Yeah! You know I'm a fatty. Anyway, they told me I wasn't the first one to get sent away. They have a bunch of random restrictions."

"Weird." I sip, folding my legs beneath me in the swivel chair. "Oh, hey, what's the deal with homecoming? When is it, again?"

"Friday. Should we go?"

"Oh, dangit," I gasp. "David just asked me to hang out on Friday! Oh my god, what do I do?"

"See if he wants to come?"

"No way, are you serious?"

"Why not?" Meg shrugs. "Just ask him casually."

"Meg, I am not asking him to be my date to a dance, that is *not* how my song goes."

"Well, we're obviously going as each other's dates, so he can be our third wheel. Or fourth, with James."

"Okay I like that better. But wait, how do I say something casually?"

"All you have to do is be like, *I'm sexy and I know it, bitches!* Let me see what you have so far."

Hello, David. I'm so sorry!

"Oh, *girl*." Meg confiscates my phone and helps me craft a normal message.

oops, I totes forgot about our homecoming dance, and *lol we should probably reschedule.*

"God, why am I having so much anxiety right now?" I hit Send with one hand and absently prod at a forthcoming pimple on my chin with the other. Closing my eyes, I exhale slowly. "Okay."

"Good job!" She pats my back. "And, like, if he's not into it, he's an idiot. You're a catch."

"You know what? I am!" I mostly believe this, minus my pesky diagnosis, the black mark on my record. "So are you, dude. Plus, you know how to play Halo! Total package!"

Meg giggles and dances in her seat. "I'm terrible, but who cares!"

I throw back my head laughing.

"You know, I get that," she offers, neatly lining up a row of paper clips and avoiding eye contact. "Anxiety."

"Yeah?" I push my sweaty palms together, awkwardly clear my throat.

"One time it got so bad I had to go the emergency room. I thought I was having a heart attack."

"Whoa, really? That's scary." It doesn't feel like the right thing to say. I know what panic attacks are. They suck.

"Yeah. They gave me Klonopin. My stepmom wants me to see a shrink. But I did that when my parents got divorced, and I'm not going back there."

"Actually . . . I, uh, see a therapist." (I regret my confession instantly, but maybe I don't even remember why I was supposed to be ashamed.)

131

"Oh, I didn't know," she says quietly. "For the anxiety?"

"For anxiety and depression, yeah." She widens her eyes. I exhale, and I think it counts for seven exhales. "I haven't really told anyone. It sounds so dramatic, it's embarrassing. Therapy does help, though."

"Well, I'm here if you ever want to talk about it. I wouldn't judge or tell anyone. You know I'm good at keeping secrets." In the moment, I realize I do know this about Meg, though I'm not sure how I know it.

I hate the squeamish feeling I have: all of my terrible worst business, right there for another person to dig around in.

"Thanks," I creak shyly.

"How is it? Therapy."

"It's not bad. I feel better than I did before."

Finally, my phone buzzes. Meg snatches it up while I burrow my face into my hands.

yesssss so perfect. i can escort you and bring flowers and the whole thing. that would be hilarious! so down.

(Hilarious because David actually being my date to a school dance, taking me by the hand and twirling me by the waist, would be a complete joke. Of course.)

"Fine," I say, nailing the whole casual thing. "If we're going to the dance I think I need new shoes."

Meg squeals, does jazz hands. At least we're in all of this together.

The Diaries of Morgan Parker

September 30, 2008

Dream that doesn't feel like a dream: I'm walking
through the mall at school, and I spot James under the
stairwell near the girls' bathroom. I'm desperate and
fed up; I grab him by the collar of his polo shirt; I'm
begging. I say, "James, I feel like killing myself." His
gaze at my forehead, for a moment, is pity. But then
he says, "I know." He chuckles, "You say it to everyone.
All the time." I step back dramatically in horror. No one
believes me.

SOMETHING LIKE A PHENOMENON

We insist we're only going to the dance because we've already seen all the movies playing, and the mini-golf place in Ontario closes early on Fridays. I'm still kind of excited about our plans: it will just be Meg, James, David, and me. Meg and I are gonna wear jeans under our dresses, and David's wearing a tie over his T-shirt. James, of course, will don a full tux.

I'm in charge of packing the water bottles full of booze, and David will drive us all from my house. He doesn't drink much, he told me; he charmingly claims everything bores him. Meg and I eventually gave up shopping for shoes—we drove from store to store in Orange Plaza with "Phenomena" by the Yeah Yeah Yeahs on repeat, agonizing over boys and blowing everything out of proportion—so we're just wearing our Chucks. (Meg's are classic black and white with impressive scuffs and a red star Sharpied on each toe; mine bright green, with the Modest Mouse lyric "I don't feel at all like I fall" written on the outer left sole. Pretty much every song on *This Is a Long Drive for Someone with Nothing to Think About* gives me feels.)

I flip my hair with the big curling iron and shred my jeans at the knees. I watch a YouTube video on the perfect smoky eye. My dress is strapless and turquoise with a full skirt. Looking in the mirror at the finished product, I avoid my face (yep, still the same, despite all efforts), but quietly decide that my boobs look fan-tastic.

Tonight, we do everything our way: paper flower corsages, disposable camera pictures with our tongues hanging out. David parks when we get to the school, and we all stare in the direction of the gymnasium. Some of the Popular Christians are shrieking and exchanging lip gloss. Jenn Hanson's geeky boyfriend, Isaiah Engelman, dutifully hangs at her side with a brain-dead smile. The Fake Burnouts, Hermit with the Korn T-shirt, all those guys are kicking soda bottles in the football stands. I spot Marissa and Jordan holding hands, throwing their heads back in laughter as they approach the school entrance, decorated with wimpy balloons and posterboard signs. They look like different people. In this moment, I want to be them. That's another thing I hate about myself—that sometimes, *I* want to be basic like them.

David's car is so stuffy, and I have the boob sweat to prove it. I glance over at him, the constellation of freckles on his cheekbones. Why can't that be us? What's stopping me from taking his hand in mine, closing the deal with that half smirk I've seen in every single teen movie?

"Hoo boy." David exhales, wiping the sweaty back of his neck. James snorts a laugh.

"You guys," Meg says.

"I know," I groan.

"Fuck it," James says.

"Okay then," David concludes, and peels out of the lot.

Someone giggles and it grows, collecting momentum into a growl of laughter. We head directly to our spot.

Our spot is a construction site on a hill above the orange groves overlooking downtown. Meg and me stumbled on it one day driving from a lunch picnic in Prospect Park, drunk on stolen oranges and spicy September wind and in no rush to go back to school. From a ledge at the center of the cul-de-sac-to-be, we can see I-10, all of Redlands, and parts of Yucaipa. The view is nothing, really, but to us it feels significant. It gives us perspective, gazing down at all the bullshit, untouchable. All of us weird and confused and trying to figure ourselves out, smoking and looking and cradling warm beer from the stash in David's trunk.

As we watch traffic light up the night air, we pass Black & Milds and water-bottle-vodka shots around. We talk about nothing and everything; we scream at the traffic below, the fog above. After a while, we get quiet, take turns letting out super-reflective sighs. I know this moment is small, that they all are, but I allow it to feel profound. What book is it—*The Perks of Being a Wallflower*?—where they say they feel "infinite"? I don't care if it's cliché in the history of teen-angst narratives, this night feels close to that. *Finally,* I think. Finally, for even just this moment, I get it, how to be light and full of love and confidence. My life looks like it's supposed to.

"Thank God," James says, shaking his head like a church lady.

I swallow my gulp and swing an arm around his neck, pulling him close to me. "Forget God."

This is the part of the night where every twenty minutes someone says, "So what are we doing?" knowing full well that our plan, our fate, is only this: hanging out. (Hanging out requires no additional guise of activity. We lose hours and hours "hanging out," trying to decide what to "do" next, and we never regret a second of it.)

Meg plays Lady Gaga on her phone and dances goofily. James is waving his arms around and shouting the climax of a long story I can barely follow, about how he and Isaiah and the other computer guys predicted the housing market crash. This on the heels of some out-there conspiracy theories about Mitt Romney. James has something to say about everything except himself.

David trades his empty Budweiser can for a fresh one and presses his shoulder into mine.

"Hey," he says into my ear, "let's go see what the view's like over there."

"Cool."

I grab my flannel and the bottle of vodka and apple juice I have marked as my own. I'm starting to feel it: freedom. It's loose and freshening, my bones and muscles relaxing under my skin, behaving themselves for once. Drinking out here in public with interesting adventurous friends and a cute boy who, for some glorious reason, wants to hang out with me— it's all so exciting. I want this to be every day, for everyone to see how chill and fun I can be, even for a depressed nerd. For a black girl. Maybe my hex was lifted with summer.

David grabs my hand as we slip away from the group and head up a small gravelly hill. The palm-side of his hand is buttery and smooth, and its grip is surprisingly muscular. It's been so long since I've held a boy's hand, I didn't realize they became guys in the meantime. I'm feeling proudly conspicuous, at once embarrassed and smug that my friends can see me grinning like an idiot and leaning flirtatiously into David. Hot, mysterious, good-natured David. Oh my freaking God, this night is awesome.

We sit on a boulder and huddle in close to each other. I take a deep meditative breath and look down at the highway view, which is no different than it was a few feet away. David lets go of my hand under the guise of scratching his patchy stubble. We glance at each other, then away, glance at each other, giggle, glance away. I don't care that it's excruciatingly awkward, or that we are both clearly blowing it, whatever "it" is. I love just being next to him, tipsy in the quiet night.

He chuckles a little, then softly hangs his arm around my shoulders. Is this it? (*Tell him how you feel!!!* Kelly's rounded handwriting commanded in the Yellow Notebook the other day, which made me roll my eyes and scoff, just annoyed at her nagging to be included and then being super annoying and using too many exclamation points.) But maybe this is it. Vodka and apple juice: courage of the gods.

"So, uh, thanks for coming tonight. I know it's sorta dumb. But I'm glad we get to hang out."

"For sure." He takes a drink and I can hear the foamy beer swish around in his mouth. "Thanks for inviting me.. This is fun." He looks at me, almost disturbingly directly, and smiles.

"Cool." And this is what I do: I lean my head into the crevice between his chin and shoulder and brush my fingers against his hand. Bold as hell.

He peeks down at me and lifts an eyebrow with a smirk and I swear to god it is the cutest fucking thing I have ever had the privilege of seeing. It is happening. To me. Bold as hell.

I crane my face closer to his, bottom lip heavy, breath heavy. *Please.*

"Whoa." His palms are suddenly on my shoulders, pushing me away. The air between us thickens.

"Oh my gosh, I'm so sorry. I just . . . ugh, jeez, ignore me."

"No, I'm sorry, Morgan, I didn't think . . . I mean I sorta thought . . ." And—he laughs.

He fucking laughs.

"I dunno I kinda thought you were . . . maybe . . . gay." Still laughing. "Shoot, maybe I'm drunk. I'm sorry. This is so awkward."

"What," I try to say, but it comes out a deflated puff of air. *Pay attention, M, be present, save yourself.*

I force a laugh.

"That's so funny! Oh-em-gee!" (Portrait of me doing what I think a hot, feminine girl does, minus the tucking back of shiny thin hair.) "*I'm* sorry for like, being weird. I'm . . . totally not, though. Why did you think that?"

"I mean—"

"I wasn't really asking," I shoot back.

"Okay. I'm sorry. It's just, I don't really think of you like that. We're friends, right?"

"Yeah!"

It's unconvincing and I know it. I showed him my cards and they are not the right cards. I'm not in a Katherine Heigl movie. I'm still just me, unlucky, marked for disappointment.

"No, really, Morgan, look at me."

I obey, wincing. Everything about me is embarrassing.

"I just don't want things to be weird, okay? Because I think you're really awesome. Like, seriously awesome. So, are we cool?"

And I look that motherfucker in the eye and say "Totally," knowing full well I'm lying.

"So, I guess this is a bad time to ask about how the ol' curse is treating you?"

"Ha." (Oh that? See *one second ago*.) "Actually, I'm kind of getting used to it. Y'know, just riding it out."

We laugh mechanically, careful not to look each other in the eyes. I am back onstage. I've successfully tucked my shame away, deep under soil, and now I shall water it with booze.

Eager to change the subject, I announce randomly, "Everything looks so unimportant up here."

"*Atención!*" James wails behind us in clumsy *español*. "You two cutie pies get your butts over here!"

Meg's changed the music to Animal Collective, and as I recognize the opening chords of "Peacebone," I feel a rush. It's like a birdcall.

(This is one of our songs. We love to lose ourselves to our little anthems, jumping and banging our heads and shouting from the depths of our bellies. I'm not conscious of how I look or anything happening around me. On Tilly and the Wall's "Nights of the Living Dead," for example, James belts "I feel so alive!" Meg shouts the "shake our asses" part, and I jump up and down like a one-woman mosh pit. I don't know what I would do without those moments of temporary escape. When I return, the world is always the dumb same.)

David and I are totally unresolved, but we need to get the hell out of this moment, so we scurry over to them.

"Gather 'round, my dear ones. I have a gift," James says, and we all huddle in a circle, as if prepped for a séance. He opens his suit jacket and from an inside pocket produces a fat joint.

"Weed, really?" says Meg. "I don't think I want any. Do you guys?"

James lifts his palm to shush us. "Listen, everyone is in on this. It's important, okay? We are owning the night! We are marking our friendship and living freely!"

Then, this dude literally howls at the blanket of sky above us. He's pretty drunk, and I am all for it. I want his energy, the sparkling night he's beckoning.

"Hell yeah." I nod.

So what if David totally rejected me? So what if the feeling of said rejection is now settled firmly into my shoulders, my fingers, my spine, eerily familiar? I can handle it. I've handled much more.

"Then, Morgan, you shall take the first hit." James lights the joint and passes it to me ceremoniously.

As the joint travels around our circle and back again, I get weird thoughts and use all my brainpower swatting them away.

David's looking at me with disgust; No, I'm imagining it; Has he always been so dumb and regular?; Ugh, who can I make out with?; Meg is thinner than usual, I'm just now noticing; Does James have a crush?; Is my medicine working?; Does everyone hate me?; Am I having fun?

After a while, James is very stoned, David's pretty stoned, I'm settling into a nice combination of full-on drunkenness and marijuana disorientation, and Meg is holding it together with—perhaps I imagine it—mischief behind her eyes. I realize we've been standing here for a while looking at smog and traffic, no one talking, just listening to Ben Gibbard tug at our ache and angst.

Meg's phone dings. "It's Kelly," she dictates: " '*Sarah from cheer just told me that a bunch of people are going to a party on the golf course. Come!*' " She pronounces "exclamation point."

"Uh, I'm down!" James tips open his mouth and pours in some vodka, sloshes it around in his cheeks.

"I don't know . . . ," Meg trails. "I am completely sober, and everyone is terrible."

"I guess I'm down for whatever." I'm mostly lying about this. I actually really want to go. Just to see what it's like and say I was there, for people to see me there. But if I go to the party, I will still be me at the party.

"Could be fun," David chimes in, trying to sound relaxed and like *whatever* about the whole thing. He looks different to me now. Like no one special.

"I don't really think I should drive though." This renders him useless. I wish he would just go home.

"We don't have to stay that long," James says. "And if you're the DD, Meg, you get to say when we leave."

Meg's acting like she's a hard sell, but it's all for show. "Ugh," she finally acquiesces, "Whatever."

I make a goofy face at her—an offering of gratitude and solidarity—and she laughs back.

James claps his hands together. He looks fantastic in a tux; I briefly wish he wore them every day. "Shall we?" he says, and cocks his hip sloppily, grinding the joint roach into the hard dirt.

OBVIOUSLY I AM STILL ME
AT THE PARTY

The pulse of a single night can change fast, like unpredictable weather.

When we get to the golf course people are already pretty wasted, and the only one of us at their level is James, who's already getting lost in the middle of his own whirling stories. The lawn is littered with girls in Hollister tank tops and boys slapping each other's butts to impress them. T-Pain blasts from someone's car. There are a couple kegs and clusters of plastic bottles every few feet. One of Jordan Jacobsen's little cronies is completely faded and driving a golf cart around in circles. It's basically a carnival of dumb people making bad decisions.

It actually looks pretty lame.

David recognizes someone from his school and says he'll be right back, to which I reply, distractedly, "Whatever." He and I are distant but civil.

James leans into me and whispers, "What happened with D?!"

"Don't ask." I roll my eyes with a pout. He kisses my cheek and goes in search of more substances.

I look at James with painful clarity, despite my blurry boozy vision. His tux looks silly here, in the parking lot of a bougie golf course where his parents have never stepped foot.

(Even I have a little butterfly in my chest stepping onto the freshly manicured green, worried I'm too provincial for the setting—we *were* only invited secondhand. My parents are squarely middle class, but they're draped in their poor Southern upbringing. They have no privileges to speak of—everything we do and see is for the first time. Plus, we're black, so by default, we just can't exist in this universe. These kids, these golf club kids, are casual about designer jeans and tricked-out new trucks. Their parents aren't forging any new territory. This is just what they were born with, what they deserve.)

What I decide to do next is get drunk. You're not supposed to drink on antidepressants, part of me knows. But the reckless part of me—the hurt part —says to drink until all the weird cheap booze swirls around in my belly with my antidepressants and lets me pretend to be a different girl.

"I'm going to try to get extremely drunk," I announce to Meg, hands on her shoulders.

"Excellent. Don't get sloppy. I'll see you later—I'm gonna try to find Kelly. Do you have your phone?" This last part she says like a stern parent who knows my phone is always dying or dead. She expects to be disappointed.

"I think it's still on?"

"I'll just come find you," she relents, and I blow her a kiss.

At a makeshift bar area, I run into Jake, one of the football guys who's uncharacteristically nice to me because he thinks my brother's funny. He catches me making a face at the few warm Bud Lights bobbing like apples in a plastic cooler.

"Malcolm's sister!" he shouts from behind me, loosening himself from a cluster of jocks playing a drinking game. (They are all humongous people. After an away game, this one guy, Mike Something, ate a 16x16 at In-N-Out, and then he even finished a cheerleader's fries, Kelly told me.)

"Morgan"—I wave—"but yeah."

"I know." He smiles. "Gimme your cup."

Jake Walker is objectively hot, like teen movie hot. I feel like someone else just being so close to him. He smells like soap and new clothes.

"What is it?"

He pours me a double shot from a plastic bottle. "Tequila. You ready?"

"Cheers, I guess." My face cinches and twists at the sharp taste—if I drink the whole thing in one gulp, I will projectile vomit. I force it down in three swallows.

"Nice," Jake laughs easily, pouring the last of the bottle into his cup. He tosses the empty into the murky warm cooler water.

"Later, Morgan." He grins.

I shout a "Thanks" as he wanders off, throwing up a peace sign. It's a strangely pleasant interaction, like in a John Hughes movie, social castes colliding.

• • •

Soon I find myself in a circle of girls from my class, dancing and giggling to several Ludacris songs. Bless everyone's flailing white hearts. I finagle another shot from someone's stash, then grab Meg's hand. We run barefoot across the grass to the artificial lake, screaming Yeah Yeah Yeahs lyrics at the top of our lungs until, like toddlers, we tire ourselves out.

After spending what feels like hours giggling and bitching about our lives, backs stretched out on the damp grass, we slowly make our way back to the group to collect the boys.

"I'm sorry the David Santos mission was a fail," Meg offers, handing me a dandelion she picked.

I crush it in my fist and blow the flurries into the night air. "Ugh, whatever. I don't know why I thought he'd be interested. I'll get over him."

"Maybe now he'll be thinking about it. You, I mean. Obviously, he realizes you are so hot right now."

"Maybe. I don't know, he's kind of annoying, now that I think about it. Whatever."

"It's okay. Sometimes we fall for pricks. It's not always our fault."

"I know. Ugh, I wish I didn't have so many feelings. Was your boy here tonight? I didn't see him."

"Nah."

"Dang."

The party's dying down now. Jenn Hanson and Kelly collect red cups, scowling at the smell, while Isaiah and Adam trail obediently behind them with trash bags. Most of the Popular Christians have gone home or to a slumber party at church or whatever, leaving only a few clusters of jocks flirting with Hot Girls, and some fake burnouts brooding and smoking a hookah.

"Oh, look, I see David." I point, and we go in the direction of his curls, his lovely, lanky lean. He tips his head back to cackle gregariously. And now I see who he's talking to, whose arm he's brushing with his fingertips. Marissa. In a cropped T-shirt and low-slung jeans, lip gloss and bone-straight hair twinkling in the night.

"Oh my god," Meg gasps as we watch Marissa's head swim backward with a flirty laugh, stumbling sloppily as she playfully smacks David's arm.

Here it is: the part in the movie where Gabrielle Union and Paul Walker tell Laney nobody really liked her all along. The bucket of pig's blood on Carrie's unsuspecting head. The plot of *Mean Girls*. Marissa ditching me in the parking lot of Carl's Jr. for Jordan Jacobsen. The prom night scene in *10 Things I Hate About You*. The letdown.

I think I might throw up.

Suddenly some bottles shatter loudly in the parking lot, and everyone's attention turns to a slurring voice shouting, "*Fuuuck youuu*, dude!"

It's James's slurry voice.

Meg grabs my hand and we rush in his direction, trying to beat the horde.

James is swaying back and forth, toe to toe with some left-back football guy (Mike Something?) while Jordan's little army encircles them, tittering at the exchange.

"Hey! Yo!" Mike baits James, who, to his credit, is trying to disengage but is too wasted and confused to find his way out of the altercation. "You Clay Aiken motherfucker!"

At the reference, I cock my head and squint.

Mike Something is also wasted, barely making sense, but he's aggressive, clenching his abs and doubling over laughing at himself. Everyone but Meg and me is laughing now. Music from somebody's Ford Focus is playing System of a Down or something, but it stops abruptly.

"Run along, idiot," James manages.

I think briefly of James's grandmother, a Greek immigrant. I think of the day someone in Drama pointed out a small hole in his shirt collar and how he shrugged it off. The Converses he sways in now, one of the soles almost detached. And watching him, so defenseless and blatant in his difference, I love him. I am him. That's how I know I can't help him. He doesn't need me to.

"Is it true?" Mike's obnoxiously loud, and I can tell he's jonesing for a scandal, something legendary that will last until Monday. "I know it's true, just admit it. You're a fag! Faggot! I knew it!"

"You don't even know . . . what you're talking about . . ." James's eyes flutter closed. He hiccups.

Mike grabs Jordan by the sleeve and leans close to him but doesn't stop yelling. "Yo! I swear to God, nigga. My mom told me. The fuckin' . . . the blood thing . . ."

Jordan backs away, shrinking from the scene, but he definitely laughs. It breaks my heart.

Mike turns to his audience, just sickeningly tickled with himself. "You can't give blood if you bone other dudes. 'Cause like AIDS and shit. Fuckin' faggots. Fuckin' pervs!"

Mike Something's finale is a lewd thrust of his hips, as if he's gracelessly humping something. I'm devastated and helpless listening to the crowd erupt—a few gasps, but mostly laughter. It all happens so fast, and both of them are completely faded. No one present is in any condition to process what's going on.

Jordan snickers scandalously, drunk and fascinated. "Fuck, dude!" He takes a couple of steps toward James, who's just standing there nakedly, with his arms crossed and a blank stare. Everyone watching gets quiet.

Jordan looks super serious and lowers his voice, as if James was just revealed to be one of those "devil worshippers" who do weird rituals in the park at night, huddled around candles arranged in the shape of a pentagram.

"For real?" Jordan spits out, slanty Sid-from-*Toy-Story* eyes all beady and red.

I'm so drunk I think I might just clobber him, curse the entire Jordan Jacobsen lineage. Pushing forward, I make sure to elbow him as I approach James, who mutters something mangled and messy. David appears at his side and links arms to guide him to the car. We follow.

"Jesus Christ!" Meg exclaims, fishing David's keys from her tote.

David throws me a look of concern, his arm wrapped around James's waist. He's still wearing that stupid tie.

"Where were you?" I hiss.

"Nowhere," he shoots back with an attitude.

The ride back to my house is silent, other than me and David alternating asking James if he's okay and him swatting our concern away. He looks like he's gonna puke, his eyes closed and leaning his head against the window. Meg cracks the window to give him some air, but she's obviously pissed— her lips pursed and stern. She plays the Unicorns, followed by Tegan and Sara; there is no negotiation. I'm trying to hold on to my buzz for dear life, especially since the vibe is so awkward.

I turn to David in the backseat, who keeps looking nervously over at James and peeking at his phone every few minutes. "Can I smoke in your car?"

"Yeah, yeah!" he gasps, looking up at me too readily. "Do you."

As I light my cigarette I roll down the window and turn up the song, "I Know I Know I Know." I look over at Meg and poke her arm, trying to coax a grin and the energy we sparked earlier tonight, barefoot and childlike in the grass.

"The same as I love you . . ." I sing between puffs.

"You'll always love me too . . ." she finishes, and we laugh.

David's rejection, James's sloppiness, Mike Something's horrible display of hate and Jordan cosigning him—all of it vanishes for a sec.

James groans strangely in the backseat, eliciting coddling

from David and more laughter from Meg. At the stoplight, she slams the breaks haltingly, teasing James's gag reflex.

"Oh my god, you're such a dick!" I squeal, drunkenly thrilled.

At the next light, she does it again, and smirks, self-satisfied. I realize how exasperating it must've been to be sober around all of those drunk people she hates, and us, too.

"Pull over!" James slurs, and David echoes him.

"Oh, come on," Meg says, speeding up.

"Dude, maybe you should," I try gently.

Meg sighs, annoyed, but complies at the next place to pull in, the gated entrance to my neighborhood shooting range. James juts out of the car and yaks, his left hand on his hip and his right clenching the gate. Meg whines impatiently. David's outside, leaning with his arms crossed against the car door, poised to run to James's rescue.

"Yo, what's wrong?" I ask her. (We were just having such a good time. Did I do something?) "I know James is ridiculous, but he *is* really wasted tonight. He's clearly dealing with some other shit."

"Fuck being DD!" she shouts, and seeing my eyebrows dart upward with worry, she puts up her hand.

"I don't really mean that. I don't feel like drinking. I just . . . I do wish I could just . . . let go somehow."

"I know," I respond, though I don't, exactly. She's still so close to the vest.

David sticks his head through the back window. "Hey, Morgan, can you bring me your water bottle?"

Meg and I look at each other with a mutual side-eye, and I

take the water directly to James, who's now dry-heaving at the gate. When I back away, David's right there, lifting his arm to scratch my back lightly. I pull away.

"I'm just trying to be your friend, I'm trying to be nice," he says.

"I'm sorry, but I don't think a friend is someone who disappears to make out with my freaking nemesis. A friend isn't so obviously repulsed by me."

"What? Morgan, what in the world are you talking about?" I huff.

"That dumb girl I was talking to?"

I open my mouth, but can't muster anything sassy and biting enough, so I go with the silent treatment.

"If you must know, she just latched on to me. She was drunk, Morgan. And we talked mostly about you. And the San Diego Chargers, for some weird reason. It was totally random. If it seemed like something else . . . I dunno, I'm pretty trashed . . . but I swear it wasn't anything like that."

I throw my head back, like, *Gimme a break.*

"I really, really like being friends. Please don't be mad at me."

"Come on, David. I'm not an idiot. You already said you didn't like me."

"Hold on," he replies sharply. "I like you. I just don't know what that means yet. Is that a crime?"

James dry-heaves some more as a plane juts through the sky.

NOTES ON THE SARTORIAL AND SEXUAL PROCLIVITIES OF MORGAN PARKER, FLAMBOYANT AND OTHERWISE

Okay, so: I don't actually care that David thought I'm gay. Even I'm only 90% sure I'm not.

(What we've learned about gender and sexuality in school is very narrow and very skewed. It just seems like more dumb rules: how to dress, how to talk, how to love. Another list of limited options I'm pressured to choose from, while I'm just trying to figure out how to be me. I've never had a boyfriend, and no one's having sex with me, so what's the big deal with clinging to a label? It all feels irrelevant.)

But this has happened before—me being misread, misunderstood, mistaken for someone else. I "seem" gay, "act white," I've got a very specific look and vibe happening. There's no word that rhymes with me. That's actually a thing I like about myself, even when people make fun of me or don't understand—and even when it's the reason for my loneliness.

All throughout eighth grade I wore baseball sleeves and clip-on ties, a jean bucket hat studded with snarky pins—those were my skateboarding days, with Dickies and slip-on Vans. Not because I wanted to dress like a boy, exactly, but because it was a look. And when I'm trying out a look, I commit. At our commencement that year—I was also really into Big Band then, I played Benny Goodman while applying mint-green eyeshadow for the ceremony—I wore a vintage chiffon dress and ivory gloves.

In ninth grade my look was a college professor, with penny loafers and reading glasses on a chain around my neck, sometimes channeling Katherine Hepburn in pants. Last year was somewhere between Enid from *Ghost World* and Zora Neale Hurston in a hat. If having an imaginative and explorative fashion sense makes you gay (for the record, to my peers who seem befuddled by basic definitions: it doesn't!), then maybe I'm gay as hell (also, mind your own business).

People believe whatever they need to in order to deal.

What I mean is, me being gay is not a totally unfair assumption for anyone to make, and it doesn't insult me. What *does* hurt about David's rejection is that I've never been an option to him. What hurts is the way his eyes bugged out, how he completely freaked at the possibility of kissing me, as if I'd just suggested we bomb the White House or something. Am I that disgusting, that the thought has never crossed his mind? Did I miscalculate or imagine our connection? And at the same time, I feel like, *of course.* Of course he doesn't want me. Why can't I ever remember the price of everything I like about myself?

I should be over it by now, but I don't hear from David all

weekend. Our hug at the end of homecoming night was awkward, all our muscles tensed up. He doesn't email, and I don't. We don't text. I don't even text him when I see a guy at the gas station who looks like Bill Murray in *The Life Aquatic*.

...

If it's any consolation prize, I was hungover pretty much all weekend, even at Greek Orthodox church with my yia yia.

I guess I might as well tell you guys the real reason I didn't give blood is because men who have had sex with other men can't give blood. I wanted to tell you before you heard it somewhere else but I didn't know how. I was scared. My sister told me someone in her class was caught being gay and he couldn't walk at graduation. So please TELL NO ONE. It's bad enough that the football team found out.

And the worst thing is I think I'm in love with a straight boy. Again. *Sigh* Our first outing was playing freaking board games at Coffee Bean and it was rediculously cute. Then we went to dinner and talked about films.

Below the entry Meg wrote:

We don't care if you're gay! We love you and you are our lover! ☺

(But of course she still corrected his spelling and added Oxford commas.)

...

I find James after school Wednesday for a hug, and we take a long walk toward the train tracks downtown, smoking and chatting.

"So, let's hear it." He grins expectantly. "Are you surprised? Weirded out?"

"No . . ." I'm not. But I don't *not* feel something. Relief? "I guess I just wish you'd been able to tell me sooner. I'm here for you, you know?"

"I know." He lights another one of his fancy cigarettes. A bright red. Where does he even get these things? I wonder if he picks colors to match his moods or T-shirts. Selection is never random for me.

"So, do your parents know?"

When James came out to his parents, he tells me, he was sitting across from them at a booth in Coco's.

"I said, 'I'm gay.' "

They said no, he probably isn't sure, maybe he should sleep with a few women first and figure it out, and by the way, does he even know what it means?

"So of course at that point I was like, *I have sex with men!* I shouted it just like that to shut them up. It was amazing! Such a scene." He swats at wild hairs on his forehead.

"Oh my god. So good." I smile, imagining all the gray heads in the restaurant turning to stare when James emphasized *sex*.

I imagine that having remained in the closet for so long makes him even more lonely and isolated than the rest of us, even though he seems unmoved by the drama of his existence. It's admirable, his ability to commit to a certain level of swagger. Still, like me, he probably removes a mask every night in front of the mirror, feeling heavy. Being a person in this world is draining.

"I just don't understand why they said you couldn't give blood. Or that you even had to tell them who you've had sex with. Is that even legal?"

James shrugs, takes a long drag. "They just don't want our gay blood, I guess."

They probably don't want mine either, laced with all kinds of chemicals and psychopharmaceuticals. Where the intake form asked for a list of medications I was taking, I only listed birth control. I don't know why.

"I'm just sorry the night got ruined." I shake my head. "I can't believe Jordan Jacobsen! We used to be really close and now he's such a dick. I don't understand how he could be part of that."

James lights my cigarette. "He's a boy. He's just acting how he thinks he's supposed to."

"Why are people always so disappointing?"

. . .

James, I love you! Who is this mysterious man? Do you want me to beat him up? Kelly, did I imagine you were a little tipsy when we were dancing to "What's Your Fantasy?" are we finally corrupting you?! I was so mad at David that night. I don't even really have a good reason. But he's been sucking up. He texted me today that he finally watched All About Eve. Ugh, I love that movie. I love when she downs a martini and says, "Fasten your seat belts, it's gonna be a bumpy night!" We should do a movie night soon. NO ROM-COMS.

MAKE A LIST OF THINGS YOU KNOW
ABOUT YOURSELF

"What year were you born?"

"Excuse me?" Mr. K scoffs, American flag pin affixed to his wrinkled Oxford shirt. He gets exasperated by the mere sound of my voice. He's just assigned us a "personal essay" about civil rights. I'm hovering at his desk being cheeky because I was mostly delightful and quiet for the whole class, plus it's the end of the day and no one's paying attention anymore.

"Well, I was just thinking, my parents were around for all this, the civil rights movement, that's crazy."

"I was young, but yes, I was 'around for all this' too."

"So, what happened after?"

He grins like the Grinch. "Well—"

"I mean, after that and *before* Reagan," I quip. He laughs smugly. "I guess I'm curious about black people, specifically. It seems like we're always talking about Frederick Douglass and Rosa Parks and then that's it. I mean, what happens to black people between then and now? We're just quiet in American history until the Obama chapter?"

The bell rings.

Mr. K shrugs. "There's a library down the hall."

Technically, the assignment is to reflect on one of the cases we discussed leading up to the Civil Rights Act of 1964, but I see it as my duty to creatively interpret all my assignments, and it's my impulse to bend the rules to see what I can get away with. Sometimes you have to be the syllabus you wish to see in this world or whatever.

The school library at Vista, incredibly, does not contain any books about black life and civil rights in the 1970s and 1980s, so after school, I head to the public library, my last remaining hope.

Unsurprisingly, as a nerd, I love libraries. Specifically, the public one near my school, with seats in big bay windows and what feels like miles and miles of wooden shelves. I'm not sure what I expect to find here, but I know there are answers in books. I find a computer with a window view of a big tree swelling with orange leaves. It's Yo La Tengo weather. I pop in my earbuds and skip ahead on *I Can Hear the Heart Beating as One,* because I must hear "Autumn Sweater" immediately. The song actually feels like wearing a chunky cable knit sweater on a fall afternoon. It's the perfect song for the trees.

I start by searching "black people" in the library's inventory portal, chewing on the inside of my left cheek and absently biting a thumb nail. Immediately sensing my mistake, I type "African American History." There are six pages of results, most of which are dated biographies and books for kids, like the only time to learn about black history is in school. Like black people are the Pythagorean theorem—they don't really come up in real life.

I lean back in the hard wood chair feeling defeated. I don't even know what I'm looking for.

A second-grade-teacher-looking white lady bustles around the room, moving books from a cart to a shelf, stopping to lean over kids and recommend them picture books or whatever. A complete and total Susan, down to the bird sweater. Her face is tight, with thin lips and wild eyes. Her hair, fashioned into a curly bob, is badly dyed red. Susans like this make me nervous for some reason. The condescending type of Susan, whose sole mission is to make me feel like I don't deserve to exist anywhere. I feel her staring at me, expectantly, but I ignore her, opening the ancient internet browser.

"Can I help you with something?"

Of course, she's also a close talker. Coffee breath.

"No, probably not." Not with anything, really.

She contorts her mouth into a grimace—I think she may be trying to smile. I pull the Black Notebook out of my back-pack and flip it to a fresh page. I don't owe this lady anything, I realize. I've spent my whole day giving away all my perfectly good minutes to people I don't like.

And I can't let her distract me.

My Wikipedia journey goes like this: Civil rights act 1964 > Civil Rights Movement > Black Power Movement. Now we're getting somewhere.

10/8/08

<u>*The Black Notebook: Research*</u>

- —*After Civil Rights Movement, Black Power Movement*
- —*Pacifism was not enough: Black Panthers*
- —<u>*Black Power*</u>
- —*Slogan for movement, Stokely Carmichael*
- —*Student Nonviolent Coordinating Committee*
- —*1965: Assassination of Malcolm X, uprising*
- —*Watts Riots in LA*
- —*Huey P. Newton + Bobby Seale*
- —*1966: <u>Black Panther Party for Self-Defense</u>*

Oh, hell yes. I'm gonna write my paper on the Black Panthers. Mr. K will absolutely hate it. I stretch my arms and my back, grinning to myself. No one ever talks about the Black Panthers, except to imply that they were bad guys. Gun wielding and reckless, angry, a distraction from true progress and unity via MLK's nonviolence. That's how they tell it, if they even tell it at all. They're a relic, a bad idea frozen in time. Meanwhile, I've heard they still hold Ku Klux Klan rallies a few towns away in Fontana. I guess some things outlive history, they get to grow into the present. Other things, other people's stories peter out and expire, or else, get buried.

I look down at my phone and see two texts from David.

hi, how are you doing?
are you mad at me?

I'm not dealing with this right now, no thank you. I'll make him wait for my response.

> —<u>Student Nonviolent Coordinating Committee</u>
> —freedom rides
> —Ella Baker
> —Freedom Summer of 1964
> —freedom schools
> —<u>Montgomery Bus Boycott</u>
> —Claudette Colvin: 15-year-old girl arrested in Montgomery for refusing her seat (little Rosa Parks!)
> —Rosa Parks!!

Good old Rosa Parks!

The one time I played Actual Rosa Parks, it wasn't a speaking role. It was one scene, on the bus, and all I did was sit there, look old, and then get arrested. I knew that couldn't be the whole story.

Rosa Parks was an activist, as a matter of fact. A radical centerpiece of the Civil Rights Movement. Her protest on December 5, 1955, was one of so many events that fueled it and the Black Power Movement that followed. Under *Montgomery Bus Boycott* I write *Emmitt Till*. I underline Till's name, put an asterisk next to *open casket*. His mother insisted on it. She wanted everyone to see his body beaten, shot, and mutilated, bloated from three days in the Mississippi Delta.

He was fourteen. It was the first and last time he felt like an animal.

Not to sound lame, but I think about calling my mom. I'm like a missionary filled with the spirit of Black Power; I want to gush about the good news. (Mom's probable reaction: asking where I am, telling me about each piece of today's mail, saying "huh?" and then pretending she hears me, giving a vague unsatisfying response. I do not call my mom.)

More David: *I just wanted to say I'm sorry if I was being shitty the other night. I knew you were upset but I didn't know how to handle it.* Ignore.

What's wrong with being mad?

In our history books, "African Americans" are always portrayed as almost saintly or Christlike. They all get hella bonus points for like, surviving racism. And even if they don't survive it—still, extra credit for suffering. That's in the Bible I think. Survivors. Joyful endurers of indescribable torture. Humble and benevolent acceptors of a lesser fate. Maybe Job was black.

(*Servants.* That's what the Curse of Ham was about, really.)

(There's a very clear moral takeaway for every Black History Month lesson, and it's obviously Biblical: Suffer in silence. Be strong, but casually. Be strong, quietly and peacefully. But which way is the right way, peaceful protest or armed and vocal resistance? How do we know what really works?)

Studying civil rights has sadly always felt stale and flat—dates and legislations without details or living, breathing people. Without the fire, the fight. I'm just relieved I'm not the only one who thinks mad is a perfectly natural response.

Notes for my manifesto: If you don't have a map, make a map.

It didn't *end* with Rosa Parks, it *started* with her. Rosa Parks is so punk!

At 6:14 PM I have a text from my mom saying that dinner's almost ready, and three more from David.

I meant everything I said, that I really, really like you!
I'm just really glad we're friends because we're awesome.
And I don't want to lose that.

I set out making a list of books to check out. When I spot the coffee-breath Susan obviously staring at me, just like the guy in the Mormon store, I give her a look right back, raising my eyebrows as she pretends to shuffle some papers on her desk.

Driving home at twilight, I'm sparking with energy, but my mind is syrupy with exhaustion. I'm feeling winded and disoriented, like I just did a Jillian Michaels workout. (Why does she always have to be so mean?)

HAVING A FIT

Dinner is meatloaf and peas. Malcolm's favorite, and a dish I hate. A dish Mom either makes when I'm out, or completely forgets that I hate it, thrilled to be able to please the golden child, her baby, the simple and charming one, tall, handsome, lean, and popular. Dinner is not off to a good start.

When we were little kids, Malcolm always got away with snide remarks or back talk by making my parents laugh, which offended my core sense of justice. It blew the whole Job thing out of the water—if I didn't have to suffer to be rewarded, then what were the rules?

My mom dotes on him, pinches his cheeks, gets the giggles at every goofy thing he says. Ugh! Pushing the stupid peas around on my plate, my skin tingles as I get worked up thinking about it. Why doesn't anyone say I'm just as funny? It's just black humor!

It's the part in the dinner where Malcolm is raving about

the food. He always gets to it before me and Dad, and we have to follow behind in agreement, finding new strings of words to compliment Mom. (It's not an afterthought, it's an always-thought—the woman has obviously never made a bad dish in her life.)

"Ooh-wee!" Malcolm hams it up. "I'm telling you, Mom, you should open a restaurant." All this for meatloaf and peas. For every A on his report card, he gets $20; since I always get straight As, I receive no monetary compensation.

"So, Mom," I blurt, "what were you and Dad doing when the Black Panthers and all those people were around? Like in the sixties and seventies."

"We were here," she says, like obviously.

"Dad, how old were you?" Nervous and antsy, I push all the words together like an auctioneer.

"Oh, I'm not sure, maybe . . ." I try to count, too, and get confused.

"Were you like in your early twenties? Like before you were married."

"I guess so. About that."

"Did you have an afro?" Malcolm holds his hands high over his head, cackling, which sends Mom into a full body giggle. So over-the-top. "Can you even grow one?"

"Yeah, I can grow one! Not like that, though." Dad runs his bear paw over his thin shiny hair.

"But, I mean," I press on trying to find my words, "what were you guys doing?"

"Morgan," my mom exhales with a loud huff. The conversation is turning against me. "What do you mean, what were we doing?"

They're not hearing me; the scene is directed all wrong. My mom's making it Just Another Annoying Episode with Morgan, bugging out her eyes. "We just told you. What more do you want to know? Eat your supper."

I clench my jaw looking down at my plate, and *really* try not to turn up my lip as I finish eating. Things are hella tense. I can feel my dad's eyes pressing on my every move.

"I was just being curious," I say quietly, trying to get a last word in. "Forgive me for trying to learn something." Man, I really messed this all up.

I know it's coming: Dad's temper, all his pent-up opinions about me, rising to the surface of the dinner table.

"Morgan, you better fix your face. Let's enjoy this dinner." He speaks through his teeth.

"What?" I whine, "I'm not doing anything!"

"You have an attitude."

(My dad always spits when he's mad. Malcolm and I used to do impressions of him, our teeth clenched dramatically, erupting in laughter behind my bedroom door.)

"I don't." I slump in my chair, and my chest burns, gearing up for a weepy explosion. A fit. I feel like a complete toddler. I breathe in and out, deep yoga breaths. Doesn't help. *I need pity!* I think. I am pitiful and sorry for myself. I clench my fists and my throat, willing my body to lock it up.

One more attempt to explain myself: "I was just reading about some of the history of the Black Power movement and the Civil Rights Era and I realized I don't know that much about your life. Like the details. You guys never tell me anything."

My mom smacks her lips, getting riled up. "Oh come on, stop that, Morgan. We do tell you things. Now enough."

"Fine," I whimper. A tear rolls, like a boulder through the front door.

Dad hits the table with his fist. "Why do you have to make things so difficult?"

"Honey," Mom interrupts, embarrassed now.

"Okay. I know." He exhales.

"This is hard for all of us." She turns to him with a low voice. I'm practically not in the room.

I cross my arms and whisper, deflated, "You guys know I can't help it. I'm trying! I'm trying to be normal!"

"Come on, Morgan," Dad sighs. "Don't have a conniption."

I look down at my plate, hold my hands underneath the table, and just sit, Rosa Parks style. I can think of nothing else to do but just stop moving and stop opening my mouth. Wait to get old and tired.

Quietly, in spite of myself and my fate, I produce a world-class temper-tantrum hissy-fit whimper.

Dad is a volcano, seconds before erupting. He screams. Malcolm cowers. I ruin every minute.

"Nothing's ever good enough for Morgan. Do you know how hard I work—"

"Yes!" The tears come, wildly.

"Stop crying."

"I'm sorry!" I wipe my eyes with the sleeve of my Henley, go back to pretending to eat the soggy meat. "I really am."

Why *do* I have to make everything so difficult?

My mom huffs as she gets up, harshly collecting dishes. "So much for a nice dinner." She snatches my plate. Silverware clangs loudly.

Rushing upstairs to my room, I'm hoping for a retreat from myself, the thing that won't let go of me. It's got its hands around my throat. I scream into a pillow so angrily that I think I feel my vocal chords vibrating. I clench my teeth and fists, release the madness in the quietest, least disruptive way. The air around me feels like needles on my skin.

I dive into my little dark closet, take root among broken hangers and shoes I should get rid of and shoes my mom would prefer I wore. I punch the pillow. Again. Again. I make a new fist and punch the closet door like I'm Elliot Stabler (with or without a warrant).

Pulling back my throbbing fist, breathless, I'm stunned. It actually leaves a dent.

I'm so tired. I get in bed and curl to my side. I'm tired of crying. I lay there as my breathing slows, I sink and get covered in the hazy waters of my own anguish.

About an hour into my quiet sulking, my dad comes knocking.

"Listen," he starts, hovering in the door jamb. "I'm sorry I lost my temper."

"It's okay." I sit up. "Me too."

"You all right?"

"Yeah. I'm really sorry," I start to crack.

"Come here." He waves me over. "Come give me a hug."

I rise from my bed, slumping like a folded envelope. The hug is awkward: he squeezes me, and I put one arm limply around him. Both of us are vessels of pure tension.

"You know I love you, right?" he says with hot breath, still pressing my cheek into his Laker's T-shirt.

"Yeah. Love you too."

I try to pull away. No luck. *He's strong,* I think, and the realization makes me love him more and fear him more. He squeezes harder and I squeeze back, sniffling.

"We're gonna get through this." He talks into my hair. He's crying. "You're my little girl. You're my little girl."

"I know." I pat his shoulder and he releases me. "I love you too, Dad."

"Good night." He's careful to close my door gingerly. Not only does it not slam, it makes no sound at all.

That's it, then the Very Special Episode is over. Just a speck of dust in the massive universe of my bad attitudes and outbursts and ruined dinners or vacations. God, I am such an exhausting person.

• • •

Begrudgingly, I pull my phone from my sweatshirt pocket to face the Very Special Episode with David. He's sent another, *I'm here if you ever need to talk.* I roll my eyes and scoff—I do have an attitude.

I pull on my PJ shorts, put *The Exorcism of Morgan Parker* on my old CD player, and take a couple library books into bed with me.

Hearing those first few chords of the White Stripes makes me smile.

Hi you
Thank you. I'm sorry I was being bitchy. I was hurt and feeling emo and embarrassed and I don't want to lose you either.
Can we please talk about how fucking badass the Black Panther outfits are.
Oh my god I love you.

I know right

I love you too

BLACK BLACK DOG

I have no clue why a therapist's office would decorate for Halloween. Aren't we all freaked out enough about our own problems?

Here I am again, the short black girl in the Dinosaur Jr. T-shirt and plaid blazer, in the waiting room of Susan's office and the waiting room for the rest of my life, agonizing over whether or not I should partake in a bowl of candy corn. The soundtrack is the Pixies song from the end of *Fight Club*, "Where Is My Mind?" because of course it is.

Even if I wanted to, and I don't, I could not describe Susan Brady LCSW's harvest-themed outfit. Let's just say there are cornucopias involved. I'm not certain my eyes don't bug out when she opens the door.

Today, her office smells like a bad batch of pumpkin spice muffins. She offers the tissues and I decline. It's our usual little silent film short.

"So, I'm off the Wellbutrin," I sort of blurt, hoping to rush through the session businesslike. "Dr. Li put me on Prozac last week."

"Oh. How do you feel about that decision?"

"Fine."

Susan puts on her peppy radio voice. "It's often tricky to find the right medication and treatment. It can be quite a transition. I'm here so we can work through the process together. But once you find the right dose, along with therapy, you'll be able to maintain. You won't have so many dips, and they'll be more manageable."

"I know." I wiggle a flip-flop.

(She goes on, says something about mountains and plateaus. Behind my eyes, I envision them as a landscape—red, orange, burning.)

"I know it doesn't feel like it now, but you're being very brave. Depression is tough. You know, Winston Churchill battled clinical depression? He called it the black dog, like a little black dog following him around."

"Hm. That's pretty much it. Except my dog is like barking in my face all the time. Or the dog is eating me." I want to say, *I guess mine is a Black Black Dog!* but I swallow the joke for myself.

Her reliably weird and empty pasted smile. "So, tell me about the Wellbutrin."

"It was working, actually. I had a lot more energy, I felt like I could do things, I didn't feel so bad about myself all the time. But it made my temper go crazy. I felt like the Hulk, like I wasn't in control of my anger."

"Are you still feeling that level of aggression?"

"No, not exactly aggression. Not like the Hulk, definitely. That was scary. It's more like annoyed."

"Mmm."

I breathe and nod slowly, concluding my report. Clumsily grab at a couple of candy corn in my fingers.

"And, do you still have thoughts about dying?"

"No!" I swallow; the sugar is like pebbles in my mouth. "I mean, not like that. I don't think I want to hurt myself."

"That's not what I asked. Do you still think about dying?"

"I'm not thinking about killing myself. Seriously, I'm not. So. You don't have to worry." I notice I've been wringing my hands in my lap.

"But, there is something you're not telling me, isn't there?"

(There's a difference between wanting to die and not wanting to be alive, but no one talks about that difference or what to do about it. Like, you can be a seventeen-year-old girl who is physically, cosmically, and innately certain that greatness and potential and the fucking sun exist in the world just for you, hanging there like a ripe avocado for *you,* specifically, to pick. But at the same time, you can be "clinically depressed," a "sinner," stuck in a skin and a landscape that feels like it's on fire. And you don't know any way out of the fire, so you just let it win, and try to remember how warm it is, and how when it covers you, you are at least, finally, not alone. Even if you're not sure you believe in God, you hope it's real. So you pray to nothing, you do everything right, just in case. Or, you say *Fuck it.*)

(I wish I could do one or the other.)

I sigh—it's more of a growl, really. I do *not* want to be doing this, and the somersaults in my stomach move all the way up to my neck.

"Okay fine," I say, unfolding my arms and flopping them like pool noodles at my sides. "It's not that I want to die, really, but sometimes, *sometimes*, I think it might be better if I didn't exist. If I just disappeared and all my family and everyone got memory-erased like in *Men in Black*. If I never existed, their lives would be better. I guess it just sucks that I'm here and now we all have to deal with that. It sucks for everyone."

"You see yourself as a burden to others."

I nod, trying not to acknowledge tears assembling behind my eyes. "And to me, too. I'm a burden to me."

"How do you feel about that?"

"I *mean* . . . bad! Guilty. I know it would be messed up to kill myself, and my family and friends would be sad, but it feels like the only alternative is being a pain in the ass. I almost think being erased from the whole world, not ever existing, would be a gift."

Susan just nods sympathetically, doesn't respond.

"Like, that's a gift I could give."

The way her eyes soften I can tell she's thinking *Cry, cry, just do it, soften and cry!*

But I am vigilant to find my words. I want to explain myself.

"You know that movie *It's a Wonderful Life*, the Christmas movie?"

"That's a great movie."

"I love that movie. I cry every time. And I can't tell if I'm crying because I love George, and I love how he's so special to everyone in town, or because deep down, I know I'm not George Bailey. I'm not this epic person who changes everyone's life. If Clarence the angel came and showed me what the world would look like if I was never born, I know that my family and everyone would be happier. I hate to say it but it's just the truth."

"And how do you know that?"

"I just do!" I snap, and cross my arms tightly, closing up again. "I mean, it's fine, that's just reality."

Susan employs her favorite strategy: silence. She loves doing it because she knows it makes me so uncomfortable, just sitting there calmly while I squirm anxiously in my seat and dart my eyes around. She makes it so I have to sit with whatever I've just said—I'm not allowed to just zoom past it and make a joke.

Ugh, she's good. I actually have to give her props.

"So, it looks like we're out of time—"

"Oh, okay," I say, standing up and exhaling for maybe the first time in an hour.

I pull a folded check from my pocket. It's swirling with my mother's loopy handwriting, and looking at the number, I think, *See? All this money they spend on me, all this stress—there's no arguing with numbers.*

"This is from my mom."

Susan accepts it but looks back at me again with probing eyes. I move mine around nervously, waiting to be released.

"See you in two weeks."

Dashing for the lobby doors, I give Framed Portrait of Bon Jovi the stink eye. What does he know? Who wants to live on just a prayer, especially if you're only halfway there—or in my case, if you don't know where there is.

Sometimes, after therapy, I feel even more lost than before. I also feel ridiculous. *What was the point of that?* I think, seeing other cars buzz around the lot of the office park, other lives just going on, regularly, unobtrusively. Other people relaxing without the aid of several doctors and medications.

Why do I have to make everything so difficult?

THE FAKE RAPTURE

In middle school, I went to church camp with Marissa. Frankly, I don't know why I thought it would be fun. I hated Vacation Bible School, youth group, chapel, Sunday services, and any other activity with Marissa's church. It's too many creepily-friendly white people. A bunch of bland food, cheesy music.

Harvest Christian Church Camp was a nightmare in this respect. Overly smiling adults, shorts to the knee, sloppy joes that didn't taste like sloppy joes, and a *trillion* group activities. I was pissed I couldn't get any reading done—the days were packed with chipper strangers getting in my face about rock climbing or whatever.

One night after dinner and before campfire worship, we were split into small groups in the auditorium and tasked with writing skits about Why Heaven Will Be Awesome. It was during this activity, huddled in a circle with Marissa and three meek strangers, that I realized I have almost no cold hard facts about heaven. Trumpets? White robes? No bad words or secular music? Is that it?

(Obviously I could never say out loud that heaven doesn't sound all that great, since it's supposed to be the literal definition of paradise and everything.)

Our skit was not a skit at all. All of us onstage looking down at the beige crowd with theater-kid enthusiasm, exclaiming about what we most look forward to about heaven.

Marissa said, "I can't wait to walk with my bare feet on streets that are paved with actual gold! Can you guys believe that?!"

"And we'll never have to go to the bathroom!" I said.

Literally that's what I could offer: the amenities seem so-so, but mortal bodies are a nuisance. My comedic pitch was terrible. I suspect the chuckles were pity laughs, or like when my cousins say they're "laughing with me, not at me" (I'm never laughing when they say that).

The next night, when they asked if anyone wanted to devote or recommit their life to Christ, I raised my hand. (Why did I do that?) Walking down the aisle, hundreds of missionary eyes on me, I instantly regretted my impulsiveness. And when I stood next to the pastor, his hand resting on the shoulder of my jean vest, all I could come up with was, "It just felt like time."

"Fantastic. And we are all here to be your witness and your strength as you renew your promise. This is a major commitment. Are you truly ready to be serious about your walk with the Lord, into eternity?"

I nodded. My stomach churned.

What if I don't even want to go to heaven? What would I do there?

One day I was coming back to our cabin from lunch, lagging behind my bunkmates because I stopped to return a Christian Young Adult paperback to the "library," which was really just a short bookshelf in the staff office. Back at our bunk, I felt uneasy when I didn't hear the usual obnoxious squeals coming from behind the door. It was silent as I entered.

The beds were made and empty, each one with an outfit arranged carefully atop the cover. Some accessories, a Walkman, a lip gloss. As if they were just deflated, drained of their bodies. My legs went limp. The walls of the cabin seemed to fall down around me. Dizzy, I started sobbing, my throat tight and airless.

I've been terrified of the rapture since I heard about it. People's naked bodies flying upward, walking like zombie ghosts into walls. What makes it not a horror movie?

And of course. Of course, I was left behind. How could this be it, my end? How could the world just stop for no reason? Was I not a Christian?

As I collapsed into a puddle of shock in a corner of the room, my bunkmates jumped out of the bathroom, grinning. Marissa, all of them, even the fucking camp counselor. I shook with fear. They rushed at me, clammy hands on my shoulders.

I pulled my knees into my chest and rocked, weeping hysterically. *I am not going to live through this,* I thought.

I had been broken. I was not like them; I couldn't laugh at it. I had been exposed. A fraud. A nonbeliever. Everyone raptured without me.

"Morgan, it's okay! It wasn't real!" They patted me like a pet retriever.

"Morgan, it hasn't happened yet!" they reassured me. "And when it happens, you don't have to be afraid, you'll be with us!"

Folding my hands over my chest, I closed my eyes. "I was so scared. I'm so scared."

"How could you be afraid of God's salvation?"

At the time, believe it or not, I wasn't appalled or weirded out by the staging of the fake rapture, like a regular person might have been. I'm me, and this is where I'm from, so I was embarrassed, even scandalized, by my reaction. That's how I know I believe in the supernatural, but not how they do. I believe in the supernatural power that spooks me, unravels me, that makes me all the plagues at once.

Years later, though I'm completely vindicated in my decision to leave church camp the following day, I still feel a twinge of embarrassment for being the girl who had to leave early because she couldn't hang, yet again. Waving at Marissa from the front seat of the Harvest Christian van, on the way to the safety and dorkdom of my parents, I felt even then that I was somehow sealing my fate. I can't even fit in where I don't want to.

MYSTIC MORGAN

I am way too stoned for this, holding hands with David and James in front of the darkened door to Psychic Visions by Nicole, in the plaza behind Spearmint Rhino. It's Halloween. Meg is trick-or-treating with her sister, the one who told me I'm brown, and we're doing this. Pretty much everything we do is to kill time, just like everything we believe is because we need to believe it, and this particular activity covers both bases. What better day than Halloween to sarcastically commune with spirits we aren't sure exist? It's all very *Teen Witch*.

The shop is filled with incense and plants. Glass cases display different-colored crystals and stones, arranged specifically, but not in any pattern I recognize. There's soft New Age music playing, Enya or something.

(*I should not have gotten high.* I am like lying-on-the-floor-listening-to-Fleet-Foxes stoned. I want mac and cheese. I'm afraid of what the tarot cards know and I don't. What my palm could spill.)

A small, deep-brown woman emerges from a private back room marked with an image of a lotus flower. Presumably, this is Nicole. She holds a bundle of dried leaves bunched together with string and burning at one end. The smell is sharp and sweet, the smoke acrobatic and blooming as it wafts in front of her gentle face.

"Hello," she greets us warmly, and we all stand up straight. "Can I help you?"

"We were hoping for some . . . guidance or something," James says, drawing nearer to her. I keep my mouth shut, still waiting for the clouds of my high to clear.

As she rattles off her services—tarot card readings, palmistry, crystal meditation, hypnosis, something about chakras—she studies each of our faces, and nods at James, smiling slyly, before resting her gaze on me.

"You have a question," she says, somewhere between an inquiry and a declaration.

"Nothing specific. Or, maybe, yeah."

I shift my stance, cross my arms like a weirdo.

"Yes," she says plainly, almost aggressively. "There is something you need to know."

Understatement of the whole damn year.

"How much for a palm reading?" I step forward.

"Five dollars." A skeptical bargain for a direct line to the spirit world, but I only have a twenty, and I want to get Cold Stone later.

...

In the closed-off room, Nicole and I sit in two throne-like chairs, separated only by a small round end table topped with a single white candle in a garish holder. I drop my bag and sit, feeling awkward as hell.

The psychic commands, "Give me your hand," and I obey.

She speaks quickly and casually, rattling off the information like a shopping list. I squint down at my hand, too (not like I can see anything).

"I see a long life—I see health and success—I see you have a gift for helping people—I see you are a communicator. I'm sensing you have recently overcome a hardship—does that mean anything to you?"

I nod yes. (She probably says stuff like this to everyone, right?)

"I'm sensing some loneliness, does that mean something to you?"

There's my familiar pain, eager to burst from behind its rightful gate. I lower my eyes, silently chide myself for being so gullible and weak.

"I hate to tell you this," she begins, her voice suddenly maternal. "I'm seeing a very negative spirit. A negative spirit somewhere in your past."

Darkness isn't a bad thing. Open casket. Black black dog.

"You mean my childhood? My parents?"

If you don't have a map, make a map.

"I think perhaps even before them. There is a dark history. Does that sound familiar?"

"Hmm." I twist my mouth and slump a little in my chair.

"I'm sorry," she says, sounding genuine. Maybe it didn't work. "Let's consult the tarot. It's on the house!"

She rises joyously toward a set of drawers in the corner of the room. She doesn't walk, she glides, as if pulled by a flock of animated birds.

"We'll pull one card to help point you in the right direction on your journey."

She nestles gingerly back onto her throne and shuffles a brightly colored deck of cards. They're pretty and everything, but they look achingly regular. (How can they contain answers? How can they, cousins of Uno cards, be magic? Or is it her who's divine? Is it me, my "energy"?) I press my lips and eyebrows together tightly in anticipation.

"Think very deeply about this darkness," she instructs with closed eyes, still shuffling meditatively. "Concentrate on the journey. What must you discover? What is holding you back? What must you avenge?"

There is a lot of stuff we don't know.

Police brutality. Harriet Tubman.

"All right." She flips a card to the table. It's a naked white lady kneeling at a river.

"The Star! This is such a joyful card!" she proclaims. She sounds surprised, which makes me feel like shit, because of course, and because I'm also surprised. An inkling of hope leaps up my spine.

"It is beaming with light, can you see?"

"Um . . . maybe." I do not (duh), but suddenly I'm obsessed with acing the quiz. I want to make the card belong to me.

"The Star is a gift, a guiding light. It is a card of hope, of inspiration and creativity. See how the woman is pouring water into the river and into the land? She is generous, and she is blessed. The Star comes to us to replenish, to offer peacefulness that will carry you on your journey, to offer clarity as you discover your true purpose."

"Whoa," I gasp. "So, what does that mean for me? What's going to happen to me?"

"That's not really the sort of thing the cards can tell us. They tell us where to look, what to remember. How to get there, but not where *there* is."

I consider this for what feels like forever, searching my brain for the meaning, I don't want to be the one in the group standing back from an abstract painting for like an hour, still insisting *I don't get it.* If the universe wants me to be happy so badly, why is life such a disappointment? Honestly, I just want her to say, *I see the end of the movie, and you win.*

When I walk through the velvet curtains I've almost forgotten it's daylight. James rushes at me holding out three necklaces with different colored crystal pendants.

"Which one?"

"Jade."

He saunters up to the counter and places a gentle hand atop Nicole's. "I would like to purchase this, please, and I am also interested in a reading of my chakras."

James and Nicole draw the velvet curtains closed behind them, and I join David under the shop's awning, where he's snickering down at something on his phone.

"Sooo? How was it?" He sings snarkily as I light a cigarette.

"Stop laughing!" I flirt. "I don't have to tell you."

"I kind of don't get why you guys wanted to come here, anyway." He says it like it's an admission, like it hasn't been obvious all afternoon. "No offense, just, maybe you're not as doomed as you think you are."

He looks away from me, so I look away from him, smirking with butterflies. Funny what passes for a compliment these days. *Not doomed* is not the same as *beautiful and amazing*, but I'll take it.

(David Santos is sucking up. He gifted me a mix for today, likely an attempt to cement our just-friend-ness. It's called "Mystic Morgan," and starts *and* ends with Sonic Youth. "Teenage Riot" and "Do You Believe in Rapture?" respectively—he is definitely sucking up. Also cleverly featured: "Ghost" by Neutral Milk Hotel, "Every Artist Needs a Tragedy" by No Age. I have to give him credit; he makes a hell of a mix.)

"Yeah" is the totally unacceptable thing I say in response.

Wrapped in a cloud of marijuana come-down, I feel a prickly, scary excitement from my session with Nicole. She saw something in me, I'm sure of it. Something dark, of course, but also something promising, something full of love. Maybe I've been trying to get in touch with the wrong spirits. Maybe there are spirits, ghosts, who are on my side.

Darkness isn't a bad thing.

There is no going back.

"Do you guys want to go see *Saw 5*?" James blurts from the backseat as soon as the car starts. He checks showtimes. I don't care about anything. I switch to the final track of "Mystic Morgan."

"So, are you like totally pagan now?" David leans into me scandalously, trying to be cute. I know why he's teasing me, but I don't want it. "Did you learn the secrets of the spirit realm, or what?"

"It was just like 'you're on a journey,' or whatever. Just like, bullshit. Anyway, none of your business."

"Bullshit," he repeats, scoffing.

I know that I basically instructed him to laugh it off, but all of a sudden, I'm disappointed that he's obeying. I feel further away from him than ever.

EVERY ARTIST NEEDS A TRAGEDY

This is a story about me, and I am the tragic antihero. Me and my bad ideas. This is a story about me believing in nothing.

It begins delightfully! In the opening shot, three sort-of-stoned suburban young adults in ill-fitting denim are gazing up at a marquee of corporatized pleasures delivered in criminal portions. All around them, children run amok in identical Halloween costumes. The soundtrack is Spoon and Arcade Fire.

"I might just get Milk Duds and call it a day," David announces to James, with his signature blend of casual and thrilled. "You getting something?"

"Oh, I'm not sure, young David," he replies. "I might be sort of obligated to Raisinets, or Sour Patch Kids. It's a ruthless duel."

We laugh our way to the counter. I get "Uh, I don't want anything, no, wait, what are you guys getting again, actually I'll have Junior Mints, yeah I'm sure, no, nothing else, a water cup."

While James accessorizes his popcorn, David looks over at me. "You really like those things?"

"Oh, I fuckin' love Junior Mints, dude. I used to eat them as a little kid."

He guffaws. "What about like, you know, sour straws or Airheads—you weren't into any of that?" He flings a hand into the air; those deadly dimples crinkle perfectly with his grin.

"Oh no, too sweet for my taste!" I play, feeling loose. "I mean, I like an occasional Trolli worm, but I have a very so-phisticated palette, my dear and darling David."

It's just terrific, gold-star banter. Then I see a Hollister polo shirt and skate shoes coming right at us. It's Jake Walker, look-ing smarmy, breezing up to the three of us like we're all old friends.

"Hey, Malcolm's sister." He smiles like a puppy, lowered head and absolutely reckless eyelashes. *Morgan*, hey."

I take the bait because it never hurts to practice flirting, right? Whatever, I can't help but do my own little bashful rou-tine and smile sweetly back. "Hey, Jake."

"How are you guys?"

"Just trying to go see a movie and you?" James blurts, sud-denly tightly at my side, the fake butter smell wafting like cologne.

"Yeah, uh, dropped my sister off at *Beverly Hills Chihuahua* and I'm going to see *Saw 5*."

"Us too," I laugh.

James looks Jake over. "How 'bout that."

"Hey, so, James, I heard what happened after homecoming, something with Mike Pinkskyzif?" He talks fast, rushing the words and flicking his movie ticket nervously. "Hey, man, I just wanted to say I'm sorry about all that shit. I wasn't there but, I just wanna like, apologize on behalf of those guys."

Skeptical, I purse my lips and suck my teeth.

"Whoa," David takes a step back. "Who are you?"

James reaches out for a handshake, his smile only slightly curdled. "Thank you, I appreciate that."

"Cool."

"Let's never talk about it again though."

Jake laughs comfortably. "Cool, cool. I just was like, I have to say something, that's not cool."

"It really wasn't," I snap, newly enraged at Mike Whatever and Jordan freaking Jacobsen.

"Should we head in?" David to the rescue. "Are you, what's your name? Are you sitting with us, or . . . ?"

"Hi, I'm Jake." He rocks on his heels. I feel him looking at me. "I'm just by myself . . . Would you guys mind?"

"Sit with us!" James grabs at him.

It begins delightfully, like in a Tarantino film. Sharp colors, good music. It feels real.

Walking into the darkness of the theater, sitting shoulder to shoulder with his Abercrombie cologne as the animated soda cup tells us to turn off our phones, I feel Jake Walker leering.

"Can I have a Junior Mint?" David's on my other side, all hopped up on sugar and loud.

The theater darkens. The volume booms.

"Can I hang on to you if I get scared?" Jake leans, whispers at my earlobe, and I tee-hee like a girl or something.

"Just, don't be annoying about it." I love-tap his shoulder. Everything feels like pretend.

In the first scene, a giant blade swings like a pendulum. Dread and giddiness fill me.

Jake Walker's wide hand is stretching itself out on my thigh. I'm not doing anything about it.

"You okay?" David shoves the Junior Mints back in my face, eyeballs pointing at Jake's fingers crawling diligently over me. No one ever asked David to come to the rescue.

Elbowing him, I nod. Jake's wet mouth is warm against my earlobe.

He purrs, "Wanna get out of here?" I weigh my options, but not long enough to consider their consequences, which I don't really care about, anyway. Exiting the theater into the light of afternoon, I squeeze his hand, disgusted with myself.

This is a story about how I end up in the parking lot of the Empire movie theater in the backseat of Jake Walker's Ford F-150.

WHAT DO YOU CALL
A FEMALE BLACK BLACK DOG?

He's aggressive, we start going at it immediately, tongues reckless. He bites my lip, kisses my neck sloppily, breathes into my ear as he palms my breasts. It's fast and exciting. We make out with vicious purpose. He leans me back onto the bench seat, straddling me, and starts taking off his belt. I glide my hand over his chest, surprised at how excited I am, surprised at who I'm being.

"Come here," I whisper, and lift my head, opening my lips. I kiss him slowly and deeply; I'm training him. I can feel how hard he is, and I'm pleased with myself. This is what I'm supposed to be doing. This is the power I'm supposed to have.

"Fuck, this is so hot," he breathes, unbuttoning his jeans.

I giggle excitedly and move my fingers across my waistband. "It's so unexpected!"

He frees his penis from his boxers. The thing is super hard, like pointing straight ahead. And it's pretty big. I smile up at him, eyes glassy with excitement.

"Oh God," he moans. "I've seriously always wanted to do a black chick!"

I almost gasp. I have no words or courage. I feel bitten, sliced.

So, I laugh.

This really gets him going, but not how I want. "I knew you wanted it," he pants. "I could tell you kinda liked me. Let me see that black pussy."

I wriggle underneath him and start to sit up. "Wait. What?"

Running my fingers through my hair, the ecstasy lifts. "No. No, this isn't what I want." I pull my sweatshirt down and wipe his slobber from my face.

"Aw, come on," he whines, sliding his hands between my legs, and he isn't gentle at all. "You little slut," he cackles menacingly. "God, I wanna fuck you so hard." It's like he's reciting phrases from a script.

He fumbles with the button on my pants, and I press my backside into the door, searching blindly for the handle. I finally manage to get the door open and jump out, and I want to shout, *You can fuck yourself!*

But I don't say anything.

Now his entire demeanor changes, and he stares down at me from the raised truck with his veiny white penis exposed. I stand frozen with the door still open, grimacing at him. I want to get the hell out of here ASAP, but I also want some vindication, an apology, anything.

"Oh hell no. You cannot just leave me like this. Come on, shit, I was just playing. Just, please."

"This is so gross," I mumble to myself, shaking my head at the concrete. I push the heavy blue door closed and pause for a moment, just breathing. In shock.

I'm not sure what else to do, so I head back toward the theater. I have no plan. I have no clear assessment of myself or what just happened. I feel tears welling up in my chest, then tight anxiety, then vivid, vivid anger. Spicy-food-in-the-belly anger. I walk faster, focusing on the light of the marquee. *Beverly Hills Chihuahua, The Secret Life of Bees, Eagle Eye.* I think of David and James and the warmth of Nicole's Psychic Visions, the afternoon sun, the simplicity of my frustrations just earlier today. Why do I have to ruin everything? I always make everything so difficult, so dramatic. I always fool myself into thinking I can be someone other than myself.

("What is it with you?" my dad said to me once during a screaming match. "You go immediately to *always,* and *everyone,* and *everything.* That just isn't the truth!")

The entrance to the theater is fairly empty, the stairs leading to the box office quiet except for a few smokers with Mohawks. At least I am lucky in this moment; I can collapse onto the steps and berate myself in peaceful quietude.

I consider texting David or James but don't. Pull my knees into my middle, feet together. Then I stretch them out. I'm totally restless. Cold. Or maybe I'm shaking?

Suddenly, out of the corner of my eye, I see Jake's raised truck revving through the parking lot, and I tense up, butterflies smack-dab in the center of me. As he speeds past I can tell through the tinted windows that his hair is disheveled, his eyes wild. He's zooming. My chest pounds like a jackhammer. Then he rolls his window down and whistles. System of a Down blasts crazy loud. What a stupid band. Even the Mohawks turn and frown at it.

"Black bitch!"

He sounds like he's speaking through a megaphone, or one of those voice-changer things from *Home Alone,* or as if all his racist neighbors and ancestors are grabbing his balls and slapping the back of his head saying *Be a man.*

I weep.

What I decide to do next is pretend like nothing happened.

The next week, Barack Obama wins the presidency. We have a black president, for real. However unlikely, a small part of me hopes that maybe this will spur some change in my life, too. Maybe things will be different from now on.

On election night, our family gathers in the living room as the results come in. We all drink champagne, even me and Malcolm, and watch coverage of people celebrating in Washington, Chicago, New York, flooding the streets. Our street, unironically named Ivory Lane, is dark and quiet. It's just Tuesday around here.

My dad blubbers silently in his spot on the couch, all snotty and breathless. My mom balances on the very end of the cushion, holding a hand to her mouth and shaking her head like she's in church.

"Kids," she says to Malcolm and me as we sprawl restlessly

on the rug. "Do you realize how important this is? All the years we have fought and fought for this? What people went through . . ."

"It's history," Dad chokes, his voice hoarse from crying.

"Yeah," Malcolm and I both reply gravely, seriously, and then we keep gawking at the mayhem.

"So important," I echo, and I try to mean it. But I don't know. Not really. No one ever wants to tell me the details.

NOW IS THE BEST TIME IN HISTORY
FOR ME TO BE ALIVE

Suburban white kids have a game they like to play: *If you could go back in time to any period, where would you go?* It's supposed to be a harmless icebreaker, a chance to disclose your love for Medieval Times or *The Oregon Trail* or the annual Renaissance Pleasure Faire ("Ren Fair" to the dorks), how churning butter at Knott's Berry Farm was always your favorite field trip. A chance to play dress up, to imagine what it was like.

I try not to imagine being a slave, but it's impossible. (Is there any clearer metaphor for my life than fourth grade, the Year of the American Girl Craze? Decades of Mollys and Kirstens and Samanthas to choose from, and the only Black American Girl is a slave.) They're always expecting me to pull the black card, take everything too seriously, disturb the fun, and be a downer once again. I try to hold my tongue and not point out the inherent flaw in the question's ramifications—specifically, for me. I just try to play along, whitewashing myself into various fashions, trying to feel entitled to any dress. But technically, right now is the best time in history for me to be living. (How depressing is that?)

During my 1950s housewife phase, for example, spurred by a new obsession with black-and-white movies and the discovery of an adorable vintage store in Laguna Beach, I tried not to think about how my dresses were probably worn by white women whose houses were cleaned by my grandmother. I tried not to imagine how it would feel to be pressed against a brick wall with a firehose, to be spit on and called a nigger.

I always wait too long to say what hurts.

If I went back in time to any period, who would I be? Would I be silent and passive on the diner stool while wiping a stranger's saliva from my eyes? Would I be militant like the Panthers? Would I wear all black and go to secret meetings in basements, would I march right up to a white cop and dare his baton to touch my skin?

If I was a slave, would I be a *Yes, massa,* suck-up kind of slave, or would I risk everything and navigate the Underground Railroad for even the slimmest chance of freedom? Would I be the version of Rosa Parks they make me play at school assemblies, or would I be like Actual Rosa Parks?

What kind of person am I? Eager to win approval from my white friends (and even foes), to play along even when I'm injured; as eager as my teachers to approve of passivity as civil disobedience, to keep the peace and blend in.

The thing is, it's never quite suited me, civility.

...

Reading Assata Shakur's autobiography made me believe. It was the first time I'd heard this part of the story in our own words, not a teacher's or a textbook's. There's no way to argue with her first-person account. The FBI targeted her, they lied in court, and she got put away for murders she didn't do. Black people were routinely framed by cops and the government as criminals and villains, when they were fighting for their rights, for their justice and liberty for all. They weren't wrong. They weren't terrorists. They had a kind of bravery, belief, and fearlessness that I'm scared to even imagine. But it was a disturbance. It messed up the status quo. Their revolution was scary—too radical, too intense.

This is why the truth hurts: all the years I've spent clamping my tongue and shrugging off the sting of being "Most Unique," all the acrobatics of attempting to blend in and be accepted by white people, all the impulses I've been ashamed of, the feelings I've punished myself for and the thoughts I've tried to correct. (Isn't that the whole point of sins? To remind you that you're always wrong? Even if they've been "washed away," they still count—you are inherently flawed.)

Now I realize I've been lied to all this time, fed incomplete and discriminatory stories, especially about myself and my people. It sinks my heart to the ocean floor.

THE VELVET UNDERGROUND
RAILROAD

My cousin Coco and I have this thing about cranberry sauce—
it has to come from the can, so when you pop it out, it has
those ridges for slicing.

"You want a separate plate for yours, too?" I ask, almost
butt to butt in Aunt Carolina's kitchen, going *in* making our
Thanksgiving plates. It's tradition for us to make our plates
together, shimmying with excitement over the buffet trays of
sweet potatoes and greens and green beans and turkey and
ham and cakes and sauces.

"Obvi!" Coco giggles and pretends to toss her hair like
a white girl. My favorite cousin, the girlie one who's only a
month and ten days older, agrees with me on the important
things, like keeping cranberry sauce juices away from the
mashed potatoes and corn pudding. "You know I hate when
my food touches."

We've been a duo since we were little: the "Caboodle Girls"
is what we were called for a while. That was back when I made

clubs for everything—mini backpacks, bucket hats, whatever—anything we were into, we had to be *super* into.

"I think I have enough for my first round." I eye the precarious borders of my dishes, suddenly daunted. "Where we sitting?"

"At the kids' table." She points, and I drop my plates down across from Malcolm, who's shoveling mac and cheese into his mouth and grunting happily.

"Two plates?" My brother gawks as Coco and I settle in, considering what to taste first. "Y'all are bougie."

"What-*ever*!" Coco sings nasally, and Malcolm pinches his nose, mimicking her. She laughs from her whole chest, loud and uncontrollable, just like her mom after a Cadillac margarita.

I smile, wishing I could muster the same revelry, but I'm too tired. I don't even have much of an appetite.

(No one in our extended family knows I've been "going through a tough time," and it was decided in the car on the way over that we wouldn't discuss it. That's our secret shame, our bond, our blemish and burden. I'm putting on my best face, teasing Coco about her last boyfriend's big head, dodging long conversations with grown-ups like a professional.)

"Morgan! You gonna make us do a play again this year?" our older cousin CJ snickers between bites, eliciting an over-the-top groan from Malcolm.

"No, I'm retired! Jeez, I was, like, eleven." I smirk. Our Christmas plays were legendary and ridiculous in their ambition. I worked on the scripts for months, assigned everyone acting and production roles, obnoxiously interrupted cocktails and conversations to demand silence during our performances.

"But you have to admit," I add, thrusting my finger into the air, "those were kinda awesome!"

"You used to be so intense!" Coco cackles. She does her impression of me, which is terrible. "Mal-*colm, your line!*"

(At least with this crew, I know my role. And yeah, maybe they'll relentlessly tease me for it, but they've always accepted my intense and difficult ways.)

I give in, laughing at all the projects and productions I was once so serious about, so committed to. "Don't worry, I'm still intense."

"Y'all are so giggly!" My mom pops over to our table, being such a mom. "Everybody good over here? Need anything?" She always eats, like, an hour after everyone else, needlessly distributing extra napkins or whatever. It's super sweet, but I also wish she would just hang out with the rest of us sometimes.

"We're good," Malcolm says quickly. She pats his head. Because we're not at home, he doesn't try to jerk it away.

Kids can never be their real selves around extended family. Not exactly. You have to be the version your parents like, the version they've approved, because you're supposed to be a little representative for them. That's what the teachers tell us before we go on field trips and stuff—we're representing God's Word. Like, no pressure.

That's why I had a whole breakdown before we came over here.

First, my mom said, "Is that what you're wearing?" which she asks every single time we're going out, and every single time it upsets me, pokes my insecurities right in the gut. I changed my shirt five times and my pants three times. I tried my hair up and down and up. Then I messed up my lipstick and just lost it. Barricaded in the bathroom, trying to catch my teary breath, I felt like screaming. I was so pissed at myself, and I squeezed my eyes shut, willing myself to get over myself. When my mom knocked, I expected a screaming match about my brattiness, about how I'm too sensitive and how I have to make everything a drama.

But she wanted to help me through it. She wiped my face and rubbed my back, and we shared a cup of Constant Comment while my breathing slowed. I wanted to let the dark cloud pass, just like I always do—and this time it worked.

Antidepressants aren't magic or anything, but six months ago I couldn't get myself to stop crying no matter what. Once I entered a mood, I became the mood. Now, sometimes on good, bright days, I literally stop and notice flowers. They're actually awesome.

The next night, after epic turkey sandwiches and mounds of mac and cheese, I'm completely taken aback when Malcolm comes to my room and asks if I want to take a drive, like old times. A surprised laugh escapes as I toss down my book, *Ain't I a Woman: Black Women and Feminism*, by bell hooks.

"Okay." I shrug. "For sure! Right now?"

"Yup. I made a mix."

Outfitted in flip-flops and hoodies, we hop into my car. The night is unusually chilly, almost like real fall weather, so I flip on the heater immediately, rubbing my hands together as the burned-popcorn smell wafts in our faces. Rudy's signature musk smells especially sweet. I love Rudy.

You can always escape.

I turn to Malcolm. "The usual route?"

"Sure."

As I back out of the driveway, Malcolm fishes a jewel case from the pocket of his basketball shorts.

"What's on it?"

"You'll see," he says, turning up the volume and rolling down his window. I roll mine down, too, and light a cigarette, speeding on the dark road toward the quiet side streets we like. Malcolm giggles as the first song comes on: Maroon 5's "Sunday Morning." Our guilty pleasure. We pinkie-swore never to tell anyone how much we both secretly love it, how we can't help ourselves from belting the chorus and the fake R & B intro. And that's exactly what we do, wind at our cheeks and our hands catching waves in the night air. I let out a long, exhilarating yelp.

We take the long way to Redlands, skip the freeway and drive over a creepy bridge we love to adventurously cross. We bypass the houses of our friends and classmates and take teeny roads as far up as we can. I have to give it to Malcolm: his playlist is damn good. Our guilty-pleasure songs are padded by Grizzly Bear, Beirut, Nico. I feel pretty proud, honestly. I taught him well, like a big sister should. We're more alike than I remember. Maybe he could understand me, and maybe he wants to.

As we near The Spot, I don't know what comes over me, but I slow to a stop and park. For the record, I am fully aware of its sanctity and a firm believer in unwritten (and Yellow Notebook–written) rules, especially when it comes to my group, but when Malcolm looks over at me, puzzled, I say, "I wanna show you something. Come on."

Maybe I want to connect with him, or attempt to. (Maybe I want to be the antidote to David's rejection. I'll try again to love and be loved, and maybe this time I'll be vindicated.)

At the ledge, the view has the power it always does: we fall silent in reverence and reflection. I search my tote for a Black and Mild; I always keep a couple on hand for moments like this.

"Want one?" I ask from one side of my mouth, cigarillo hanging from the other like I'm James Franco playing James Dean or something.

"Nah, not during the season. Sometimes I'll do chew with the seniors, though."

"Whoa, really?" I manage to laugh but feel a pang of disapproval.

"Want some of this?" Malcolm—two years my junior, whose head my family teasingly refers to as a cantaloupe, whose birth angered me so much that I bit his infant forehead—produces, out of nowhere, a water bottle. One of *those* water bottles: undecipherable liquor bathed in Gatorade. I seriously almost choke.

I know I can't go all prudish on him, though I weirdly want to, so I stifle my shock.

"Uh, maybe just a sip. Since I'm driving."

"Be my guest."

"Where did you get this?" I take a swig and my mouth puckers at the sweetness. "And what is in this?"

"I swiped a little vodka from Mom and Dad's cabinet. It's my recipe: vodka, orange Gatorade, and cream soda."

I laugh and shake my head, staring down at the few cars on the highway. I'm speechless. Finally, I manage, "Dude, you really love candy."

Malcolm takes back the bottle, grinning mischievously, and indulges in a nice, long drink.

"So, what's up, little brother? How's life?"

"It's cool."

I shift on the ledge to adjust my butt. My flip-flops are filling with gravel, but I don't care.

"What about girls?" I nudge him goofily with my elbow. "How about Sarah Yates? She's cute."

(Sarah and Malcolm have been tight since the fifth grade. She's smart, kind, and it's obvious she has a crush on him. Once, when they were studying together in the living room, I saw the way she giggled at him, and to my surprise, I thought it was sweet. They make a cute black couple. Maybe at least one of us can have a normal healthy relationship. She seems like the type of girl who would try to be my friend, too, try to blend in with our family. She wears these cute flouncy skirts and her hair is in long braids. She is so not punk, but cute for Malcolm, I've always thought. I've always been jealous of both of them.)

"Naw, we're just friends. She's cool, don't get me wrong. I just don't like her like that. Besides, I'm not really into black girls."

He says the words so easily, like they don't mean what they mean.

Here it is: knife to my heart. The letdown. My whole stomach leaps into my throat.

"What do you mean?"

"I don't know . . . I guess I'm just not attracted to them. And they're always so loud."

(What I know everyone is thinking when they see me: No. Or something even grosser, if they're "into black girls." "Black pussy," Jake had whispered, spraying his saliva all over my neck. I don't know which is worse.)

I nod solemnly, quickly advancing through rage, embarrassment, horror, and finally settling on disappointment and grief. I swallow my pain and hold my tongue and try not to make everything so difficult.

(*Even Malcolm,* I think, heartbroken.)

Malcolm doesn't seem to notice my wheel of emotions. He goes on.

"I mean, there's only two black girls in my class, anyway."
I laugh inadvertently. It's more of a cough, really. "True."

"I don't know, there is someone I've been talking to. Maddy
Walker? I kinda like her. But I don't know, we'll see."

"Like, Maddy Walker like Jake Walker?"

"Yeah, you know him? He's in your class."

I grab the bottle and gulp the disgusting cocktail. Whatever.

"Oh, I know him," I say, nervously lighting another cigarette. I'm gonna have a sore throat tomorrow. "He is . . . he's
not a good guy."

"What do you mean? He's always nice to me at football."

"Yeah. Nothing, never mind. Forget I said anything. Maddy's
nice! I mean I don't know her, but she seems okay." I stiffen.
Dangit. The same word vomit and bad attitude that ruins every
moment.

"We should probably go after I finish this, I guess," I sigh.

"Yeah, probably."

"Are you better? Like, cured?" Malcolm asks earnestly on the
drive back, lowering the volume on American Football's "I'll
See You When We're Both Not So Emotional."

"It doesn't really work like that, Malcolm," I say quickly.
Then I add, "But, yeah, I guess I feel a little better right now."

"Cool, cool. You seem better than before."

At a stop sign, the van in front of us has a license plate that
says *In Case of Rapture, This Car Will Be Unmanned!!*

"That was scary," he adds, lowering his head. "No offense."

"I know. It was scary for me too." I turn onto a residential street that looks almost exactly like ours and slow the car, glancing over at him. "I'm sorry you had to go through that. I know I'm not an easy sister."

We're quiet as the song fades, and the Velvet Underground comes on, "Candy Says." We are almost home.

"I hope you keep feeling better, sis. It's gonna suck when you leave for college."

It's so abrupt, I don't know how to respond.

"Ah, come on." I smile slightly, cruising ahead and letting the achiness of the song wash over me. "At least you won't have to deal with me bossing you around and being so intense all the time."

"Well, that's who you are," he snickers.

"Yeah," I sigh with a snort, "I guess it is." I've heard some people talk about a part in the cycle after grief—acceptance.

I sneak a look over at Malcolm and notice his eyes are welling with tears, his mouth slack. "I'll just miss you," he says quickly, wiping his eyes in one swoop of his sleeve.

"I'll miss you too." I get a little smooshy—wind chimes sing in my chest. "But that's not for a while. We have some time."

"Truuuue," he sings, then busts up when I join on the highest note, shaking his head and begging me to close my mouth.

I have no idea if I have the hypothetical and figurative balls to be a Black Panther, or Actual Rosa Parks, or to risk my life leading hundreds of slaves to freedom. I don't know where I'm going when I die, and I don't know where I'm going after graduation, and sometimes I don't even know if I want to keep being alive. But as long as I'm here, and I'm me, I will definitely be intense, ridiculous, passionate, and sometimes hilarious.

THE ROAD TO FREEDOM

The Diaries of Morgan Parker

<u>Monday, December 1, 2008</u>

I'm in detention for the first time in my damn life. My whole life. And my life has been pretty long. I mean, you might not think so, but I do.

I don't really know what I'm supposed to do in detention. The only other people here are two fake-stoners that I'm pretty sure are here every day, and they're just sleeping with their heads down on their desks. Mr. Howard is at his desk looking bored, grading essays about Thoreau. I know because he already gave mine back. A+. At the top, next to the title, "Solitude Is Better than Society: Thoreau Transcends at Walden Pond," he wrote, "You are an excellent, talented writer!" It was a helluva good essay.

I love writing, even though I never do it anymore. I used to, pages and pages of stuff like stories about girls my age with terminal illnesses. Most of it wasn't stories, though. It was just about me and how I felt. So full of emotion. I loved it. I think I just like the way words sound and how you can make them do whatever you want. Reading beautiful words makes me feel like the world is so big and amazing and painful. That's what I liked about Thoreau. That guy really knew how to talk about loneliness and how everything about modern society is so full of crap. But he was optimistic, which is more than I can say. I liked when he said, "I did not wish to live what was not life." Dang.

Am I supposed to think about why I'm here? Well, I'm here for no good reason. Technically, for being "disrespectful and disruptive" in Government class this morning. Well, you know what I think is disrespectful? Only teaching the parts of history that you like. Whatever. This is what happened:

Harriet Tubman.

Did you know Harriet Tubman carried a gun? I've never realized it before, or else I was not encouraged to consider it. But, you know, of course she did. You can't escape slavery (several times!) armed with just quick wit and street smarts. (Or slave smarts.) It's not like those footprints in the sand could do anything to protect her. The other guys had guns, so of course she did, too. In pictures she's always standing still in her shawl, and the only thing in her hands is a lantern and some kind of walking stick—like she's actually Moses from the Bible.

White people really take things literally.

. . .

Pop quizzes on Mondays are perhaps the biggest treachery I have ever endured from a non-familial adult. It's only something the asshole teachers do, and only when they're feeling particularly lazy and spiteful. It's an easy way to punish us without doing much work at all. They'll begin the class with a pop quiz, feeling haughty as they pass warm sheets of paper down each row of desks, and basically chill until we're finished. After that we're instructed to stare at a horrible film or read the next chapter of our textbook in complete silence as they grade our haphazard answers. Totally unfair, and completely hellish.

This one's fill-in-the-blank, which, in Mr. K's class, is obviously a complete trap for me.

Here are some sample questions from today's quiz:

Harriet Tubman's nickname was _____
because _____.
(Bonus points for Scripture memorization.)
Harriet Tubman was a _____ during the Civil War.
Slaves used _____ to communicate instructions about the Underground Railroad.

216

Slaves were freed in _____, as a result of

_____.

Because I'm not an idiot, and I know exactly what the deal is, I resist the urge to write: "Harriet Tubman's nickname was *Minty* because *her real name was Araminta*," a fact that I only just learned. Must have gotten lost in all those years of "African American History" Months that drilled her abridged and approved biography into my memory.

Just like with Rosa Parks, I've always weirdly assumed Harriet Tubman to be matronly and unassuming. Unsatisfied with the usual blurb on Harriet Tubman from our Christian school textbook, I decided to do some more research. Turns out she was a boss. In addition to being a fugitive during the civil war (the "Moses" Mr. K's looking for, with extra credit for Exodus), Harriet Tubman was also a nurse, a cook, a scout, and a spy for the American government. She also carried a gun and vowed to use it on anyone in the way of her freedom. We never learn any of that in school.

Anyway, I don't write what I want to on the quiz. I don't write anything on the quiz. I guess I do it out of protest. I'm just not in the mood to play along.

I look around at all the diligent bowed heads and quickly try to put on a "serious" face, eyebrows all scrunched. Staring down at the half-sheet of printer paper, I try to move my pen around to make it look like I'm writing, but I'm not.

"Time's up!" bellows Mr. K, appearing smugly at the first row of desks. "Hand your quizzes up."

Pages flutter, and I sneak to mix mine in with some others so no one sees my blank page; the only markings are my name and the date. That's gotta be worth something.

For the remainder of class, we watch a movie called *Amazing Grace* which no one has heard of because it's a Christian movie for distribution only in Family Christian bookstores and youth group movie nights. This movie is all wrong, dude. It's not about American slavery at all, and Harriet Tubman is nowhere to be found. Instead, it's about some white British Parliament guy. It's so random and super boring, so I zone out for pretty much the whole time.

The bell finally rings and I'm more excited than I have ever been to go to Calculus.

"Morgan, can you please stay after class?"

I stiffen, a notebook half into my backpack. "Uh, okay. Yes, yeah."

Shoot.

Meg darts a worried look my way and I shake my head.

"I'll see you at lunch," I say. I pretend not to notice how she keeps hanging out in the doorway for a few more seconds.

I sling my backpack on my shoulder and suddenly Mr. K's hovering right behind me, creepily. He's so tall, I'm just now realizing, as I stare up at the patches of prickly gray on his chin. I *hate* hovering, everybody knows that. I hate it almost as much I hate P.E.

"So, let's hear it."

"What?" I cross my arms, sigh heavy, and bend my head down. I'm prepared for a condescending, right-wing-tinged lecture.

He sighs back at me and places a pale hand on his doughy waist. "Morgan, I know we have our differences."

I open my mouth to snap back, but he holds up a finger to stop me. I slump and try not to roll my eyes. I have learned from experience that rolling my eyes, even inadvertently, *really* sends pissed-off grown-ups over the edge. To curb my bubbling aggression, I try to think of something else. Assata, Harriet, David, the Curse of Ham, Jake Walker, my Bummer Summer . . .

Turns out I don't have very helpful material for Zenning out.

"I know we have our differences, but you've always been one of the brightest students in your class. I would hate for you to jeopardize your grades just to spite me with some liberal protest. Now, tell me what's going on. Why didn't you complete the quiz?"

I part my lips, but I have no words. I haven't thought this through, so I just stare down at my shoes.

"I'm trying to reason with you, Morgan. I know you know this material. These quizzes are worth ten percent of your grade." He lowers his voice gravely. I can tell he's trying to soften his face like one of those concerned and super-involved teachers on *Degrassi*. But he sort of looks constipated. "Is everything okay at home?"

"Everything's fine at home, yeah. I just . . . I didn't do the quiz because . . . I didn't feel comfortable."

(This my best impression of an adult sentence.)

Clearly running out of patience, Mr. K tips his head back. "What could have possibly made you uncomfortable about these questions? I thought the African American History unit was one of your favorites! Is this a feminist thing?"

"*No,* it is not a *feminist thing.* It's just . . . It kind of . . . wasn't the whole story. So, for instance, did you know that Harriet Tubman was a *SPY* for the government during the Civil War?! And, did you know that Harriet Tubman wasn't her real name, and that there was a bounty on her, and she was armed? We don't talk about that. I know that wasn't on the quiz, but I'm just saying."

"Exactly, young lady, you're right. Those weren't questions on the quiz."

"Well, they should have been." As soon as I say it, do I regret it? Do I want to stuff my words back into my mouth while they're still hanging in the air? Or does saying it feel good?

"Excuse me? Miss Parker, I'm frankly very tired of your disrespect and sassiness in this classroom. It's distracting and unacceptable."

He trudges to his desk and opens a drawer, still talking in a high-pitched, reprimanding tone. "You'll go to detention today, and if we have another problem, it will be suspension. And I shouldn't have to tell you that you will also receive a zero both for the quiz and for class participation today." He scribbles something on a pad and hands it to me. "You're dismissed."

It's a detention slip. I've never even seen one before. It says *Insubordination*.

"And, Morgan, you don't know everything."

I stuff the paper into my back pocket and leave without saying anything. *Neither do you.*

YEAH, BUT NOT REALLY BLACK, THOUGH

I didn't ask Meg and James to wait for me after detention, but when I'm released through the school's double doors, there they are, my own Ponyboy and Sodapop rising from the steps to meet me.

"Welcome back." James slaps my shoulder.

"Ugh, that was a waste of an hour of sunlight vitamins."

"Coffee Bean?"

"Sure, okay."

While I drive, James riding with Meg somewhere ahead of me, I pout and stew. I feel myself sinking into the misfortune of the day, to a place I'm terrified I won't return from.

I'm so out of it that I go to the wrong coffee place, in the wrong plaza altogether, and it takes me forever to get to the Actual Coffee Bean, craning my neck to check every identical shopping center I pass. James and Meg are already at a table on the patio when I finally arrive, anxious and out of breath.

"Sorry." I slump into my chair with a grumble.

"What happened?" Meg ogles.

"I went to the completely wrong plaza."

"Oh. Well, that's understandable."

(Every strip mall here follows a very specific and formulaic pattern: chain grocery store (Vons, Albertsons, Stater Bros., Ralph's, Trader Joe's); chain drugstore (Walgreens, Long's, CVS, Rite Aid); chain coffee shop (Starbucks, Coffee Bean, Peet's); nail salon; and one to two miscellaneous storefronts—usually a See's Candies, a Mail N Copy, a pet spa, or a dry cleaner. It's not uncommon for residents to misremember specific groupings, such that one might pull into an Albertson's shopping center expecting a pet spa but be met with a Starbucks instead. It's a lot to keep track of, with very few identifying visuals to help one discern any difference at all, which is another thing I hate about it here.)

I stretch my legs, willing the sunlight vitamins to work their magic and repair my mood. Meg offers her drink, but I pass. I don't feel like anything.

"You okay, buddy?" Meg chirps with a long face.

I snap, "I'm fine," and look down at my Docs. I hate my stupid socks and I hate that I feel bad and I especially hate that Meg knows it. I wish I could "fix my face" as my mom would say—it's like my attitude is tattooed all over me. I suck in a deep breath and when I exhale, I imagine that I'm lighter, chiller.

"Um, what'd I miss?" I reach for Meg's drink, trying to start over and just be normal. It's too sweet for me.

"Soooo," James starts, smacking his lips after a sip. "It's

straight boy crush's birthday next week and I have absolutely no idea what to get him. Like should I go super friendly, like a David Lynch DVD, or flirty like chocolates and essential oils?"

"Okay well, first of all," I snort, leaning over the table like we're the Sisterhood of the Traveling Pants. "I don't even know what essential oils are, so definitely don't do that. Second, it's amazing that you just called David Lynch 'friendly,' I totally agree obviously," I chuckle, counting out my points on green nails. "But, this is a hard one. What does he like?"

"I don't know. . . . He's sweet, and straight. . . . He has a nice broad chest."

Meg snickers, "And you're saying we *don't* know him, right?" There is not an inch of subtlety.

"Maybe chocolate and a movie?" I squint, guessing in the dark. Meg lets out an *Oooh.*

"That could be cute, and you could invite him to watch together? No, sorry." I shake my head. "Don't listen to me. I have no idea what I'm talking about."

"Ugh, whatever. I'll get him DVDs. Or maybe I won't get him anything. It's not like he'll care." He slumps back into his chair, and it is the slump heard around the Inland Empire. Meg reaches over to stroke the side of his face, what we call a "hard-pat."

"I'm super sorry he's not into you, dude," I say softly. "You should be with someone awesome. I wish we could all find someone awesome."

"Me too! My goodness, a relationship would be good right

about now. Even a short one. But real boyfriends, not just Yellow Notebook conquests. Speaking of—"

She slips the tome out of her tote with a pen, opens it to the inside front cover.

Sometimes we fall for pricks.

She glances at me as she dictates. It stings, but I let it.

"Amen," James agrees.

"I know, I know," I spit, raising my hand in concession. "I'm moving on. I just need a distraction, except everyone basically sucks."

"We need to meet new people." James nods with wide eyes.

"But what about Coco's Waiter with the Hair? You never updated the Notebook."

"It's not a big *deal* or anything." Meg smiles down at her acid-wash jeans, suppressing excitement. "But he is very into me. Like, I am definitely hot right now." I love Meg's pleased-with-herself grin; it's inspirational.

James and I squeal dutifully, throwing jazz hands up. I almost lose balance in the unstable chair at the surprise of good news.

"Um, we need to know everything!" (Truthfully, I'm a teeny bit stung that this is the first I'm hearing about the development. But I keep ignoring my feelings.)

"Well, okay. So, when we played Halo that one time last month with his friends, it was super awk, he said basically seventeen words to me, but he's been randomly texting me quotes from *Gilmore Girls,* which he apparently loves, so I think he's pretty much perfect."

"Oh *God.*" Months ago, it was one of our little bits: me overdramatically complaining about *Gilmore Girls;* Meg offering spontaneous recaps of that week's episodes. This time, for some reason when it leaves my mouth, it feels sour and cruel. Am I bitter? *Just keep your mouth shut for once.*

"I know, I know. But I really like him. I think we could be good together. Don't you think, Morgan? How good would that be?"

"Yeah, totally, I know, it would be super good." [(!)(?)]

"We're having lunch this week we decided." She adjusts the child's barrette in her side-parted hair—a penguin—and quickly adds, "I think I'll make a move."

"Great!" I squeak, clapping my hands together. I can tell it sounds insincere, but it isn't, I don't think. "You got this!"

"Definitely make a move," James insists. "He probably has a huge crush on you and is intimidated."

To think—I once thought that about David Santos. I was so stupid. It stings, and I don't want to let it. ("Whatever, I don't really care" has been my official stance; all I have to do is keep repeating it until it's true.)

"You guys are right," Meg swoons cheerily. "He's gorgeous and when we hang out it will be fantastic. I don't know why I always expect everything to go horribly."

"Ugh, I feel you. Lately I'm reaching mountaintop levels of

misfortune." I fake a laugh and cross my arms; the same move I pull in therapy to undercut the grief.

When my friends don't jump to refute and assuage me, I'm washed in relief—I don't want pity, I just want someone to hear me. Meg looks over, offering her hand, and I take it. We braid our fingers together and wince into the sunset, like two middle-aged women at the end of a Lifetime movie. James hums the bridge of a Fiona Apple song and starts playing a game on his phone. I feel my exterior soften as the bad attitude relents.

"I'm starting to feel kind of crazy," I say slowly, hesitant to unleash who I was this summer. I could revert back to that raw, emo puddle any minute. "Not crazy—just, I can't make anything go my way. Who gets detention? I don't know why I didn't just write the answers on that stupid quiz." I shake my head at my shoes, sighing through my nose.

"Yeah . . . ," Meg tries gently. "Why didn't you?"

"It's not like me, right?!" We exchange wrinkled foreheads before I drop mine back in disgrace. "I don't know. I guess I just got frustrated with how dumb our school is."

James snorts a smile, tips his head into his palm. "What do you mean?"

"I mean . . ." I loosen my hand from Meg's and huff. "Do you guys remember last year, when Jenn Hanson said she thought the Underground Railroad was a real railroad?"

Meg rolls her head, "Oh my *LORD*! Yes, that was completely ridiculous!" They cackle, and I grimace.

"Shit like that," I snap. "And it's like everyone's totally fine with being ignorant. The only people who get rewarded are the football players and the Popular Christians. And they're just basically mean, conceited people in Abercrombie polo shirts whose parents go to church with all the teachers. Anyone who actually wants to learn stuff is labeled a freak. And it doesn't matter what I do. I'll never have blond hair, so I'll never be cool enough." I mumble the last part, leaning my cheek against a fist.

"Those people are not cool," James concludes definitively.

"I like being weirdos!" proclaims Meg with fervor. "I don't ever want to wear a dress. Or wear pink. Or be one of those girls who draws her eyebrows. Why do they do that? They look like cartoons."

I'm not in the mood to giggle. "It's not the same, though, Meg." I suck my teeth dismissively. "It's harder for me because my skin color is different."

They don't rush to placate or correct me, but now they're just staring blankly. Relief has vanished; tension is thick in its place. Meg sits on her hands, looks down at her shoes, sniffs. James shifts in his chair and it creaks on the pavement, clucks his tongue, squints at the sun. I'm definitely not being heard.

"You guys really don't understand what it's like to be black in this country. Even at our school! You know what? *Especially* at our school!"

"Yeah but, you're not *really* black," scoffs Meg. "Not like 'ghetto' or whatever."

"I have black skin, so I'm black, okay? Black does not mean 'ghetto,' or 'urban' or whatever. I hate when people say that."

James chews on his lip, eyes ping-ponging between us.

"That's what I'm trying to say," she says in her arrogant "practical" voice. She's never used it on me before. "You're not *just* black, you're you. You know what I mean." It makes me feel ridiculous.

"I do, and I don't agree with it!" I stand up, press fists against the mosaic tabletop, trying to formulate a final word. "It hurts my feelings!"

"That's not what she meant," James says, reaching to rub my arm. "We're just trying to help you feel better—"

"And like, feel better about what? How I was born? Why should I always have to be the sad one?"

"We're sorry, Morg," Meg pleads as I collect myself. I hate that she uses an unapproved abbreviation of my name, trying to tame me with fake intimacy. (I'm pretty staunchly anti-nickname. One thing I actually like about myself is my name.) "For real. I really didn't mean to upset you so much."

"Whatever. It's fine. I have to go." I wave manically, mumbling "See you tomorrow," and nearly crash into a sandwich board advertising eggnog lattes.

In the parking lot, I lean against my car window. "Rudy," I whisper, "sometimes I think you're the only one who understands me."

Without hesitation, I send a quick *SOS* text to David and fold myself into the front seat. I have zero desire to go home and face the parental shame of my detention or the reality of my suburban imprisonment. I flip through my CD case for something comforting, mashed potatoes for my ears. I put on Elliott Smith's *XO* and skip immediately to "Pitseleh," and I listen to the whole sad and elegant song while the car idles and the sun fades.

At my last session, over Thanksgiving Break, Susan gave me a holiday-themed exercise to do. Gratitude. When I feel hot with frustration and angst, I'm supposed to think of five good things that have happened to me.

Won essay contest ninth grade.

Trip to Hawaii with Malcolm, Mom, and Dad when I was twelve. How Malcolm and I couldn't stop laughing when Dad went crazy at that sushi buffet.

TGIF sleepovers with my cousins when we were little.

My fifth birthday party, the Beauty and the Beast cake.

I stop at four. It takes effort to recall those good moments without attaching them to some horrible memory that came before or after them. It is actual deliverance when I look down to see a text from David: *Say no more. Come to 7-Eleven parking lot on Florida Ave. Just finished band practice with some buds.*

He's in a band?

MAKE A LIST OF THINGS
WORTH FIGHTING FOR

David Santos is sitting in the trunk of his mom's station wagon, red Vans swinging, drinking a Slurpee.

"Hey."

"Hey." Pulling at the waist of my black skinny jeans, I hop in and scoot next to him.

He slings a loose arm around my neck. "So, you had a tough day, kid?"

I exhale, surprised to find that this—commiserating with my friend David in the back of a station wagon in the parking lot of a 7-Eleven—is exactly what I need right now, like I didn't realize how pent-up I've been. I launch into the gory details of the day, glad to have a soapbox for my woes that isn't Susan for once. Or my parents, or anyone I'd have to be delicate with, bend the truth with.

I tell him all about how I got detention because of Harriet Tubman, about how I feel like the world is conspiring to keep me from the real truth about stuff.

"Gnarly," he replies gravely. "What are you gonna tell your parents? About the detention, I mean."

"I have no idea, dude. I don't even want to. They'll be pissed, but they can't be mad. My brother's had a million detentions and this is the first one I've ever gotten. They know my teachers are assholes to me. It's not really *that* big a deal, I just wish I could stop doing the wrong thing."

"Oh, Morgan." He grins. "You might not know it yet, but everything you do is the right thing."

I lean my head onto his shoulder and sigh. "Then this other thing happened . . ." I start to tell him about being "not that black," but I don't want to feel the words in my mouth. I just want to be glad the day is over.

"Ugh, forget it. It's not even worth talking about."

"All right . . . ," he says suspiciously. "I'm here if you ever want to talk about it."

I swat my hand as if at an obnoxious housefly. "It's just, you know, white people."

"Gotcha," he says quickly with a laugh.

"Wait," I gasp, sitting up to yank at the sleeve of his *I <3 NY* T-shirt. "Back up. Uh, where's your band, and also, you're in a band? What the hell?"

"Okay, I mean, not really." He puts his hands up, cowering in embarrassment. "I can play two and a half songs on the guitar. We've never played a show or anything, or even like in front of anyone. We don't have a name. We just hang out every month and mess around. Anyway, they're getting peach rings . . . and actually, here they come."

Two guys are approaching us from the illuminated oasis of the 7-Eleven: one kid with long blond hair on a skateboard wearing a wrinkled white oxford shirt and a wide dad tie, and the other—light-skinned with a short, unkempt afro—holding a skateboard under his armpit, and an open bag of peach rings in his other hand.

"Morgan, meet the band without a name." David gestures. "Overdressed here on the drums we have Matty, and the one with his mouth full, you already sort of met on the phone. This is my cousin Sean."

Yep. He's as hot as his voice sounded over the spotty speakerphone.

"Favorite cousin." He flashes dimples just like David's when he smiles. I laugh to myself—Coco would say the exact same thing, and just as immediately.

Sean's light brown eyes are flecked with amber, and they shine. It kills me. I stupidly grin and wave.

"Hi, Morgan, a pleasure," he croons as I shake his hand in a totally uncool way.

(Confession: I love skaters. Not that I've ever dated one, or really know any, but in my mind, they're somehow my people. I know they're not too far off from the football guys, but they seem chiller and kinder, if not just too oblivious to be cruel. I can imagine no Jake Walkers among them. This is a simple class of bro, with simple needs and pleasures. Shaggy hair, lean muscles in their arms, a breeziness in the way they move. Like bro ballerinas.)

"What up." Matty nods and high-fives me.

Sean tosses the candy into David's lap. "Overdressed and Mouthful, by the way, is not a bad band name."

"We'll add it to the ever-growing list." David pulls on a gummy with his teeth.

Matty jumps off his skateboard and leans on it in one graceful move. "Okay, but we should probably also, you know, learn a song?"

"That does sound pretty important," I offer.

"See, she gets it!" Matty presses, as David and Sean instinctually wave him off. "Morgan, any interest in joining a band?"

"Oh, come on!" David shouts. "You can't just trade us in!"

I'm trying to be in on the joke as much as I can, but unfortunately, I happen to be an extremely awkward teenage girl, also clinically diagnosed with major anxiety and depressive disorders.

"Sorry, I don't play any instruments."

"Neither do these idiots!"

(I excel at being one of the guys, always have. There's no mistaking my energy as feminine or flirty. I'm a total nonthreat, too emo to exist on a plane of cuteness. And despite my boobs, my body's stocky and weird—sometimes I feel like my shoulders are perched up to my earlobes, masculine and out of proportion. In pictures, I always look . . . sturdy. Like my emotional baggage is showing. While the downsides to my asexual aura are copious—see: Operation David Santos—guy friends are an undeniable perk.)

"Hey," says Sean. "I write all the songs and design the album artwork. That's a thing."

"Whatever, Basquiat," Matty teases back, relenting. "Anyway, I gotta go. But seriously, dudes, let's meet again in two weeks to work on that chorus, okay?"

"Yes, Dad." David rolls his eyes at Sean, snickering. The boys fist-bump each other. Their intimacy is cute.

I force a chuckle, but even though I just met him, I'm on Matty's side—I have to root for my fellow intense people.

"Lata. Good to meet you, Morgan."

"Yeah, you too."

Once Matty's out of earshot, Sean leans in toward me. "We give him a hard time but it's only because he's like, a legitimate musician, and also because we love him."

"Plus," David adds without lowering his voice, "he's our token white."

Sean snorts and I giggle, "Of course."

"Listen up!" David exclaims. He's hype. "Do you guys want to make a fort in here or what?"

And suddenly he's peak zany David, doing the most. He crawls up to the front seat and turns on the car battery to play *Devotion* by Beach House, rustling through all the crap that lives in his car (what I call "a mess" and "garbage," he calls "a system of alternative organization" and "supplies"), and tossing towels, throw blankets, and half-eaten candy bars back at us. We assemble ourselves in the wagon bed, blanket over our legs, a patchwork of dirty shoes and chocolate wrappers and our reeking feelings. It's getting dark, the 7-Eleven is having a slow night, and I think maybe this is what camping is like. If it weren't for the smog, there would be an ocean of stars up there. If it weren't for the parking lot, and everything just beyond the parking lot, the night might feel romantic, inspiring.

(I've gotten very good at pretending I have more than I do. Or maybe, in some moments, I have everything. That's what I mean about stopping to notice the flowers, as dreadfully and sickeningly corny as it is. It shocked me. I hadn't looked, really looked at one in forever.)

David pulls a joint from his jeans pocket. He lights it between two fingers and inhales dramatically, holding the smoke in his chest and emitting a croaky cough. Bows his head, offering it to us. Sean accepts, but doesn't smoke it. When David finally looks up to face us, he's deadly serious. "So, okay, I have to tell you guys something."

Sean has an immediate good-guy reaction, burrows his thick eyebrows all concerned and gently reaches out to touch David on the shoulder. "What is it, buddy? Everything okay?"

He passes me the joint and I take a little bit, careful not to inhale too much. I'm not in the mood. I chew on my lip, stay quiet, like if my body is still, my mind will be, too.

David shakes his head, gingerly accepting the joint from my fingers. "Naw, I'm fine, it's just . . . Do you guys ever feel like you have no purpose? Like you're just here taking up space for no reason?"

Sean's chest seems to expand, like his heart is trying to escape. "Hoo, buddy, do I! I actually thought I was the only one who's totally clueless about how to do this life thing. I keep expecting it to just click one day, but instead, I just get older." He laughs nervously at himself.

Of course, I'm completely swept up by his vulnerability, by David's. Of course, I want to scream *Yes! What is happening?! Are we going to be okay?!* But I don't want to bring up the events of July 22, 2008, because I don't want them to be real. I don't want to carry the darkness around; I don't want to face my shameful secret. I just want to move on and be like everyone else, not sick. So I just go, "Yup."

"Actually, Morgan, you got me thinking about all this stuff. You know when you were telling me about that poem by Assata Shakur?"

"'Affirmation.'" I nod and recite the first line: *"I believe in living."*

David leans into his cousin. "Do you know about her? She was a Black Panther and part of the Black Liberation Army."

"The FBI arrested her for a bunch of murders she so totally did not commit," I add. "I was just reading her autobiography, and it's awesome."

"Whoa." Sean smiles. "Wasn't she Tupac's aunt or something like that?"

"Yeah, his godmother!" I lock eyes with Sean and immediately look down with a shy smile.

"Dope," he says, hands folded over his knees.

"So, anyway," David continues, "I was mentioning this stuff to my dad, and out of nowhere, he tells me how he got beat up by the cops back in the day."

"What?" Sean blurts.

"Yeah," David says flatly. "When we lived in San Diego, when I was a baby."

"What happened?" I gasp, and David's chest rises as he closes his eyes in a deep breath, as if at a pulpit.

"So, my dad was speeding, I think? Or maybe he was doing nothing. I don't know. The cops pull him over, and then they didn't just arrest him, they beat the hell out of him. Like, with freaking clubs, their pistol grips, but also just shoving him into his car with their bare hands. He had bruises all over, his eyes were swollen." David exhales.

"Jesus," I utter at some point.

Sean shakes his head like he's seriously going to cry, but I think it's just the way his eyes shine. "Poor Uncle Ron."

"He spent the night in jail. As soon as my mom bailed him out, he pledged to take down corrupt cops. He wrote this op-ed for the newspaper, he held a meeting with all his neighbors, it was like his *thing*. But after a couple years—and mind you the whole time my dad is like getting way deep into it and my mom is taking care of me, which as we all know could not have been easy—people in the city started getting aggressive toward him. Someone left a note on our doormat. Someone else spit in my dad's direction while he was at the mall. He's just shopping for khakis at the mall like a regular dad!"

"Wow." Sean looks devastated, slowly shaking his head, but I'm beginning to think all of his reactions are big ones. "Just, I had no idea about any of that."

"Dude, same. I don't even know if your parents know all about it. And obviously my dad stopped trying to kick up dirt like that. That's like, a hundred percent not what he's like now.

Anyway, I guess that's one of the reasons we moved out here when I was little."

"That's crazy," Sean says, and a gust of wind floats his hand my way a little, brushing our thumbs. I pretend not to notice. "I guess I could see Uncle Ron getting fired up like that. Like, for something he cared about."

I say, "That is super crazy. It's awesome, though."

"It really is," David says, "and the thing is, I wish I knew that version of my dad. The badass version. On some level I get why my parents moved and became all suburban, but I also want to know more about those rebels."

"Totally," I say. "It would be cool to know I have some bad-ass in my genes. That's how I feel reading about the Black Panthers. What was it like to be so committed to the cause?"

"Exactly!" David throws his hands up like spaghetti to a wall. "That's what's bugging me! I just keep thinking, what do I care that much about?"

I'm nodding emphatically. "For sure. Sometimes I feel like I could have that in me, but I don't know what to do with it."

"So, let's figure it out already. Let's do this." Sean says this so firmly, it startles me.

"Do what? Take down cops? Right now? I gotta go home, dudes," I joke, my weird impulse in the face of sincerity.

"No, I mean let's all make a pact to figure out what we wanna fight for. Look, the whole country is all cranked up on this 'hope' stuff. The president is black! Anything can happen."

"True." I raise my eyebrows at David in consideration, and he shrugs back. "I guess there's more possibility now. . . .

maybe." I hate that I can't stop thinking too much, about everything that's wrong.

"So why should we be left out of all that, out here in the middle of this wasteland?" Sean gestures empathically at our particular wasteland. "Stuck being depressed in the 7-Eleven parking lot . . ."

I feel pricked by the *d* word. *Anything can happen. You can escape.*

"Hey, I love this 7-Eleven," quips David, and Sean elbows him, laughing.

A small, sleepy smile creeps onto my face. I wish I were a different kind of person. I wish I could look ahead, be hopeful. I wish it with all my heart.

"We can call it an end-of-year resolution. Anyway, that's what I'm doing," Sean concludes. "I am so tired of being so bored, man."

If this guy isn't in student council, he really is doing things wrong. I'm totally swayed.

"Okay," David sticks out a hand for his cousin, "I'm in. If Ron Santos can fight for something, then so can I, right?"

"Absolutely," I agree, and I think I mean it. "I'm in, too."

My whole life other people have been telling me what's important, literally telling me what to care about and who to root for, how to behave and think. I've been a good student, obedient and determined to do everything right. But what if I could follow Harriet, or Assata, and refuse to play along? What if I could be in charge of myself?

HARRIET TUBMAN COMES
TO ME IN A DREAM

Harriet Tubman comes to me in a dream. She's on a talk show set, with a glass coffee table between her and another black lady.

"Harriet Tubman?" I ask.

"Yes, I am."

She sounds kind of like Beyoncé in interviews. I turn to the other lady.

"Are you Oprah?"

"I'm you, in another life."

There are other people scattered in the audience bleachers— kids I recognize from school, some moms from my art class, David and Sean, but Harriet Tubman and Other Me are only talking to me.

"Harriet Tubman, are you also me in another life?"

"No way. But I could be."

Other Me becomes the only person in the room. She leans

in so close our noses are almost touching, and everything around us goes black.

She's just as annoying and dramatic as I am.

She says, "What are you doing?"

(NO SUBJECT LINE)

From: aaaaaaahhhhmeg@yahoo.com
To: daria_but_black@gmail.com
12/1/08 6:17 PM

Lover,

that was messed up today, I know. I'm so sorry we hurt your feelings. We seriously didn't mean to offend you. I love you. James does too. I owe you In-N-Out. I'm sorry everyone in our stupid town is a boring idiot. At least we're way cooler and smarter than pretty much everyone.

    <3

From: Sean.something42@gmail.com
To: daria_but_black@gmail.com
12/2/08 10:24 PM

Hi Morgan,

Dave gave me your email, hope that's ok. It was great meeting you last night! I'll definitely have to check out that Assata book. I was wondering if you might wanna hang out sometime?

Text me 909-555-6500

Peace 😊

Sean Santos-Orenstein

From: davidneedsahaircut@yahoo.com
To: daria_but_black@gmail.com
12/4/08 1:08 AM

Hey btw forgot to tell you I gave my cuz yr email, figured it was ok since u are both huge nerds

ttyl

ds

THE DIARIES OF MORGAN PARKER

December 3, 2008

*listening to Steely Dan—Two Against Nature (forgot how good this is!!!)

It's me again of course, old crazy me.

Meg and I made up because why not. Everything else sucks. A lot of things can be fixed with cheese fries and laying in the grass. Even when my friends don't understand me, they love me at least.

They'll probably drop me eventually or we'll drift away. That's just how things go. But right now, here we all are.

This year has been crazy. It's the year where nothing is as it seems. Everything is different: my friends, my style, my ideas about the future. Most importantly, my idealism and romanticism have shifted to the dark realm of realism, which leaves me with a bleak view of life. Nonetheless, here I am, five foot nothing, scared to death. I wish I were in control, but I am who I am. I like to be sure, except I cannot in fact recall a time in which I was actually sure of myself. I am stressed, inquisitive, immature (I admit it), confused, discouraged, and obnoxious. But quietly and secretly, I think I am a grand, passionate hero. I know that sounds super dramatic.

DO YOU KNOW HOW MANY WAYS YOU CAN FEEL YOURSELF EXPLODING?

In this moment I feel particularly suburban. I'm aware that my world is small and today is only a sliver of my life, a blink. Meg and I are chewing on iced coffee straws and browsing the little boy's shirts at our favorite Salvation Army, across from the Stater Bros. where Coco works. We hopped in Meg's dusty car after school feeling silly and light. It's a sunny windy day, and there's nowhere else for us to be. I'm almost nostalgic for how boring it all is.

"Oh my god," I say wryly, holding up a heather-blue shirt with neon lettering. "I must have this." It's from the church down the hill from my house—Marissa's church—and it says, "Fantastic Journey with Jesus." I giggle with utter delight.

"Oh, most definitely," Meg bellows across the aisle. "That is fantastic!"

"What'd you find?"

"Well, this I'm getting for sure," she models a bright yellow tee that says *OK* in thick block lettering, gives her best Zoo-lander face.

"Yes!" I laugh. "Actually, it kinda looks dope with that out-fit." She's wearing a black and red flannel, skinny jeans, and what she calls her "shit-kicking boots."

"So, um," she starts, shuffling hangars indifferently. "I'm sorry again I was being such an ass on Monday."

"I know, dude." I nod. "I'm past it, really." We mosey around the store, bopping to "Heart of Glass." (Is it just me, or is Blondie always playing in a thrift store?) I'm pulled as if by a magnet to a row of blazers.

"I just wanted you to know . . . I felt really bad. . . ." She hangs at my side chewing her lip.

"I know," I whine. "And like I said, I forgive you, and we're cool, I promise." I hold up a houndstooth number that would swallow me; return it to the rack. "It's just . . . I get really tired of people trying to tell me how it is to be me. Like, there are some things you just can't understand. And that's okay! Like, that's good!"

"I know." She lowers her eyes. I shouldn't keep pressing, but it's as simple as this: I want to. I want to say my piece—I owe at least that to myself, to Harriet and Assata and all of us.

"That's the thing, though. You don't have to pretend to know. You could ask me stuff, you know. Or just listen. Like, if I wanted to know something about heavy metal bands, I would go to you. I wouldn't try to speak on that, you know?" I stumble on a marvelous velvet navy jacket that's almost too good to be true at $8.99. I pull it from the hanger as I keep wax-ing philosophical, keeping my tone even (no one will be telling me *Don't get so emotional* today).

"Sometimes I feel like white people can't bear to be left out. Like, maybe it's an A and B conversation, you know? Okay, what do you think?" I adjust the lapels and stand up straight.

A smile creeps to her mouth. "Damn, that is perfect."

"Isn't it!?" I squeal, gathering it in my arms with my other goodies. "Anyway, I'm sorry about all my feelings," I say to her face.

"You and your feelings." She rolls her eyes, and the way she smiles, I know we are family.

"Okay, but what about this one?" I present a green plaid Tommy Hilfiger blazer.

Meg scrunches her nose. "Don't you already have one ex-actly like that?"

"Ugh, fine, you're right." I slump. "It's probably time for me to cut myself off on the blazers."

On our way out, plastic bags weighing down our wrists, Meg halts to marvel at us in the storefront window's reflection.

"Let's take a picture!" she dives into her tote bag excitedly.

We stand there in our small town, heads tilted like clink-ing glasses, me in my sweater and button-down, so stumpy in my Vans next to Meg's long spindly form, and looking in-describably cool in shit-kickers, disposable camera held out next to her face. We strain to hold cheesy smiles as an old car screeches past, blaring Lil Wayne. I'm fairly certain we're cackling or blinking in every frame she snapped. I'm fairly certain that we're glowing in every shot.

In her car headed back to the school, we shoulder dance to "Tainted Love," one of our jams. I goofily sing along in a ridiculously terrible soprano until she's begging me for mercy.

"So, can we finally have a movie night this weekend? Before you get all intense again about finals like you were about PSATs."

"I was not intense!" she snaps, and I cower apologetically.

"Some of us have to study, Morgan," she says with a voice. "Straight As don't just come easily to everybody."

It pinches. She's right, but I never really thought about it.

"I know, er," I pivot, "I'm sorry, Meg, you're totally right."

"There's some things you don't know about, too," she snarks. "That was actually a really hard time for me. I didn't want to talk about it then, but . . ." She shifts gears merging onto the freeway—though we're getting off at the next exit. (This is the logic of our home.)

I say, "Are you okay?" just as she's starting to say, "I don't know." We let ourselves laugh at ourselves.

(Do you know how many ways you can feel yourself exploding? That's what living is like—you inflate, deflate, you ask and answer at the same time. Everything happens at the same time. That's something I realized ever since I decided to keep existing.)

"I think I'm okay now," she explains, and my eyes soften with encouragement.

"Good," I say softly, "that's good." I don't know what else to say—I want to go back to shoulder dancing, and I want to go back to September and be a better friend. "I'm sorry you were having a hard time. You know I'm always here if you want to talk."

"Yeah," she says flatly, exhaling. "I'll be fine."

I nod and take a deep breath, just trying to let my body exist without my mouth messing everything up. (Why do we do that thing, let ourselves lie to ourselves and each other? We act like it makes things simpler, but it doesn't.)

Back in the school parking lot, Meg parks next to my car, where James is sunning on the roof. My car has an excellent roof for sunning. Meg whistles at him and I stick out my tongue as we get out of her car and I collect my bounty.

"Hello, dearies!" James shouts without opening his eyes.

"Time to wake up, sir!" I say, tapping my keys on the hood.

"Ah, but I was having such a lovely dream!" James hops off the car and brushes dirt from his camo cargo shorts. He taps Rudy's hood like it's a pet. "Who's a good boy?" he squeaks at the super-dirty backseat window.

I'm giggling watching his theatrics when he quickly drops his hands to his side and stiffens. I turn around; walking toward us is the asshole himself Tim McCloud, in a corny Dave Matthews Band T-shirt and some dumb khakis. I didn't notice his red Chevy parked nearby. Narrowing my eyes in his direction,

I make a big show out of fumbling for my keys and ignoring him.

"Hey," he says softly, and his car beeps.

"Hey," James says weirdly. It startles me—I guess I didn't even realize they knew each other.

They keep eyeing each other as Tim slips into his front seat. "Later," he says, slamming the door shut with a smirk.

James exhales as if he's been holding his breath underwater. I glance at him quizzically. "What was that?"

"Huh? Nothing."

"That guy is such a tool." I give him two quick pecks on his cheeks. "Bye, darling!"

He gives me a tender, sleepy smile.

James can sleep *anywhere*. He famously fell asleep drunk in my bathtub once. The story goes that he was taking a shower to sober up, fell asleep with the shower on, and all he can remember is my mom grabbing him by the hair and pulling him up. That's the way he tells it, that she saved his life, but my mom denies the whole thing. In general, we always prefer to repeat the better story rather than the truth. Maybe, eventually, the real truth won't even matter.

MADNESS AND CIVILIZATION

Therapy is especially horrible today. Mostly I'm just not in the mood to be here, and also, I'm bored out of my mind with myself and everything around me. Now this Susan lady is so obviously ready to be annoying as soon as I walk in. I raise my eyebrows at her like, *So?* and she returns the look with stern, pursed lips.

"So, everything's pretty much the same," I say, folding my arms and sinking back into the ugly couch. I've gotten so comfortable not trying to impress her—just coasting through each session. I'm light-years away from the heaviness of last summer.

"Morgan," she says, tilting her head all serious, "do you realize you've been coming here for five months now?"

"Huh. I guess I hadn't thought about it. That's kind of a long time." I sniff; the flowery Auntie smell sticks to the inside of my nostrils.

"It is, quite a bit of time."

I nod and bite at the inside of my cheek. I don't have anything to say.

"Do you think these sessions have been helping?"

I unfold my arm and futz with the hem of my skirt. For some reason, I keep eyeing the spine of a book called *Madness and Civilization*, glowering at me from the center of her bookshelves.

"Um, yeah I guess." I regret that my voice gets high; she'll notice I'm lying. That much I know from *Law & Order*.

"I mean I guess the Prozac is working. It's easier to get up and go to school and hang out with people and all that stuff."

"You don't sound too convinced."

"No, no I definitely feel better. It's just, I still don't know what the point is."

"The point of what?"

"The point of anything. I just feel empty." I hate how it comes out. "Not to be dramatic."

"Well, I can tell you that you aren't alone in that. That's something most people have asked themselves at some point or another."

"Yeah, I know, I know I'm not, like, special."

"That's not what I mean. It's important to ask these questions. It helps us learn more about ourselves and challenge ourselves to live our lives to the fullest, and on the most righteous path."

(And yet: Madness and Civilization.)

"But what do I do? I feel I'm always on some kind of path— maybe not a righteous path but like, self-discovery. I just feel like I'm searching and waiting but not doing anything. Like, I'm passionate, but it all just stays right here, in my chest." I press my fingers to my sternum, hard, focusing all my pain and frustration right there.

Susan manages a pitying nod, and I ramble through the silence. "I don't know, I feel like there's some purpose I should be focusing on. But other than my writing, I don't know what I care about. All I know is what I'm told to care about. I just go with the flow because I'm afraid of really being myself."

A little tear collects, and I wipe my eyes before it drops, but Susan sees me. I'm pretty sure I've never articulated these words in quite this way. They scare me.

She makes me stew for a minute. Damn Susan.

"And what would be so scary about being yourself?"

"Uh, judgement, I guess. My depression. I can't be regular without taking pills. Last summer—that was the real me," I boom, declaring it for Susan and for myself. "No one can deal with that person. I can't even deal with that person."

Susan takes a deep breath and *fine*—I give in and take a tissue. I'm crying openly in therapy and I hope everyone's happy.

Susan leans in, inching to the edge of her chair and speaking softly, like she's my first-grade teacher and I just skinned my knee.

"That's not you."

I blow my nose. It is a honk, the opposite of dainty. Another thing I hate about myself: I am an extremely ugly crier.

"That's not you," she says again.

"I know." I slump and roll my eyes. "I know it's not."

254

"Say it, come on."

Though I'm obviously mortified at the corny after-school special that is my life, I guess this is who I am now. I accept the role and say my line.

"That's not the real me."

"You are not your depression."

"I am not my depression."

Ugh, I half-expect Dr. Phil's studio audience to golf-clap at my vulnerability. I hate myself right now.

"Morgan, before you go," I follow her eyes to the clock— somehow, we're over time. "I want to ask that in the next week you consider the possibility that you have touched lives in ways you may not realize. Think about your impact. The ways you can use that creativity and passion to express yourself, instead of hiding yourself. Just as an exercise. Think about it."

OMG so corny. I say, "Okay," and stare at the door, but she keeps talking.

"And also," she says, standing up and revealing a million wrinkles in her linen potato-bag dress, "if you feel you haven't made a difference, then make a difference. No one is saying you can't."

Every time I hear things like this—hopeful things, encouraging things—that evil part in my brain reminds me that stuff like that only applies to other people.

In the lobby, Framed Portrait of Bon Jovi has been replaced with Framed and Signed Headshot of Mel Gibson. That really pisses me off.

NO ROM-COMS

On Saturday, after a deeply awkward but adorable attempt at bonding with my dad over coffee, I meet Sean Santos-Orenstein at the foothills of Prospect Park's winding dirt paths and orange groves, our closest approximation to "real" nature, to the outside world. He's standing on a blanket under a big oak tree with two paper Stater Bros. bags at his feet. Even with his black Ray-Bans on I can tell he's google-eyed as he grins, and right now, all of a sudden, I realize exactly how cute he is.

Still, I haven't thought about whether this is a *date* date or not, and secretly, though I have no business feeling this way (as beggars must be beggars), I hope it isn't. Since Jake Walker, I can't really care about boys. They're clearly not the solution to any of my existential crises, and also, they're not that great. (Life is really not the way anything in *NYLON* magazine says. Or at least mine isn't, and maybe that's why I'm not in *NYLON* magazine.)

If it's boring or weird, I'll just go home. If (when) it's

embarrassing and awkward, I'll flee the scene like I usually do and drive around crying to Rudy and Morrissey.

"Heyyy," he calls as I make my way over to the tree.

"Hiii." I wave, and he gets to work pulling stuff out of the grocery bags.

"Wow, this is a whole spread." I eye the bags of grapes and chips, the little thing of salsa.

"I mean, I thought I might as well go all out." He grins and lands his long body on the blanket, which, actually, is more of a throw. "Glad you could come."

"Me too," I unfortunately squeak. Plopping down, static hits the backs of my thighs. (How is it December and almost 80 degrees? Shorts are the least interesting article of clothing, and they're extremely hard to work with. I hate it here.)

"Sooo . . ." I fidget hesitantly. "What's up? I mean, how are you? I mean, I don't know anything about you."

He laughs easily and pops a grape into his mouth, smirking at me.

"You're hilarious." He smacks on a grape. "Hm, about me . . ." He pauses, and I patiently stretch my legs in front of me and lean back on my palms.

(For posterity, and because I'm pretty proud of getting creative with khaki shorts that are a little too big for me, the whole outfit is: a red vinyl belt, bright red lips, espadrille sandals, a white oxford shirt pushed up at the arms, and a pin of a Gustav Klimt painting. It's very class-mom-on-field-trip-day. Or Black Diane Keaton on vacation in Italy.)

(By the way, this is an example of a look my mom goes

crazy over. I think she wishes I was Black Diane Keaton every day, shopping the racks of Ann Taylor Loft with her. "You can't beat a nice, crisp white button down!" That's one thing my mom is passionate about.)

"Well," he finally says, "I don't play any instruments and I'm in a band with no name."

We both crack up and he jabs me softly in the arm. "Shut up! What about you?"

"Well, personally I think Overdressed and Mouthful is a perfect name."

"No, for real," Sean laughs and smirks sharply. "Tell me about who you are. I want to get to know you."

He's wearing a Hawaiian shirt and long tight cutoffs, printed socks, and simple low Adidas. Dad-on-field-trip-day-but-dad-is-in-TV-on-the-Radio. He scratches at patchy sideburn stubble. I believe I am being seduced.

I consider lying, flirting. But whatever.

"Hm. *Who am I.* Well I like reading books, writing. Music, obviously. I like the color green and apples and thrifting and movies . . ." This is the part where I usually stop talking, but today I disrupt my own peace.

"I mean, I'm kind of a mess, I know it. So many things are wrong with me. But there's so much I want to do and be; I have a feeling I could be this grand, passionate hero."

I don't know why I quote myself, but I do. I just want to say it out loud, almost as a joke.

"Wow," Sean whispers.

"Except," I sigh, "I'm trapped, and I don't know what I be-lieve or where I'm going." I pull some grapes from their stem with a self-deprecating chuckle. "Sorry, that got real dark, didn't mean to be a downer!"

He laughs, but not at me—it doesn't make me feel stupid or weird.

"You really hate small talk, don't you?" He pretends to elbow me.

"You asked." I shrug with a pout, blushing under my black girl.

Sean quickly looks down, drags his hand across his fore-head and through his puffy hair. I notice his dimples. He pulls off his shades; his eyes do their happy glistening.

"No . . . I don't think you're a mess," he mumbles, squint-ing. "And I don't think you're a downer. I think you're smart. And what you just said was actually really beautiful."

I smile and try not to ruin anything because I don't know how I'm supposed to be. "Well, thanks." I reach to surrepti-tiously pick a blade of grass.

"Seriously," he basically marvels. "Everything you say is like a little poem, it's amazing."

I snort shyly. "Maybe you're just easy to talk to."

He grins and shrugs proudly. He's good at saying a lot without words. He's sort of intense—but it's working for me, there's instant intimacy. I feel like I've known him for years. I bend my head back over my shoulders and look up at the sky, its shapeless clouds.

"So, tell me a story about you," I insist.

"Hmm . . ." He tilts his head to join me in cloud-gazing, folding his knees up to his chest and drumming them absently with his fingers. "I think about living in Italy one day. Last summer I tried to teach myself Italian. You know, with Rosetta Stone? I pretended to understand all these Italian poems— I thought I'd pick it up by osmosis, eventually. Anyway, I gave up after two weeks."

He throws a grape into the air and tries to catch it in his mouth. He doesn't.

"That sounds awesome! I've never been to Europe."

"Sparkling cider?" He extends the Nalgene to me and I prop myself up on my elbow.

"Ooh, sure!" It's lukewarm and sweet, but a charming touch. (Who thinks of that?)

"Maybe not live there. There probably aren't too many other Black Jews in Italy."

I swallow, snorting with surprise. "You'll be one of a kind, then," I try.

"Oh, I already feel that, believe me I do."

I take another drink and pass it back. "So, what's it like? Or, I mean, I don't know much about Judaism."

He offers me a chip. I wave it away, listening intently.

"Well, I'm not that religious actually. We celebrate High Holy Days, Rosh Hashanah, Yom Kippur. Passover is pretty dope. But that's pretty much it. I don't do anything special."

"But what do you believe?" My voice cracks; I cough

nervously to cover it. "Or, I guess, what do you have to do to be saved from hellfire or whatever? You pray?"

(People are always telling me to pray about my sins, saying they'll pray for my sins, talking to me about damnation.)

"Yeah, we pray. I pray sometimes but not, like, frequently. I believe in rituals and family and all that stuff, being a good person, basically. Jews don't really believe in hell."

"Oh, whoa." My eyebrows furrow tightly as my face tenses into a pucker. It's like my mind can't wrap itself around the idea of a life not ending in eternal flame. "Wow," I absently repeat, like I'm trying to memorize the information.

"Oh!" he hops up from the blanket and I'm stirred from my mind's somersaults.

"By the way," he announces, rifling around in the shopping bags excitedly. "In the spirit of our new friendship, at the suggestion of one David Santos, I made you a mix." He tosses me a jewel case.

"That's so nice! I wish I had burned you one." I adjust my eyes to his handwriting; I think the mix is titled "Anthems of a Seventeen-Year-Old Girl." I think my lips and my whole body might cover him any second, I can't fathom how perfect it is.

"Ah, *yes*! A track listing—you really are different from David."

He grins as I scan the picks—there's some Atlas Sound and Broken Social Scene, but also some stuff I've never heard of, like the Blood Brothers, and some old-school Marvin Gaye and Nina Simone. Weird, but super good.

"Thanks so much, dude."

"For sure. My pleasure." He exhales and lays his body like a paper doll on the blanket, and I lay back next to him. "That's better. So, let's talk resolutions."

"Yes. How's yours going?"

"Uh, it's not? I don't know, I was super fired up last week, but the truth is I have no plan. It's like I'm trapped in this tiny world of my brain and I can't get out. That's why David and I spend so much time goofing off and we don't even have a band name."

"Aw," I croon. "Or look at it this way—you have many band names. Infinite possibilities!" I chuckle half-heartedly and run a hand through the grass. "I know what you mean, though, about being trapped in your own brain, thinking too much."

"It sucks," he sighs, looking up at the periwinkle sky. "And it's not just that. I'm going to college next fall—wherever I go—but I just don't want to wait that long to get started."

"On what? You mean studying, or working?"

"No—just living. Sorry I'm not making sense. Erase that." He swats at his forehead.

"Crazy talk."

"No! That completely makes sense. I feel that way too, for sure—like I want to just grow into myself already, to know who that person is and what she's all about." (I always talk so much with my hands. That's a thing I know about myself.) "I just don't have the freedom to do that right now. So, yeah, trapped."

He hums a little as he sighs. He smells like salt and dryer sheets. He turns his face to mine, but clumsily. (That's a hundred percent not this movie.) "Well, what is it that you're passionate about?"

"Um, writing, I guess." Something flies into my mouth. Of course, I spit it out loudly, sticking my fingers up to my lips. Sean snickers. "Also—" A fly buzzes around me and I try to dodge it, cursing. (I'm very good at dates.)

Sean is cracking up now and I laugh too, sitting up and collecting myself.

"*Also*, the truth."

"Ah, the truth. That old rascal."

"Man, you're so lucky you go to public school. Vista is an alternate universe. We're completely cut off from reality."

For a minute I think I'm getting chilly and rub my arms, but the weather hasn't changed.

"I have a cousin that goes there," he offers. "She's a freshman. Dude, she really is in her own world. I feel like all she does is go to youth group. It's dope that she's so passionate, but sometimes when I hear her talk I worry that she's passionate about the wrong thing. You know what I mean?"

"God, totally. It's kinda scary. Like, why am I the freak, just because I'm not really sure what happens when we die?"

"Well, first of all, we become dogs, obviously!"

I can't help it—I get the giggles, and Sean, trying to keep a straight face, eventually erupts in laughter too. I laugh so hard my sides start aching—about the joke, but also about everything. It's weird to feel so close to someone so fast, like we just met and decided we'd be besties.

"But, all right, second." He elbows warmly. "Do you *really* think you're going to hell?"

"I . . . I don't know." I drop my head. "I'm not perfect."

"Well, you know, no one—"

"No one's perfect, I know, I know."

"No, I was gonna say, no one cool goes to heaven. You can't do anything fun there."

"Right! So, hell, I guess."

"To hell!" he shouts, wielding an imaginary goblet.

"To hell." I jut my raised fist into the bright sweet center of every orange in California. "To the church of raising hell!"

"Oh, shit!" Sean gasps wildly, and I smile, prouder of myself than anyone in their right mind would be, like I just gave birth to an icon.

"I know. That is an incredible fucking band name and you should definitely use it and give me credit, obviously."

MANIC PANIC

I'd forgotten my ringtone was "Kool Thing" by Sonic Youth. Man, I love that song.

"Is that your phone?" We're standing by a tree examining our freshly picked fruits for bugs. Sean darts over to feel around the blanket. "Catch."

(I obviously don't, but whatever.)

It's Meg calling, and I think about not answering, but I check myself. "Yo dude."

I can barely understand her. She's doing that kind of breathless crying, choking out tears and blubbering. Her voice is erratic and wild and it's terrifying.

"Ugh . . . I don't know . . . Laura . . . it's not fair . . . I wasn't . . . I don't know what to do."

"Meg, slow down, calm down." I widen my eyes and shrug at Sean's look of earnest concern. I have no idea what's going on.

Meg takes a deep inhale and whimpers.

"Are you hurt?" I ask, but before she can answer, I say, "Where are you?" because she definitely needs me right now.

"My dad's. Can you come over?"

"Sure, yeah. I'm on my way. Take deep breaths and stay put."

This seems serious. I know about serious. I just didn't have anyone to call in my moment, and I desperately wish I had.

I hang up the phone, shaking my head wildly, and look longingly at Sean. "I'm so sorry. That was my best friend, I don't know what's wrong . . ." I start gathering my stuff, collecting myself. "Something's going on, I was having so much fun, but—"

"Say no more. I'll drive."

Sean Santos-Orenstein has the most normal car in the world, a Camry or something, and it's eerily clean. It's kind of sweet— I can't help sneaking smirks at him as I navigate to Meg's dad's. When we turn onto the rural street, it's already darkening, and Meg's in the driveway throwing a bunch of stuff into the trunk of her car, all the doors open and Metallica playing from the stereo.

"Oh no," I say as Sean parks across the street.

He grimaces, "Is that Metallica?"

"Meg listening to Metallica is a Bad Sign, Sean. She lets Metallica speak on behalf of all of her aggression." I close my eyes and inhale as I open the car door.

"Uh," he softly lays a hand on my knee then quickly pulls it back, "I'll just wait right here. You go take care of your girl. Call me if you need anything?"

"Thanks." I squeeze his shoulder and nod with a smile as I get out of the car.

Speed-walking across the street, I foolishly look both ways even though it's completely deserted. In front of a corner house are two broken tricycles and, inexplicably, a covered wagon. It's Klan country out here, for sure. As much as I've been raised to love and desire whiteness, I can't get down with "hick" culture, even ironically. People just love forgiving racism because they like music or values or whatever.

Meg turns around to me, holding a box of Manic Panic hair dye, looking absolutely crazed.

"Dude!" I rush at her. "Stop. Wait, what is going on? Breathe. Actually, I'm gonna breathe too, I don't even know why." I laugh because what is even going on.

Meg does one of those cry-hiccups, her shoulders heaving up and down. She puts the hair dye in her car and turns it off. Without the Metallica, the night is quiet and still—only crickets sing in the air.

"Can I have a cigarette?" Meg finally says, and shivers a little as she shakes her head. "Effing bullshit."

She doesn't smoke, but it wasn't a question. "Here. Did something happen?"

She only sighs in response, and I light our cigarettes.

"Start at the beginning," I say, steering us to the curb. We squat down and fold over into our laps, tip our heads into each other. We just sit and smoke and stay quiet.

"I hate my parents," Meg groans after a while, kicking her pointy-toe Target flats at the pavement.

I scrunch my face sympathetically.

"So, apparently I'm obligated to go to Bible college. My parents won't pay for it otherwise." I gasp as she goes on. "All their fighting over the years, and the one thing they definitely agree on is making my life a nightmare."

I shake my head and suck my teeth. With sudden choreography, Meg stands up from the curb, clasping her hands together, announces, "I have to tell you something," and sits back down on the curb next to me, her face a landscape of worry.

"You know how you said I was all intense about the PSATs and stuff?"

"Meg, I didn't mean—"

"No, listen . . . I was taking Adderall. Like, 'recreationally' or however they say it." She makes air quotes, nervously bobbing her head.

"Oh," I breathe, befuddled. "Plot twist."

"I know. It was actually my prescription, from the time I went to the hospital before. I actually did see a shrink then, just once, and he gave me a prescription. I went off it because it made me feel all coked out. But then I started taking it to study. . . ."

"Dang. Jesus, Meg," I exhale, feeling lost. "You mean . . . a lot? Like that episode of *Saved by the Bell* with Jessie and the caffeine pills?"

"Kind of a lot, yeah," she admits with a bowed head. "But that's over. I have one left and I'm saving it for babysitting."

"Are you sure you're all right?"

"Yes, I suppose," she sighs. "I was feeling so . . . out of control . . . you know?" she squeaks, turning to me. I put my arm around her shoulders and squeeze a hug. "I, like, made a little schedule, like one of Kelly Kline's anal spreadsheets. I thought if I studied for this many more hours, I could raise my GPA this many percentage points. Whatever, it was stupid."

"Hey." I turn to look her in the eye. "It wasn't stupid. You're not stupid. Everyone gets overwhelmed like that sometimes."

I have good advice—I should listen to it.

"Yeah. That's true." She smiles sadly. "But it doesn't matter, because it's not like I'm applying to any big colleges. They said I'm *obligated* to Bible college for my first year. If I don't like it, tough shit, and I can transfer when I can pay my own way."

"Jeez. That's really harsh."

"That's what she said tonight, *tough shit*," she mocks her stepmom in a bitchy voice. "I just, like, lost it. I said *Fuck you.* I never, ever say *Fuck you.*"

"Oh, babe, I'm so sorry," I commiserate, but I have to smile imagining it, Meg slurring, "Fuuuuck youuu," like that scene in *SLC Punk!*

"I just think," she goes on, looking straight ahead in the dark, "I'm just so sick of all their rules. I just want to live my own, simple, boring little life—is that so much to ask?"

When her tears start to fall, mine come, too. I gather her in my arms and we drape ourselves around each other, and I can feel how small she is, like she could snap in pieces. We have needed to do this for so long.

As Meg pulls away, she wipes her nose with the back of her hand. "Jeez, we have so many problems."

I laugh because I know my lines. "Honestly, dude? It could be worse. It's not great, for sure, but really—you'll get through it. We will." I squeeze her shoulder. "I should probably go check on Sean." I nod toward his Camry.

Meg gasps, bringing a hand to her mouth. "I totally forgot about your non-date! I'm sorry, I wasn't even thinking when I called. . . ."

"Oh, he's fine," I snicker. "He's probably listening to a podcast or something like that." I stretch to my feet and help Meg up; we both swat at "nature" on our butts.

"But hey," I speak carefully, "I really think you should go talk to someone. I mean, it can't hurt, right? You probably just didn't have a good one before."

"Eh, I don't know if it's for me." She says it glibly, like she's talking about seeing a superhero movie. It stings but doesn't leave a mark.

"I know it seems that way, but I still think you should try therapy. My lady is hella corny, I'm just warning you, but I can get you her number if you want. I just . . . Maybe it will help, to work some stuff out."

"I won't go off the rails again, I promise. Not everybody needs therapy forever, you know," she concludes. Her words are neat and precise. "Sometimes people just bounce back from things and move on."

I open my mouth but close it. My body absorbs the words like a sponge.

"No offense or anything."

"Oh, yeah." I start in Sean's direction, muttering, "Yeah, I know, I know. Yeah. No big deal."

I need to switch from one mask to another. I need a version of myself that feels different.

"Oh, and of course, her name is Susan." I roll my eyes at Meg with a broad, self-deprecating smile.

"Obviously." She grins. "Such a name for a therapist. I think the one I had when I was a kid was named Martha."

I cackle and knock on Sean's window. I can make out the shape of him leaned back in the front seat, earbuds in and fingers laced over his chest. Meg and I titter as he startles and hurriedly gets out of the car.

"Hi, hey." He reaches out his hand to Meg. "I'm Sean."

"Meg, Sean. Sean, my BFF, Meg." I grin. They shake hands and Meg cracks up loudly at the formality.

"Everything okay? How we doing?" Sean sidles over and lightly taps my back. I look up at him, and he smiles back like Meg's not even there. It's amazing. I feel safe.

I squeeze Meg's hand. "What are you gonna do?"

"*Oh*, I'm good. I'm gonna go to my mom's for the night."

"Word. Are you sure? After we get my car, I can meet you somewhere?"

"David just texted that he's at Coco's," Sean offers, a temptress, climbing back into the front seat.

"Aw, thanks, no, you guys go. Tell darling David Santos I

love him. Thank you so much for coming." She looks at me. "I promise, I'm gonna get out of this dumb city before I go crazy."

I press my hands into my best friend's shoulders and look her in the eye.

"Congratulations. One day this will all just be an anecdote."

CORRESPONDENCE BOTH DIGITAL AND ORIGAMIED

From: Sean.something42@gmail.com
To: davidneedsahaircut@yahoo.com, daria_but_black
@gmail.com
Subject: Bam!

Here's the notes I typed up from our "meeting" the other night at Coco's. Good stuff. Mediocre pie. Morgan, I know you were just joking but I seriously think you should do the [REDACTED] thing. Will you send the names of the books you mentioned?

David, you talk to Matty? He is psyched about the name HOW TO RAISE HELL. You're right, we should just commit.

here's to punk and protest,
s

...

Hey,

How are you? Like, for real? Saturday night was really scary, and not just seeing you that way but the fact that I had no idea. I feel bad that you didn't think you could talk to me about how much you were struggling. Maybe I can't even talk. I've definitely made my own bad choices, probably as recently as this morning. I've been through some really dark and scary stuff.

Ugh, I just wish everything could be simple for us. I wish every day were just picking oranges in Prospect and giggling about crazy recipes for tacos. Dancing to Le Tigre. Making "margaritas" with Squirt and tequila.

If nothing else, can we just pinky promise to look out for each other, no matter what?

Sean said this cute thing in the car after we left your dad's, about friendship. He said, "Sometimes friends are just people who aren't weirded out by looking at you." I don't know, I thought it was kinda deep. Not to be mooshy, but, you know. Anyway, Gov is almost over.

loveeeeee you loverrrr

. . .

hello my lover!

I'm better, yeah. I'm staying at my mom's and we had several long family "discussions" about my many "issues." They're making me go to church every week now, and babysit every Sunday too, and I'm getting a therapist. <u>You were right.</u> I guess that's all I wanted to say about that.

I'm not even grounded, probably because I only ever really end up at your house, anyway.

I'm looking forward to having a shrink actually. Stuff is hard, man. In conclusion, I'm not gonna become a druggie. And now Bible college has been "opened back up for discussion."

Thanks for coming and watching me freak out. It really did help. I think I didn't even realize how out of control I was. Mostly it's just embarrassing that I was so crazed about the PSATs. Everyone knows no one looks at those. Because they're PRACTICE. So dumb.

Sean is . . . cute! Is that a thing now? What about David? It kinda works, though.

I have a new crush, but I'll save it for the Notebook, because if I don't, James will FREAK OUT.

What are you doing Friday? We should watch movies after school and paint our nails, or some dumb girlie stuff like that.

love ME(g)

<3 (still so bad at drawing hearts)

THE BLACK NOTEBOOK

The plan

*Wake up early, even before [REDACTED]—ridiculously
early, like 5. So nervous-excited, I probably won't sleep,
anyway. COFFEE. Prep. Finally figured out how to get into
[REDACTED] before [REDACTED]. During any given season,
some sports team or another wakes up at the butt crack of dawn
for training—in my opinion, a small price to pay for small-
town popularity and school-wide dominance. I'll just sneak
in through [REDACTED]—enduring the [REDACTED] smell
will be my penance. Set up across from [REDACTED]. Wait.
No one will know anything about the [REDACTED] or
how they actually started, because not even I did, and I'm
black (surprise!). They'll all be scratching their heads at the
[REDACTED]. It's kind of like History Day, when all through
the school the seniors have booths where they act out historical
moments—Nazi Germany, Alabama in the 50s, Women*

Suffragettes. But this time we don't have to all awkwardly
pretend the black kids aren't there.

Supplies

Two LARGE trays (pile high!); Hundred-pack of Smart 'N
Final paper plates; Fancy-seeming plastic forks leftover from an
ancient Thanksgiving; Tongs; An emptied grape jelly jar; Scotch
tape; Posterboard signs; old, rickety card table, scooped from the
garage and likely not important.

Playlist

Couldn't sleep so I just made this (Morgan—in your tote bag!).
It is excellent. Starts with Marvin Gaye's "What's Goin' On,"
and goes right into "I'm So Bored With the USA." How good is
that transition!

CAUSING A SCENE

I wash my hair. I don't flat-iron it. It's Chapel Wednesday, and I'm ready to raise hell.

Fresh out of the shower, looking in the bathroom mirror at the soggy carpet on my head, I'm filled with melancholic regret. How can it be that this is the first time I've done this? Do I really not know how to wear my hair regular, naturally?

I don't even let myself ponder the metaphor. I find a comb of Malcolm's and plow through the hair as it dries. If it doesn't stand up in all the right places, no one will know the difference. Besides, the actual execution of the hair is way less important than the outfit.

The outfit is and must be: black skinny jeans, black turtleneck, black boots. No compromises. I don't have a leather jacket, so I put all the concert pins I can find on my jean jacket and flip up the collar for a little added rebellion. This part is less for the optics—(it doesn't take much to stand out at school)—and more for me. For attitude.

After I get dressed and get my eyeliner just right, I go back downstairs to the kitchen. Damnit—I'm too late. My mom's already here in her bathrobe, an elbow propped on the counter, coffee mug in hand, basically waiting to chew me out. When we lock eyes, she clears her throat and slowly scans the disaster in the kitchen, making A Face. She doesn't have to do anything more than that. I get it. She might as well save her breath.

"I *knowww,*" I whine. "I'm sorry, I was gonna clean up!"

I start rushing to secure tin foil on trays and throw pans in the dishwasher. She laughs, satisfied that she's gotten to me. (It's like she delights in rubbing her cheery morning disposition in my grumpy face.)

"Is this a class project or something?"

"Uh," I grimace. "Or something?"

"All right." She raises her eyebrows and waves in surrender. "As long as you kids clean up after yourselves, I'm not gonna get into your business."

(In my particularly relevant experience, this means, *I will almost certainly get into your business in the next four minutes.* Besides me, my mom is the least subtle person I know. She's a backseat driver, a backseat cook, a backseat launder, a backseat makeup artist—and all while chanting, "I'm gonna stay out of your business.")

"Your hair is cute like that," she winks before turning toward the stairs. "Let me know if you want me to show you some natural styles."

"Oh! Cool. Thanks, Mom." I smile, off guard. (My mom

has a weave and it was my understanding that weaves, not afros, were the current Black Mom Political Stance.) "You had an afro?"

"Hell yeah, everybody did. Your dad really did have the best one." She throws her head back at the thought of it, cackling. "Have a good day, wonderful daughter."

I completely have the jitters driving to school. I take my time at every single stop instead of barreling through the intersections California-style. I know I should be doing this. This is what the end-of-year resolution is all about. It's hilarious, and I don't really have anything to lose. If I do, I clearly don't know what it is. Six months trying to get unstuck, and all I do is keep adding layers and layers to the impossible math equation of myself. It's like in *A Beautiful Mind*, when he steps back and is like *OMG, I am nonsense*.

I sneak in through the locker rooms as planned. I'm carrying pancakes under one arm and the card table under my other, so I don't get to hold my nose as I scurry through the B.O. and Axe-scented corridor. I'm a little shocked how easy it is for me to make it into the main hallway undetected and set up camp. The school is totally dead, lit only by the early morning light, misty and gray—for some reason, the quiet fills me with excitement.

I station myself just across from the doors to the gym, where everyone will be funneling in first thing for chapel. (Today's message is supposed to be about obedience—they're gearing us up for the annual retelling of "the true story of Christmas.")

My posterboards are totally ridiculous, I know, but I love them. One says: *FREE BREAKFAST. POWER TO THE PEOPLE.* Then I veer off from the Panthers theme and enter "Morgan at Vista Christian in 2008." The other posterboards say, in bubble letters taught to me by Kelly Kline in 4th grade: *TOUCH MY HAIR: $1* and *ASK A BLACK GIRL: $5.* And then, just for good measure, I have one other poster with printed-out pictures of the Black Panthers—I just need everyone to know how incredible their outfits were.

I hang up the signs behind me with tape and I set up my card table and all the pancakes (so many pancakes); I fluff my hair (it feels so weird like this!) and leave out the Smucker's jar for cash. Then I wait. I eat a pancake. I think about going to make a cup of coffee in the teacher's lounge, but it's not a day for that kind of conspicuousness. I start to get nervous and consider scrapping the whole idea. I feel my heart pounding even in my ears. But I don't expect anything too dramatic, and at least I'm doing something educational. This is going to be hilarious. Right?

It's a complete mob scene by the time the ten-minute bell rings. Some of the jocks and popular girls are at the back of the crowd making fun and taking pictures with their phones, but some of them are also eating pancakes, and most kids are actually listening to me as I'm telling them about the Panthers'

Free Breakfast program. The yearbook photographer starts to rush up to me with his camera around his neck, but I give him a stern look in the eyes and say, "No. We cannot do a story about this."

(I don't know what I'm doing, if this is technically a protest or some kind of performance art or what, but either way I know it shouldn't be documented in a school publication. I've slipped in some risky stuff before, much to the chagrin of our advisor, but politics is completely off-limits—even in an election year, and even with a black president.)

After a fake stoner asked, "Why do black people like chicken so much?" I ditched the *ASK A BLACK GIRL* service, but I've already made sixteen bucks or so on hair touches. I should really charge for this all the time. (If I had a dollar for every time a white person has touched my hair *without* permission, I could buy a two-day pass to Coachella.)

Jordan comes up for a pancake, and he can't resist saying, "You're so weird," as he stuffs a bite into his mouth. Then, chewing, he says, "This is kind of tight, though."

When I spot my crew coming toward the gym, I stick out my tongue at them. Meg and James speed-walk over, their faces bright with giddiness, and James is even applauding.

"So, explain!" he commands. He and Meg are both wearing white T-shirts, black Converses, and black jeans. Meg's shirt has a dinosaur on it.

"Welcome to the Black Panther Party free breakfast program. For a dollar, you may also touch my hair."

"It looks amazing," Meg and James chime almost in unison.

"Oh my gosh!" Other Black Girl Stacy Johnson pushes her way in, looking totally confused. "You are so crazy, Morgan! Did you just come up with this?"

"No, it's a real thing. Or it was a real thing, when the Panthers were still around. Before most of them got killed. They had breakfasts, and ran schools and community education programs, too! Isn't it weird that no one talks about that?"

"Yeah, I guess, um, if it's true . . . Uh, are you guys going to chapel, though?"

"What?" I'm barely listening to her, distracted keeping an eye on the growing crowd, and also, I sort of can't believe I just revealed an epic piece of black history and she is asking me about *chapel,* of all things. Poor Stacy. She can't be saved.

Kelly Kline disbands a group of JV cheerleaders whispering and mocking me on their way to the auditorium. They roll their eyes as she shoves them and scans the setup, impressed and Class Presidential. She drops a five into the Smucker's jar.

"Keep the change." She laughs. I nod in authorization. She runs her finger through my kinks and her eyes widen. "It's really incredible! How cool!"

The group around us is getting unwieldly and loud. I'm almost out of pancakes, but people just love spectacle. Any excuse to break up our routine for even a minute.

Meg grabs me by the hand and heads for my spot behind the table. "Let me help."

James uses his theater voice to direct the crowd: "Please form a line, ladies and gentlemen. No peace, no justice; no justice, no peace. Thank you from the management."

I feel so close to my friends right now. They're looking at me for the first time, a new version of me, and they're not even flinching.

(I'm surprised this is actually happening, that some uptight faculty member hasn't already pushed through to shut me down. This is not the sort of chaos I imagined would spring from my plan. I guess I didn't know what to imagine.)

If nothing else, a group of nerdy freshmen are totally getting schooled, and it's awesome. One of them croaks, "But I thought the Black Panthers were a terrorist group," and I'm psyched to launch into a lecture about everything I've learned. I explain that *they* were the ones being terrorized, by the police, and their jaws drop so wide I can see their braces. I get louder, even though the kids from my class are pretending not to be listening.

"They protected their people and their neighborhoods! They stood up for themselves and their rights! They wanted revolution because they were tired of getting so much less than anyone else, of being beaten and shot by the cops who were supposed to be protecting them. That's why they had education programs and organized their communities. They had to protect themselves, help each other, right? Does that sound like terrorism?"

I've got a little group of dedicated listeners—quiet kids from a bunch of different grades—nodding their heads and raising their eyebrows at all of my points. I'm energized by the attention, by my own command over the crowd. I can't believe how good it feels to be heard instead of gawked at.

One of my pupils, a blond girl even shorter than me and wearing a yellow polo shirt, asks, "But they *were* violent, right? I understand self-protection but . . . isn't it always wrong to fight violence with violence? What about turning the other cheek?"

"Yeah, I thought you were 'little miss pacifist.' Now that communist Barack O*sama* wins, you go all Malcolm X?"

I'd know that new voice anywhere—of freaking course Tim would appear with his irritating air quotes.

"You are absolutely right," I respond as calmly and civilly as I can. This wretched asshole. "And listen, nonviolence is incredibly noble and amazing. But—"

"Absolutely not!" A commotion. Kids scatter. Mr. K runs screaming down the hall, or jogs, whatever it is he can manage. Mr. Howard waddles behind him, trying to look serious, but I can tell he's excited by the disturbance.

"Everyone to the gym for chapel, immediately!"

Mr. K waves his arms around as if he's parting the Red Sea. Everyone scurries, my friends and a few other nosy folks hanging back on alert. Mr. Howard looks practically amused, but Mr. K is livid as he stares me down.

"Principal's."

A FIT, A SCENE, A RIOT, A PRAYER

What I learn in the principal's office: I'm suspended pretty much until Christmas break, which means I have to miss all the good-time movie-day class periods that teachers slide into their lesson plans in December. I basically just come to take my midterms. I also have to miss that final, glorious, sugar-filled afternoon when all the cool girls get in trouble for wearing sexy elf costumes and everyone exchanges gifts and even the teachers are in a good mood. The "insubordination" will be added to my transcript. I can kiss Columbia goodbye, the college counselor says, because even radical liberals wouldn't want someone with behavioral problems. I am never getting out of this town. ("Figures—Ruth Bader Ginsburg went there," Mr. K said to me once. "You'll love New York City. It's a disgusting pit of immorality.")

The principal's office: you would think this would be the one room without a Footprints in the Sand ghost-story poster, but it certainly is not. I can't take my eyes off it. But if I did, I would see Mr. K, the principal, the vice principal (literally Mr. K's brother), the counselor, and, for unexplained reasons, Jenn Hanson. (Something about her being the class "morality monitor"? I thought that just meant she sang in chapel.)

When I first sat down across from my judge and jury, the spirit of Footprints in the Sand hovering over us, I was riled up, fueled by inexplicable adrenaline, like after a punk show. I came right out and asked them to explain exactly *why* I'm being suspended (not that I'd want them to consult the code of conduct—*that* would be extremely thin ice). But all they did was stutter and flounder and spit out the words *un-Christianlike* and *Disturbance* and *Inciting Speech*. All of which does not sound like serving free pancakes to the student body and graciously supplementing the school's lacking curriculum. I truly don't get it. Last year a group of seniors wore Halloween costumes and started flash mobs pretty much once a week.

Now, back at my car, reality is a bitch. The weight of my sentence is sinking in, and it's like all the blood leaves my body. Like part of me just drains away.

Fuck.

I feel red-hot and tiny. The familiar slump descends upon my shoulders, and all my worst critics take the stage in my head. *How could you be so reckless? What were you thinking? What is the point? Who do you think you are?*

I rip up my posterboards and shove them into Rudy's back-seat. I'm wrecked with fears and complaints and worst-case-scenarios. Part of me thinks I'll never come back here, and the other, more terrified part knows I will.

I'm so angry and harried that I don't see Mr. Howard come up next to me, cartoon weasel with a heart of gold.

"Oh, hi." I'm out of breath, my eyes still misty and puffy.

"Morgan, I'm so sorry—"

"I know, it's okay. I'm sorry, too. I guess it was a bad idea."

"I just wanted to say it's bullcrap. Completely. But it's not their fault. Honestly, I think you're probably right, you're probably smarter than them, but this is where we live. The black thing is just not familiar to these humble idiots," he says dryly, sardonically. His mouth twists into a Cheshire cat smirk. "Don't pay too much attention to them."

I can't help but snort a little at that one, sardonic and bitter. "I'll try. Thanks."

"Oh, and before I forget—"

"Right, I'll email you the midterm paper. It's due on the fifteenth, right?"

"No, I mean, yes, but what I was going to say is, this essay . . ." He holds out a rolled-up paper, and it's dog-eared, not stapled, so I know it's mine. "This is worth something. Merry Christmas, Morgan Parker."

As he saunters away like he has nowhere to go, I look down at the curled printer paper and cannot believe what past-me has done. I smirk in spite of my woe, rolling my eyes and shaking my head. It's my poetry paper, titled "The Black Girl

Speaks of Rivers: Finding Myself in Langston Hughes and Assata Shakur."

It is a tremendously excellent essay, even if it's completely wrong for this place.

If I were the school, I might kick me out too. *The black thing,* Mr. Howard said.

The black thing. The black elephant in the room, the black swan, the ugly Oreo, the weird one, the difficult one, the drama queen, the loudmouth. ("You're just unique," everyone says, wincing.)

And I can't help it: As soon as I snuggle into the worn leather of Rudy's front seat, I close my eyes, inhaling the thick scent of cigarettes and brand-new yellow air-freshener tree, and I start to cry. My heart clangs around in my chest cavity and into my stomach—I feel sick.

I am not understood. I do not belong. No one can ever fully get my jokes or understand what I'm trying to say. Not even Susan, not even my parents, not even my invented versions of Harriet Tubman/my future self. They probably never have.

Everyone probably takes pity on me, rolls their eyes when I leave the room, secretly shakes their heads about how it's too bad I'm so weird and I'm not white.

HOLIDAY FOR HELL-RAISERS

Meg and James come by afterschool on Thursday and Friday, but I don't want to talk to them. I don't want to talk to anyone. I'm back at the bottom of my hole, my sadness womb, all Interpol and Elliott Smith and *no one understands me*. All week I'm in a depression—the dark, quiet, resigned kind.

My parents were seriously pissed when I first came home with the official suspension notice, and as I sat at the dining room table and told them everything, they still had their stern faces on, but when they went upstairs to their room, I heard my dad muttering "fucking pricks" and my mom shushing him. Now they're encouraging visitors, trying to lure me downstairs with movie-selection privileges.

Everyone is powerless to my depression. I remember this. I know this feeling. I spend days pacing the teeny square footage of my bedroom, crying off and on, and sometimes so frustrated I start stomping or throwing pillows. At night I feel a ball of fire rush up from my belly to my chest and back again, like the Supreme Scream at Knott's Berry Farm. This feeling is me. I wonder if I'll die, explode with complete self-disgust.

"Your mom let me in." Meg stands at my door with a hand on her hip like a soccer mom, keys in her fist. I grunt.

"And I've got David and James in the car."

"Meg." My eyes plead with hers, thick eyeliner and a bouffant ponytail topping her wiry form. "I seriously don't think I can be social today. I can't handle it. I don't mean to be a dick. . . ."

She just nods and opens her arms to beckon me, and I crash right there. That's how it feels to be me—crashing into heavy feelings, reaching for lifeboats. Meg is good at being quiet, and there.

"Dude, it's okay. We'll give you time." She rubs my back while I sniffle. "Just take your time."

I actually smile. "Thanks. Sorry. I know I always have to cause a scene," I joke, wiping my eyes. "Call you after Christmas? I have to wrap your present."

"Sure! We can do our own exchange, our little weird family of freaks. It'll be great."

I grin widely. "How's everyone? How are you? Anything new?"

She shrugs. "We miss you. Everyone's actually oddly normal at the moment. I mean, for us. Oh." She unzips her backpack and digs around. "Kelly asked me to give this to you," she chirps, presenting me with an intricate piece of origami, labeled *Love you Morgs! From Kelly Kline* 🩶 in those cheery purple bubble letters.

"Aw," I giggle. "Tell her I said thanks."

"And, of course, from David." I accept the unlabeled CD. "And here, James's mom's baklava. I guess his mom says to tell you 'fight the power.'" I laugh loudly and roughly, surprising myself.

"Thanks so much. And thanks for coming to check on me. I really mean it."

"And I brought you *Teen Vogue* and silver nail polish because sometimes you just need girlie things!"

She shrugs, tilts her head in a grin. I squeeze her tight.

My friends check in with me every day. Meg live-texts me from church (because she's a germophobe, it's mostly about how she hates having to hold strangers' hands), and then from babysitting the little freak (all kinds of wacky pictures of Barbies and G.I. Joes). David calls almost every night and lets me be awkward while he regales me with stories about random daily encounters with a woman who looks like a Linda or a kid who looks like the little boy from that thing we watched on YouTube. Sean emails me song drafts or book recommendations and articles about black writers. James comes over one day, and we watch movies in silence, but eventually I go up to my sadness womb and he stays downstairs cooking dinner with my parents.

But eventually everyone disappears to tend to family

Christmas stuff (and Sean's family's Hanukkah, then their half-hearted attempt at the first few days of Kwanzaa), and eventually, miraculously, I rise and perform my own family duties. I am trying to ride it out, to outlast my mood. Maybe I can get stronger. Maybe next year can be easier.

A few days before Christmas, my mom is doing my hair in two-strand twists while I sit patiently cross-legged on the living room carpet. Her iPod dock broadcasts a Christmas sermon by a gospel preacher with a gregarious and musical voice. Coco's over here "supervising," aka holding a bag of Lays and chatting giddily with my mom about hair and makeup and boring stuff like that. I see my same old face in the mirror. I think about the "true meaning of Christmas" the preacher recounts, the story of dozens of school plays and church musicals, the Holy Night of happenstance and myrrh. What a wild story, way more surreal than the Dickens story.

I think about Mary. Who just wants to have a baby for no reason, not to mention get run out of town, scandalized? And furthermore, what pregnant lady wants to ride a camel?

The thing about the Christian Christmas story, and all the drama Mary had to go through, and all the stuff we kids have to go through—midnight Mass, endless pageants, pretending we don't care about presents or those tree-shaped cookies—is, who said we needed to be saved? Not all "sins" sound that bad at all. I mean, murder, yeah, but—doesn't everyone get jealous? Why does Jesus need to be involved in our "intercourse"? Why shouldn't homosexuals just get to be homosexuals? And how did I get here, where even curiosity is punishable?

Don't follow rules you don't understand. I pledge allegiance to myself and my rebellion. I get it—consequences hurt, and mine will always hurt a little more than everyone else's. But it's worth it to stand by my own rules. I see my hair in the mirror, its delicate kinks glimmering with Blue Magic hair grease, and I see myself differently.

So even though I'm depressed as hell, on the night of our family's Christmas party, I'm feeling in control of myself enough to just be easy, let everything and everyone around me fall as they may. Even me—I even leave myself alone. In the seventy-degree weather of sunny Highland, California; my aunties cackling in the too-small kitchen; my dad shouting at basketball on TV; my mom, tipsy and shouting for me to get my iPod and pick out a song for the electric slide; my brother across the room, catching my gaze for a shared eye roll; my cousins laughing *with me, not at me;* the way my cousins and uncles and fake-cousins love me even though there's so much about me they don't know.

I help myself to another glass of wine, and I smile, because it feels good to be warm.

CLICHÉ ROAD TRIP MONTAGE

15 Hours to 2009. Montage to the soundtrack of Regina Spektor's "That Time," where James always exclaims the line "so sweet and juicy!" in a pitch that pierces the whole coast of the Pacific, and I laugh so hard I cry.

Bright and early on the last horrifically lovely day of hellish and legendary 2008, James, Meg, David, Sean, and I are in my dad's Man Van on our way to an apartment in San Luis Obispo, a trail of cigarette butts and empty peach ring bags in our wake, tasked with cat-sitting for James's sister's friend. James suggested I invite Sean and David "as arm candy," and my parents are going out of town for the weekend, anyway, and Meg's mom is feuding with Meg's stepmom.

After five hours and just one stop for $5 per gallon somewhere along Pacific Coast Highway, we drop our backpacks on squeaky beds in maritime-themed bedrooms.

It's a pretty sweet deal: when we arrive, there's a note on the counter from James's sister's friend, with the contact information of an of-age gentleman who's agreed to buy us "supplies"—to assure our adult comfort. James rides with him to the liquor store in his Toyota Tacoma.

9 Hours to 2009. While the rest of us decorate the back patio with leftover Christmas tinsel and lay out on our beach towels with a few Coronas smuggled from the Man Van, James rides with the guy, Jack maybe, to procure liquor, and is misunderstood.

"So, what do you want me to get?" says Jack maybe (and his Caesar cut) to James on the eleven-minute ride to the strip mall Ralph's.

(We were like, "Just get whatever you can!")

"Oh, you know, um, just some beer, wine . . ." James pushes his luck because you miss all the shots you don't take. "And vodka. And also whatever."

The guy laughs, "Nice. You're gonna have a pretty good time with those two girls."

"What? Oh. No, we're um . . . It's not like that. They're just my friends."

"Can I give you some advice? You can't hit the ball if you don't swing the bat. So just go for it."

James nods, hands clasped tensely in his lap, raising his eyebrows and probably grinding his teeth with restraint.

"Swing the bat," goes the guy. "Swing the bat."

. . .

8 hours to 2009. James is delighted to re-enact this conversation for us when he returns, bearing gifts of every kind of liquor.

Each of us is holding secrets and tensions, but out in the beachy air, things are easy. I know Southern California is my personal purgatory, and when I see blue skies for a hundred days in a row I'm convinced I'm going to choke on the sun, but I can't imagine not wearing cut-off shorts on a holiday.

6 and a half hours to 2009. Sean, James, and I go through hell turning on the tiny red barbecue on the apartment patio.

For dinner we make grilled swordfish, mashed potatoes, and asparagus. David, being difficult, opts instead to eat three Hot Pockets.

We raise white wine in real glasses and toast "to the freakin' New Year," or rather, to the end of whatever this year was. "Good riddance," we shout.

5 hours to 2009. We get down to business taking shots.

I get drunk pretty fast because of the Prozac in my system, and Meg gets sloppy drunk real fast because she never really drinks.

"Lover!" she shouts at me. Drunk Meg should be on You-Tube.

"I can't feel my face!" she shrieks, grabbing at her cheeks after her second vodka, and I laugh so hard I cry, filling and refilling a water glass I keep pushing on her, glad to repay all the nights of her playing Mom.

James turns on some random *Now That's What I Call Music!* and twirls his hips in another room.

3 hours to 2009. David corrals us into the kitchen, the whole world simmering with nervous anticipation of the ball drop.

"One more shot, guys!"

It's shot number three, I feel like Cuervo is in my nostrils and my tear ducts and my pores.

"After this one," he adds with urgency, "we're getting baptized in the Pacific."

I love him with those inspired, swimming-pool eyes. I almost forgot how warm and exciting it is to be his friend.

"Amen!" shouts James, wielding the human-baby-sized handle of alcohol.

"Should we say resolutions or something?" Sean holds up his shot glass. I notice some muscle in his bicep and internally blush. I really like his "Cassius Clay" T-shirt. I like *him,* maybe. Another high-drama but probably-dead-end saga for the Notebook—it's thrilling.

"Nah, screw resolutions." David Santos should become either a motivational speaker or a camp counselor or the host of *Fear Factor.* He would be good at exactly these jobs. "Let's say what we're leaving in this garbage year. Oh!"

He dodges, a sweaty gazelle, to the iPod dock, the rest of us rapt and expectant but impatient to drink. Usher's *Confessions.*

"Oh, so, a for-real baptism?" I follow up, trying to swallow the weightiness suddenly attached to a dumb shot of tequila. "We're washing away our sins?"

David rejoins us around the table, squeezing in between me and Meg, and takes my hand. "Better than an exorcism," he elbows.

It is super cute.

"So, you go first, darling," I flirt for the hell of it.

"Okay, fine! I, uh . . ." he scratches the back of his neck nervously but tries to look casual. It's like he's deciding whether or not to lie. Or run. "So, when I met you, Morgan, art class?"

He starts laughing, but not with his regular laugh.

"I don't know why I took it! I took a bunch of those classes, too, and guitar and karate and I was even in a book club with a bunch of retired nurses. It was crazy. . . ."

He trails off somberly. (What's going on with him? Why didn't I know this?)

"So, my parents were fighting a bunch, and I was starting to think I was the problem and I just, couldn't be in that house last summer. And the worst part is," he sighs, the rest of us listening intently, not sure how to respond, "I didn't like any of it. I don't like anything. I don't . . . know what I care about. I guess my sin was running away from figuring it out."

I wince as his pain lands like a bee sting on my own skin. To me, David has always been so certain, so firmly sure about himself and the world.

But maybe when we were trying to break my curse, we were on a mission to break his, too. Get him unstuck. Find something bigger. While I want to giggle to the Yellow Notebook about how intimate the moment is, make everything light and surface-level, all I can focus on is how much I care for David. How much I genuinely want only good things for him. How close I feel to him, and how important he is to me.

Darkness isn't a bad thing. Darkness is just real.

"Anyway,"—he glances over at me with a particular look—"you guys have really helped me with that stuff." He drinks, contorting his face and wagging his tongue. Sean reaches around to clap his back.

Meg extends her glass ceremoniously. "I know I'm probably supposed to say popping pills, but that's too easy. So, popping pills, yeah, but also: I stole something. I know I shouldn't have but . . ." She shakes her head and giggles, twisting her arm around to reach into her back pocket.

She opens her fist, and in it is Mr. K's American flag pin.

"Is that—" My eyes bug out, and James and I completely crack up.

Meg smirks. "Yep."

"How did that even happen?"

"It was just sitting on his desk!"

James slow claps. "Amazing."

He amps up while Meg swallows her shot, jaw clenched. "Okay, so you know that guy Tim McCloud?"

I get a pang of shame and rage and roll my eyes. "Ugh, yes."

"So. I . . . gave him a blowjob." James downs the shot. Meg and I go crazy gasping and screaming.

"How did *that* even happen!" Meg is breathless.

James removes the lime from between his teeth. "Well, I met him in a nerdy video game chat room and . . . yada yada yada, I gave him a blowjob behind the GameStop in Sunshine Village Plaza."

Everyone freaks out, the room is roaring with laughter. I jab my shot in the air and blurt, "Oh, so, um!"

"Okay, okay," David yells like a kindergarten teacher, waving his hands. He would not be a very good kindergarten teacher. "Everyone shut up. Morgan, then Sean, then holy water!"

"So, okay, um," I repeat, hardly containing my laughter. "I also gave that guy a blowjob!"

I can only sip the shot because we're all laughing so hard. Everything is ridiculous.

"In the backseat of his car. In the orange groves. After mock trial." I frown theatrically, finish with my lime and shrug at James. "It was just okay, right?" He gives me a high five.

"It was a hard year," I mutter to myself.

"I cannot believe this!" Meg shouts. "You both have to write about it in the Yellow Notebook so we can compare and contrast."

"Yo, who *is* this guy?!" Sean blurts, totally clueless.

David's laughing just because. "Yeah! Is he like the Jared Leto of your So-Called Christian School?"

"I wish!" I cover my face, cringing and giggling. "That's the thing . . . he sucks!"

"Oh my god," Meg squeaks, darting for the iPod. "We need to dance to 'No Scrubs' *right now*!"

"Wait!" I stop her. "Sean's confessional!"

Sean takes the floor. "Okay, um . . . Guys, I don't know anything about Kwanzaa. Like, I don't really know what the hell it is!"

I cackle as he brings the shot glass to his lips, and just as he's about to drink, he chuckles, "I don't know a lot of things, man."

He goes straight for the shot, no salt, and bites into the lime like it was candy.

"Let's dance!"

1 and a half hours to 2009. We're two verses into our '90s R&B sing-along when someone rings the doorbell. Things get sloppier and sloppier as the New Year countdown ticks.

EXIT MUSIC FOR A FILM

New Year's Eve is unquestionably my least favorite holiday in the history of the world. It's just so much *pressure* to make one night both foreshadow the year to come and memorialize the year that's ending. That's too much responsibility for one night, especially since most nights are pretty terrible, anyway. I hate setting myself up for disappointment. It's just pointless— the universe already has that covered.

When midnight comes announcing 2009, someone's entire glass of sparkling cider is soaking the front of my jeans, and someone else is in my face asking if I'm okay, and I don't know who any of these people are.

I'm drunk, but not the right kind of drunk, not the happy kind, but the stressful confusing kind. I look up from where I'm absently wiping my jeans with my own T-shirt, pushing an anonymous white hand full of KFC napkins out of my line of vision, and all I see is a blurry idiotic mess. I dart for the back-door, pass all my friends swinging arms and dancing in circles with that Jack guy and some other random strangers, forming ill-advised drunken bonds.

It's all closing in and I pretend no one can see me, my tight face, all the clanging going on in my skull.

Out on the apartment porch, I close my eyes and the party is only in the distance, and the air is cold and crisp. I hear the ocean a few blocks away. I taste the air and let it settle me.

The world is so much bigger than me, than all of us, than my moods and my fuck-ups and my bad memories. It is wide and beautiful, I remind myself. Without the noise and crowd around me, I smile a little bit. *You made it*, I think. I'll be damned. Never mind the terror of what could happen this year or even tomorrow, I am a survivor.

I jump when I hear the sliding door creak open.

"Hey." It's Meg. "You all right?"

"Yeah it's just . . . a lot going on in there."

She nods in agreement and steps out on the patio and stands next to me looking out at the bay, passes me a bottle of gas-station champagne.

"Happy New Year!" I say obligatorily, raising the bottle before swigging from it.

She puts her arm around me and we stay, just breathing.

"Can I tell you something and you promise not to get mad?" she says eventually.

Jesus, this is a triggering question.

"Um, I guess," I say quietly, passing the bottle back.

"I read your essay, from Mr. K's class. The one about the Black Panthers and Rosa Parks?" I start to bury my face in my hands.

"Oh God, so embarrassing!" I creak as she goes on.

"He gave it to me to hand back to you while you were out, and I promised I wouldn't read it, but I did, so I'm telling you."

(This is a story about how my body is a brown paper bag getting crinkled. I know that becoming a writer would require other people to read my writing, but I thought I'd just figure that out later. Right now, I'm too mortified of all my feelings being exposed. So. Many. Feelings.)

"No, no!" she rushes to grab my shoulders and looks me in the eye. "You're really good, dude."

"Really?"

"Yeah, seriously. It's like you put into words exactly what I'm thinking! You're really deep, and you're so good at explaining the Black History stuff in a way that's actually exciting. Like, dang."

"Wow, thank you. I'm so shy about my writing! That's why I never shared it with you, even though my dream is to be a writer."

"That's so cool. I know you're gonna do it. I can definitely see it. You have something to say."

I chuckle a little, loosening up and unfolding my arms. It suddenly feels so cozy out here, on a stranger's patio on the first day of the year.

"I have way more to say than you can even imagine," I mutter with a *pfft*.

"What do you mean?"

I'm quiet. I want to say everything, start the New Year without the secrecy of last summer weighing me down. Over the past few months, I've watched my two best friends open up about their darkest secrets, but I still can't talk, really talk about what really happened last summer? I keep thinking it's not a big deal, but also, what if it is? That's the pro-con loop ping-ponging in my head right now.

"Morgan?"

I didn't even notice my eyes have welled up with fat tears. I didn't even register Meg taking my hand. With my Kelly-green Chucks back on firm ground, the air misty on my face, I squeeze, blink back the tears, and inhale.

"Um. Well, you already know about my therapist, Susan . . ." She snorts at the name and nods for me to go on. It's like I'm trying to formulate the sentence in Spanish.

"I started seeing Susan because last summer, it got so bad . . ." I feel myself getting choked up, but I push against it with all my might. I don't look at my best friend, though I can hear her gasps and whimpers of concern while I talk—I focus on the beach. "It got so bad that I wanted to kill myself last summer. So, I have clinical depression and anxiety disorder, and I'm on medication for it, probably, like, for the rest of my life."

I breathe in like I'm about to say more but realize—that's it. That's all.

"Oh. Whoa. Are you . . . doing all right?"

"Yeah, yeah!" I turn to her, knock the heaviness from my shoulders. "It's not that bad anymore. If I take my pills. I guess it's pretty common. But I hate it. I hate that I'm like 'ill.'"

"Wow." She takes a deep breath against the ocean air with a little *hmm*. "Since last summer?"

"That's when it was really bad—I don't talk about it but I, um, I tried to hurt myself. That's basically 'how I spent my summer vacation,' actually." I barely bother with the air quotes and the jokey voice. My nervous laugh borders on villainous, deep and knotted. "So embarrassing."

"And no one knows this?"

"Uh, not that last part, nope." I feel heavy, a syrupy mess of guilt and regret and shame.

"Oh, Morgan, I'm so sorry." She pulls me into a close hug, resting her chin on the top of my head. "You shouldn't be embarrassed! I just wish you didn't have to deal with that on your own. You know we're all here for you, right?"

Okay, so now the tears have busted right past the ducts. I wipe my eyes with the sleeve of my hoodie.

"Yeah, I know. It's not your problem, though. And I didn't want you guys to look at me different, like I'm crazy."

"Psh, we would never. I care about you. Those idiots in there singing off-key Elton John? They freaking love you. Dude, we're your friends."

"I know. And it's not that I don't want you guys to know, exactly, it's just . . . talking about it is scary even for me. And if I talk about it, if I say that I honestly wanted to die, like it

307

was that bad, then it's true. I guess I just didn't want it to be the truth."

Letting my head rest on her chest, I feel so incredibly safe. Finally comfortable, not at all anxious.

When we unlink, she lifts up the dregs of the champagne in cheers, and I accept.

"Hey," she squeaks casually, "if it's too hard to talk about, maybe you should write about it. Your depression."

"Yeah," I swallow. "I've been journaling about it."

"No, I mean . . . Didn't you say you have another feature story to write for the yearbook?"

The patio door groans open again, and James is posed in the doorframe, donning plastic 2009 glasses.

"Happy New Year!"

"Happy New Year!" We throw our hands up, giggling.

"So, our rando guests went back to their friends' party down the street. One more shot, then we're going to get baptized. Come on."

"Yo." I swat his arm on my way back inside. "What was the deal with that guy? I don't even really know his name!"

James just scoffs mysteriously, shakes his head. What I decide to do next is let go.

Sean and David are sitting at the kitchen table playing drunk Jenga, which is just building weird robot figures with the blocks. David's wearing one of those Conehead party hats, with *DICK* written on it.

Sean claps and rubs his hands together as we all crowd in

around the pile of Jenga blocks, noisemakers, beer cans, and red cups full of floating cigarettes. "What are we drinking?"

I start clearing the cups from the table.

James buzzes around the TV tray we've propped up and called a bar. "Well, I think those girls definitely finished off the tequila. Captain Morgan?"

He turns to look at me for approval, and everyone giggles in their syrupy haze at the nonsensical pun.

"Huh?" I puzzle. Then, like a light switch, I remember where I am and who I am.

"Oh," I gasp, "I hid a bottle under the sink!"

Everybody shouts in joy as Meg discovers it.

"Brilliant!" David claps. "To our sins!"

We traipse the few blocks to the ocean, drunk and giddy, talking too loudly, laughing at everything. I stop when we step onto the sand, awestruck.

It's like that heroic orchestral ending to Bright Eyes' "False Advertising" or those slow, steady guitar riffs closing in on the final perfect chords at the climax to the Best Weezer Album.

The world is enormous. It is incomprehensible. It's the best argument for God I've ever seen. Or maybe, I think, this is God. This, not memorized proverbs or parables. This, real beauty, better and bigger than all of us. The fogged-over moon lights the surface of the water in a translucent blue-black. The waves are like every song I've ever loved.

I walk toward the shoreline. My friends are all distracted in their own ways. Sean and James stand together wading and talking quietly; David and Meg build sand mountains. I don't know why, but I start taking off my clothes. It's cold and weird, like my skin knows some parts of it aren't supposed to be in the open air. I get a rush. I follow my own rules. I run into the Pacific until I am completely immersed.

IF YOU DON'T HAVE A MAP,
MAKE A MAP OF YOURSELF

After that, it's easy to write.

The next week, in the yearbook room, it's almost eleven at night when I finish. I've listened to Modest Mouse's entire discography, eaten two mangoes, and drunk a Venti mint green tea from Starbucks. I save the file and pledge not to think about it until it's published. I know it's not as dramatic, as big, as it feels to me. I know it's brave, but I also know that the world is wide, that when I'm finally out of this place, when I finally get a good view, this won't be much of a story. Nonetheless, here I am, five foot nothing, an individual, scared to death.

Darkness isn't a bad thing.

Don't follow rules you understand.

There is a lot of stuff that no one knows.

Anything can happen.

You can escape.

If you don't have a map, make a map.

...

Soon it will be just another bright and annoying day, dogs and car pools waking, sprinklers showering manicured lawns in unison, everything in unison, daring you to pay attention and do something. This is a story about what happens after that.

If you don't have a map, be a map.

AUTHOR'S NOTE:
THE OTHER PART OF THE JOKE

That's kind of it. I wanted to say Morgan gets the choice between two mysterious and interesting boys, and even though she knows one of them will break her heart, or she'll break theirs, she jumps right in because this is what all the songs are about. I wanted to tell you she's cured. I wanted to say that I figured it all out, and every single tear I shed had a triumphant purpose.

That's not exactly what happened, but it's what happened-ish. I went to Columbia and then NYU; I wrote some books. I kept being alive and grand and passionate. My depression is just part of me, and I talk about it all I want. I take my pills, I go to therapy and love it, and every breakdown is a tiny bit easier, because I know it will pass. It has to. Because that's how you do this life thing.

Here's the thing about time: we can't see it. We understand the straight line that turns present into past and future into present. But what about déjà vu? What about the moments that seem to keep repeating—did they ever really end?

We are the continuous and swerving line. We are the present progressive. We *are*.

This year I'm turning thirty, and no matter what age you are, you're probably cringing reading that, either because it sounds super old or because it sounds like I'm still so naively young or whatever. It's a pretty weird age to be. When I was a teenager, I thought that at this age, I'd be typing away at some Great American Novel, gazing out at the Pacific Ocean from my beach house, wearing a white linen pantsuit with a satisfied, peaceful look on my face, and just behind me, in a gorgeous kitchen filled with stainless steel, my beautiful and caring husband is finishing up the dishes, and my two beautiful children are finishing their math homework before bed, everyone careful not to disturb Mom, the glamorous genius.

That is decidedly not what's going on.

And maybe that's why I had trouble writing this. Maybe I didn't want to admit that, deep down, I'm still just as naive as I was back then, in search of a movie-script ending. I didn't want to squash my young dreams or yours, my perfect and precocious reader, because that's not how literature works.

(Right?)

This year I packed up my apartment and moved out of New York City, the huge, mythical place I've called home since I was eighteen. Moving is never not intense—it's like a flashback montage of your entire life, but in objects. I had to take stock of every book I've ever read or pretended to read, every concert T-shirt and jean size I've worn, the person I was when I was wearing them. And as I was going through my "archives" (which are definitely not, as my friends would say, "trash of hoarder proportions")—my yearbooks and essay assignments and the Yellow Notebook and my notes to Meg and James and Kelly and everyone—I began to see a story unfolding. I found the novel I'd been trying to write, and it turned out I'd been writing it for longer than I realized. All the stuff—scraps of paper and crayon drawings and lists of songs and pictures and so many feelings—if you take a step back from it, you can trace a kind of life.

I didn't get the guy. There was no guy. I don't even remember who I was talking about. They didn't matter. They aren't in the kitchen as I write this, kissing my children on their foreheads. I have no children at the moment. The guy could be cool, but he wasn't really the prize. I mean, let's be real. The stakes are higher than that. They have to be.

I also didn't lead a social or political revolution. I'm not secretly Toni Morrison or Angela Davis. But I am sipping out of what could only be referred to as a goblet, and it's pink, and I'm looking around at my apartment, which I inhabit all on my own, and it's full of books and music and colors I love, and I know myself. I know where I've been, and I know what I want to say to the world. I know my flaws; I know what hurts me and why. And I know what makes me beautiful. Even when other people might not. When the world tells me I'm wrong, I know when to say *nope*. I guess that's what I have now that I wish I'd had then: the confidence to know when my instincts were right all along.

I never got suspended and I never preached about the Black Panthers, because I didn't know, when I was seventeen, who they were. Not the whole story. I didn't find out the whole stories of Fred Hampton and Emmett Till before I went to college, and that pains me. I know their spirits were part of me, only dormant and waiting to be found.

I do know that I felt isolated, that I adored my Vans and Sonic Youth, and that every single feeling of sadness and hopelessness and ugliness was, and is still, true. That's the part that I can break to you—the part where I'm still just me: hero and antagonist, hilarious and gross and flawed and well-meaning and corny and pretentious and obnoxious and thoughtful and complicated.

I saw "James" just last week. We both live in Los Angeles now, minutes from each other. In his apartment, late at night as usual, I uncorked wine and joked with his boyfriend while James finished preparing an elaborate three-course dinner. At the table, I couldn't stop smiling at their PDA. Mr. K doesn't teach anymore, and folklore has it I ran him off. My brother traded playing sports for music and social justice, and remains way cooler than me.

Everyone has fucked up. Everyone has been brilliant. Both of those things are true.

I saw "Meg" in Portland, Oregon, on my last book tour. I wore a full suit. Meg had purple hair. After my reading, we went to see our friend Luke, who isn't David or Sean but who definitely drove me around playing Modest Mouse and wrote me heartfelt notes about how we saved each other, and how the music did. Luke had a party that night, and after a while, rolling our eyes at everyone there, the three of us slipped away to his room, video game controllers strewn all around, and fell asleep in his bed.

In the morning, Meg and I sat on his porch, hungover and waiting for cabs to different places, and he brought us coffee. We were almost adults. Meg said, "I remember what you said to me that one time when we were eighteen. I was crying, and I felt like I really messed up and you just took me by the shoulders and smiled and said, 'Congratulations. One day this will all just be an anecdote.'"

We aren't always our best selves. And even if we try to be, sometimes life is just too hard. But the thing is: we're all still here. We still shared laughs and cried together and watched each other throw up and fall head over heels for the wrong person. We made dumb choices and then smart ones and then dumb ones again.

It gets better, but then it doesn't, and then it does again. That's the thing that's not so interesting about living: it's just living. *That's* the story, and it's actually not so bad.

Anyway, you'll see.

ONE MORE THING: DON'T WAIT TOO LONG TO SAY WHAT HURTS

It will surprise zero readers that I have grown up to become the sort of person who holds up their own book-signing line (sorry!) to help someone find therapy resources (not sorry!); who shrugs off deadlines or my own care (working on it!) to spend a day researching psychologists for a friend in another state (not sorry!). What I mean is, I waited so long. Far too long. If there's one thing I can say to anyone reading this: admit when it hurts. When it hurts like that, when it's unbearable, the kind of bad that's so bad you don't even talk about it—you don't have to go there by yourself.

I like to email folks what I call a little "therapy starter kit," with a few resources I've used and some tips about how I search for a good therapist. It's not extensive or official or anything, but it's something. And when I can, I like to offer to help search or call doctors for appointments. Just, something. I know this is a scary thing. But I also know how bad it hurts. (And I don't know about you, but the last thing I want to do when I can't even get out of bed is call a bunch of strangers and tell them I'm sad.)

The point is, I want to keep you alive. But there's actually no therapy cheat code or insider secret—we should all know where to turn and where to turn each other. So I'm going to put a little version of my note here. For folks who are struggling— and also for our parents, our siblings, our friends, and anyone, really. Because it's that simple, that easy, to help each other keep being alive.

Begin Forwarded Message

_____

the little therapy tool kit i send to friends:)
    It's been a rough year
    ps I made a bunch of sweet potato pie, it is here,
come over

_____

hi love,
    so so good to see you and hang last night!! I know I know I owe you another email about book things but I'm sending this stuff before I forget!
    Ok, so, this my therapist, here's her email address.

Like I said, I love her, and I think you'd like her. She also has a lot of colleagues she's happy to recommend. Also, a friend highly recommended this woman.

I usually use *Psychology Today* to search for a new psychiatrist (if I'm looking for someone to also prescribe my medication) or psychologist (if I'm already working with a doctor prescribing my medicine, and I'm looking for talk therapy). You can filter by insurance, by gender, by specialties, by faith, etc. Therapy for Black Girls (therapyforblackgirls.com) is also AMAZING. Both databases have doctors' bios, information about their experience and their approaches to treatment, contact info, and sometimes rates.

If you let me know specific things you're looking for, I am happy to help search, because I know this is the WORST part, especially if you're, like, *in it*. And remember, it seriously is like going on a first date or a job interview or something; you're seeing if you can work together, get each other. You don't have to just settle, and it's worth taking the time to find a good fit— trust me.

When I'm searching, I find it helpful to write a little paragraph about what I'm looking for when I reach out for a consultation. That way I can just copy and paste, and it doesn't feel like a whole uphill thing every time.

Here's the one I used this last go-around, just as an example:

I'm searching for a psychiatrist to aid me in talk
therapy and medication management. Though I've been
in therapy and taking antidepressants fairly steadily
for the past fifteen years to treat my depression and
anxiety, I recently moved and I'm looking for a new
psychiatrist. Collaborative and long-term treatment with
a doctor is very important to me, and an ideal therapist
for me is one who is insightful, culturally sensitive/
aware (as a black American woman, my place in society
intersects with my depression), and sensitive to my
busy and unpredictable schedule as a working writer.
If you're accepting new patients and think we may
be a good fit to work together, I'd love to talk about
your method/philosophies and costs. If you do not
prescribe medication, I'd also like to know if you work
with any psychiatrists to collaborate on my medication
management. I can be reached at this email or the
number in my signature. Thank you!

I'm happy you're doing this. I'm here to help in any
way I can. I'll check in soon!

xoxoxo love you

mp